MW01126436

Women
Are
Gods

Women
Are
Gods

James E. Grant

To order additional copies of this book, contact:
Xlibris Corporation
1-888-795-4274
www.Xlibris.com
Orders@Xlibris.com
53215

Contents

Acknowledgements

Tabitha Grant, it all began with her and through her own Spiritualism, I was born as her son. Rose Grant, thank you for sharing your love with the family, because of your love for your family you have given me a better life with many choices. Jean Fleming, I am sorry that it was late, but I am glad that you are my sister, you have showed me this in more than one accusation. Marcia Grant, thank you for being the sister that you are the no nonsense sister. Judy Grant, thank you for sharing the love that you have shared for our Mother. I love you, that would always be remembered throughout my life. Marilyn Grant, thank you for all that you have done for me. Olivia Grant and James Grant, you are the life and light of my life. Shawn Grant, keep doing what you are doing, and it is going to get better. Brian Grant, I need to see you more often. Michelle Grant, you are like the sister I never had. Paula Fleming, continue doing and achieving in your business.Charline Wilson, I know you want twins. Rosemary James, I appreciate your friendship over the years. Nelson Albandenz, the man who like his son. Alex Asare, thank you for teaching math in college. Rosco Baker, thank you for being supportive to me when I was growing up. Loraine Mundy and Goldsmith, you have touched my heart more than anyone in life. You taught me about unconditional love before I was able to read it in the Bible. Rod Mundy, thanks for everything you have been supportive to me. Oscar Reed, you have to get it together. Mark Jones, it is good knowing you, you are always ready to teach. Roderick Thomas, thank you for your support as well on the book. John Carter, you are the baby brother I never had, thanks for telling me what I should major in college. Adrience Dancy, you have always been an inspiration to me. Ron Hobson, thank you for teaching me how to become a better teacher. Andrea Bynum, thank you for always being there and being supportive and loving. Lisa Dixon and family, thank you for being good hearted.Shawn and family, it is good being a father. Marvin Bynum, it has been a good year knowing you. Keep up the good work and progress. Carol Bynum, thanks for your support over the years after my high school years. Terry Fleacher, thank you for being my friend over the years. Ron Walker and family, thank you for teaching me how to sing. Crystal Haynes, keep teaching the children of the world. Kenny and Donny Haynes, thanks for being my extended brothers. Most of all, Vincent and Rachael Harding, both over the years have given me the inspiration to write and turn it into a book. David Barnwell, thank you also for being my friend. Erick Forman, thank you again. Make sure that you are able to out your fires, be careful when working. Rosemary Reeves, thank you for being my friend over the years, you are a true friend. Malachi Israel, thank you for just sharing the knowledge of inspiration with me. Michael Gray and family, you have always been a good friend over the years. I have to give great thanks and support to the men and women in the Massachusetts Department of Correction. These men and women have the most stressful and dangerous job in the world. A lot of people in our society do not give them the credit they deserve as Law enforcement officers. Their lives is at stake every day when they leave their families to go to work. This is the only job I know that the employees do not know if they would be able to see their family again when they leave to go to work. These men and women need to be paid a lot more than what they are getting right now. People who work for the D O C are the most courageous people in law enforcement. Keep up the good work our society might not appreciate you but they cannot live and exist without you as a society think about it . . . you are the greatest. Sergeant Maudy Mullum, I also thank you for supporting me in order that I would be able to complete my education and call me your son. Tracy Huston, thank you for your insights and your enlightenment. Valerie Marrocco, thank you for looking over the book before it was published. Peter Brown, thank you for supporting and looking out for me during some difficult times. Paul Craven, thank you for understanding me and being a voice when I need someone to talk to. Windel Williams, thank you for your support and effort in the department. Cynthia Lewis, I also thank you as well. Ernie Gareno, you are the greatest and latest inspiration of all times. Jerleen John, I do appreciate you for teaching the children. You are a very good person of inspiration. Cliff Azee, I do appreciate your love for teaching our children to develop a better future. Howe Harrison, I also appreciate the time you actually put into these children in order to develop in them a better future. Michael Tabb and family, thank you for being a good friend over the years and looking at the book. Rick Thomas, thank you for loving our children enough to educate them. Susan Turner, you have been a good friend over the years. Tracia Grant, it was refreshing to know you. Darry Henderson, it is always good talking to you. Butch Reid, thank you for being very supportive when I need someone to talk to, keep the faith. Cheryl Belfry and Elanor Chalonus, their inspiration for the children will be very well appreciated in the future. All the staff at Smith Leadership Academy, thank you. Also Glennis Ogaldez, thank you for your support teaching as well the children of our world to become successful in life. Aime

Rigaudert, thank you for the support over the years. Milton Paige, I also thank you for your support in life and guidance in life. Lamount Penn, please tell your mother I am sorry for eating all of her food. Ronald Spratling, thank you for supporting me as a student and even now. Dr. Michael Rees, I thank you for being the doctor that you are for me and my family, you have supported my family in their time of sickness and death. You are the true physician that has enough passion and love for your patients. You are the true doctor in the medical profession. Barbara Nee and Molly Henderson, you became like a mother to me and I thank you for being so supportive to me. Robin Hunter, thank you for all of your support while I was working on this. Keep up the good in you. You are the greatest person in the world. TCB Cooperative Bank-a friendly bank with a family flavor thank you for supporting me over the years. Janelle Hoffman, thanks for inspiring the hearts and minds of our children. Jane Cole, Sam Daniels, Joseph Remulta and Sheila Sanders and to all the staff of Xlibris Corporation. Thank you for making this possible. Michelle Merdarea, I want to thank you for giving me the first start as a teacher, and however great I become I have to give you all of the thanks. Thank you for everything. I also appreciate you reading the manuscript before it was published and thank you for putting me in a positive perspective to publish my work. Ms. Nora L.

Toney, keep up the good work of educating our children for their future. Wesley Cameron and family, thank you for your friendship over the years. Rudy Dottin and Blue the sound master. Kevin Richardson, it is good that you are still teaching the children to stay positive, stay in school along with playing tennis. Don Garner, the master of music, keep your music inspirational. Sherry Smith, thank you for the long friendship and support when I was in school. Sarah Y. Daniels, thank you for the support. Dominique Astier, thank you for your information and support in allowing me to become a better teacher. Felicia Jordan, I thank you for being an inspiration to the children's future. Frank Scanga, thank you for you and your family's support all through the years and you have been a tremendous friend. Marcella and Ricky Hardman and family, thank you for helping me out and giving me my first start in my career. Dana Lyman, keep working hard. Atty. James Smalls, I really appreciate all the help and for trying to lead me in the right direction. Derek Livingston, Michael Maxium, Denise Marion, Michael Gray, Butch Reid, Richard Lynch, Bill Crowly, Tara Cabral, Pat Prescot, Evette Prescot, Diana Prescot, Norman Grant, Grantly Grant, Debrea Grant, Janean Grant, Larry Robinson, Steven Sullivan, Ywain (sido) Engerman, Mary Pola, Curtis Howe, Eugene Fleming These are the people who really care about the education of our children's future, that have touched my heart and became an inspiration in the lives of these children. Pamela Sherwood, Thea Stovell, Larry Dean, Michelle Dean, Randy Willis, Howe Harrison, Linda Solomon-Key, Denise Washington These are some of my students that I enjoyed teaching over the years Spencer Graham, Kevin Arroys, Zachary Hurt, Celine Then, Mayari Velasquez, Ashley Borris, Angel Sanchez, Lilya Kuusipalo, Natlee Sheets, Sabrina Valeri, Trey Bradleywhite, Randy Cheam, Toyin Eghareuba, Bismely Moreta, Jomary Feliciano, Gisselle Harris, Junioris Jimendez, Sandy Alexandre, Daniella Toussaint, Yeraldine Guerrero, Jermaine Thomas, Jeffrey Pena, Cerone Davis, Jomary Feliciano, Rashad Goode These are the students that gave me the inspiration to become a teacher, I love you and I want all of my students to become successful in life. Students, this is your future go for it, and demand everything you can from life. Toyin Eghareuba, Watson Jean Pierre, Edison Peguero, Sebastian Tirado Medesto Sanchez, Raymond Gray, Yeraldine Guerrero, Daniela Nova, Manuel Feliz, Jermain Thomas, Jeffrey Pena, AdamFarah, Awilda Pimental, Adnan Tahlil, Leanna Armstrong, Siggi Sanchez, Akeem Mooltrey, Anthony Cruz, Norberto Cabrera, Lesley Amaro, Felipe Soto, Jonathan Basile Angel Sanchez, Angela Lugo, Raymond Serrano Jr., Ashley Burris, Mayari Velasquez, Erika Torres, Marcus Diaz, Joanne Salazar, Jewell President, Raymond Zapata, Gilberlyn

Perda, Gisselle Harris, Spencer Graham, Wildania Pena, Marquis Barnswell, Jazmarie Burgos, Patrico Lara, Siggi Sanchez, Kevin Arroyo, Nauchaliz Castillo, Lillyabelle Echevarria, Randy Cheam, Wildania Pena, Pasha Dzemianok, Wilfredo Flores, Shawtyanna Davis, Luisa Matos, Sebastian Tirado, Junioris Jimenez, Brandon Valdez, Edison Peguaro, Earl Jackson, Tasheena Church, Fabiola Rodriquez. These are some of the people that have some how bring me to the spiritual level of my life. These are some of the inspirational students. Cedric Woodson, Quahtayvia Wallace, Brain Lawrance, Elizebeth Singletary, Jawuana Freeman, Federic Arroyo, Isis Merrick, Laniah Jackson, Chistopher Andrade, Jerron A. Jacques, Lamount Arroyo, Charlis Jones, Marcus Vilian, Dimitria Singletary, Jamila Sealy Norvin, Maccua Vilain, Shaquilla Williams, Jawvana Freeman, Karina Santana, James Pina, Louis Santos, Houssan Booth, Naisha Wood, Jaynia Henderson, Irkleris Gomez, Skaliada Robertson, Deandra Turner, Shawntell Themes, Michelle Montgomery, Rosemary Mc Clue, Marcus Fergus, David Carrasco, Adonis Acantara, Laniah Jackson, Dorin Bazmore, Ashly Campbell, Sadae Clehorn, Jarron Jacques, Luis Christeea, Christopher Ramirez, Reddick Sedeeg, Seldon Jordan.

Foreword

No one can have an appreciation for life without first understanding what life is. The question I have to ask is what happened to those people who are trying to understand what their meaning in life is? Defining their meaning in life is based on how some people used their lifestyle in order to define what their true meaning in life is. Although a person's life can only be determined by the circumstances and obstacles that they are face with or events that take place in their lives, these cause them to change those events to make people's lives better. Just like we come into life and not know what it is; as we progress in life, life starts to reveal itself to us, and so is our purpose and reason for defining our true existence.

I would like to ask people, "What is life?" Most people might say I have lived in the nature and essences of life, which they might refer to as the physical existence of life. But how much of life do we know as we continue existing in the true realm of life, or how much of life do we understand as human beings? Many people use God as a means to justify life; many people go as far as to use God in order to understand the nature and essence of life. Still we seem to know more about life than we actually understand what is the true essence and meaning of our life. Some people would say that because I lived in the physical existence of life, some people would admit that I still do not know or actually understand what life is, even in the physical manifestation of my existence. Those are the people who are the true enforcers of life. They know that there is more to life than what we experience on a day-to-day basis, or every day.

Yes, although we live in this thing we call life on a day-to-day basis, most of us still would admit that we do not know what life is. What is it about life that keeps us constantly existing from generation to generation? What is it actually?

Second, no one is in a position to interpret life without first knowing who they are in life. Then life is nothing more than energy that brings matter into the creation of itself, which we refer to as life. Now how can we live life without first defining what life is? How can we understand life without knowing what life is? How can anyone have the truth about life if life is not defined through the power of God? Now maybe we should ask ourselves this question, and that is, who is God, who created God? Did man actually create God, or did God actually create man? The question still remains as to who created the purpose for life to exist, even in the physical existence of its creation. Then look around you and ask yourself, why are we here, and what is our purpose? Most people who are traditional thinkers would never ask people or think of those questions; still and yet, these questions affect us every day. Many people are still searching within their subconscious for their meaning in life. This question goes way beyond the mere physicalness of our life existence. It is the spiritual existence that we live with every day that is battling what our purpose in life is.

What is our purpose as human beings to exist? Now there is something that is important that bears a strong witness to the energy of our souls, and that is no one should give someone else enough power over them in order to influence or dictate to them who or what they are as a person or who they should be in life. In order for us to understand or interpret life, we must first understand who we are in life, because if we do not know who we are in life, we then give others total control over who we are and our existence, and this is when we become mentally entrapped to the control of other people's influence and that is what creates our weaknesses in life. We as human beings must always be very mature in our thinking. For example, a mature thinker is a person who, if they are wrong, and when people tell them that they are wrong, they accept it and move on with their life. People become weak when they let others influence them. Remember this: life only has meaning based on how we define who our God is in life, to ourselves.

Now this leads me to a more understanding of the essence of life, and that is to define through the elements of life what is the truth of life. Could it be that all of the truth we believe in leads to nothing more than theories and what we believe in is nothing more than an honest lie? How do we remain steadfast in this life? In other words, how could we exist in a world living in nothing more than theories? And these theories honestly makes people believe that the lie we know is the truth, and the truth, as it was told to us, is a lie. In other words, does anyone know what is actually the truth in life that pertains to God, man, and woman without first understanding who they are as a person existing in the physical manifestation of life?

Most people define God based on how they define what life actually is to them. Most people are not ready to define life because most people do not know enough about what life is, especially when they try to define life on the foundation of who God is. Remember that life itself only exists because of the woman. For example, the hate mankind has for each other in their hearts comes from how they defined who their God is; it is always God's will for people to hurt each other only when someone has to protect their life in order to survive, but in the written words of God, man and woman should love each other, and this love alone sometimes become the most painful emotion known to man and woman. This same emotion we call love has brought nations together and caused nations to go to war, still it brought families together and broke them up with so much hate. I do guess there is a slim line between love and hate, and in order to understand love, we must experience the hate that comes with love.

It is amazing, but God can only be defined in the physical manifestation of life because it is within the physical manifestation of life that we depend on knowing who that God is, as well as defining who God actually is. The only way a person can define what the truth is as it pertains to God and man is by first knowing what it is about the truth that others do not want you or me to know and why. Now the question I ask is how much of the truth is being hidden from the masses of people and why, and how much of the lies about God is taught to us as the truth of life.

The only time people can appreciate who they are is by first recognizing who God is. I mean that God that exist within us and gives us the true spiritualism of life. Where does our true spiritualism of life comes from? Now as we begin to define who we are in our own presence of existence, it is within our own presence of existence that the woman gives our life its true meaning, being, and existence.

The key to life is being able to define who we are as a person before you can even comprehend who God is as a divine creator of life. No person can define God as a divine being, especially to become his or her personal comfort zone for the rest of his or her life, where they could live in peace and harmony with themselves. Because the deception of all life sometimes lies in what we think peace and happiness is. The perfect peace in life is being able to recognize who you are in the realms of all the pain and suffering that you go through in order to survive in your life today.

Now the strength of who we are comes from when we are able to experience our own pain and suffering in life and uplift ourselves through our own power of mind transgression in order for us to have complete control over our own destiny in life, and that is when we are able to understand who we are in the spiritualism of our life.

We must always remember that no man can define life without first defining the woman as his God. When we as men begin to define life, we must first give the woman the thanks that she deserves for being able to manifest man from substance, matter and then transform man from the substance of life into the nature of a potential human being with the creation of a heartbeat. That heartbeat becomes the rathemy of all life's harmony. Where does all of that power come from? It comes from the energy of the woman's mind, body, and soul. The question I would like to ask is who is the true God of man?

The Ha'oba'cka'

When we speak about the woman, we cannot deny the fact that the woman is the most powerful force that exists within the human creation, as well as the most compassionate person when it comes to caring and preparing for life. It is within the woman's womb that all human beings experience the beauty of life, as well as the pain and suffering it takes in order for the woman to bring life into existence. This is the beauty of life that no man would ever experience or claim as his own creation.

The pain and suffering that the woman experiences to bring life into existence men cannot claim that experience as their own. Nor can men say that their genes are the dominant of all creation. The truth of the matter is, men do not actually experience the same pain and suffering that women experience when it comes to creating and bringing life into existence. That is what makes women the most powerful force in the universe. The pain that every woman embraces at every man's birth of existence is what I refer to as the gift of life. That gift of life is what I refer to as the most powerful element in the universe because the pain and suffering that the woman experiences contributes to every human being's spiritual connection to life and their physical existence. The question is, what is it in creation that causes women to have pain and suffering even when they have the power to bring men into existence? I do believe that all of God's divine inspiration is in the pain and suffering it takes to create the spiritualism of life that women already have bestowed upon the existence of life. That same pain and suffering is also embraced in the power and energy of the woman's mind, body, and soul. And that is one of the woman's true contribution to life—creation and being a true God of men. Men have also taken that right away from women just because we are supposed to be living in a male-dominant world. How can women's hands that care so desperately for life become so submissive to life? Please let a man answer that question. I will take the responsibility to answer that question. I honestly think that men have always been insecure about the divine power that is spiritually bestowed upon the woman as God for the people in the world to worship her as God. Do you, men, know how much pain and suffering psychologically, emotionally, and physically you afflicted upon the women in order to remove her from society as the most powerful and dominant God of all? The world would never become complete if we do not give the women back their true divine right and purpose as God. That is why even today and tomorrow, the world will continue in so much chaos because our true God is not revealed to the masses of people as God. Women are revealed to the masses of people as sisters, daughters, wives, mothers, aunts, grandmothers, but not Gods. We can use all of the theological philosophies about Christianity we want. We can even try to convince the world that God is in the skies and that the God in the sky is our true God. But the true God is the woman, who is the true God of men and the world. So why would we refer to the woman as the weaker vessel? So why would we refer to the woman as the weaker vessel? Instead, to me, she is the stronger vessel of life, even the true essence of what we define as spiritualism and the creation and existence of life, it all begins and can only be defined and experienced through the woman.

Yes, the woman is the stronger vessel. The woman to me is a stronger vessel than man. It is a fact that people, such as churches or academic institutions, do not want to admit the true power and creation of the woman. The woman is the true divine essence of life that people in society has overlooked because we are focused on the idea that God is the most powerful force when in actuality it is the woman. Let us look outside of the religious dogma for a minute and focus on the reality of life and its existence. We might say that God from the biblical perspective actually created Himself; that is one of the many things that God has done in order for Him to become God. Now when we think about that theory of God being able to create Himself, I always asked the questions "how much of that is true?" and "how much of that is fiction?" Actually, how much of that do we know to be true?

Now if God is able to create himself or, just like human beings who are able to create themselves from the power and energy of the woman's soul, we must ask one thing, and that is where did God get the power from to create Himself to be God? Now that power that God gathered to create Himself as well as human beings, I refer to that as the most powerful force in the universe called the Ha'oba'cka'. Let me continue, now, the Ha'oba'cka' is a transcending power that becomes the true energy that creates all human life from substances, matter, and then forms that life into its own original nature; please let me elaborate. The original nature of a thing is what that thing was created to be from the essence of its life creation. We all exist as human being based on what our essence predict us to become. For example, we must recognize that everything that exists in life has its own nature, reason, and purpose. Now even when we look at the existence of God, and believe that God actually created Himself, we must admit that it was the Ha'oba'cka' or energy that actually created or caused God to create Himself from nothing to something.

The key to life is being able to recognize what our true nature and purpose is in life and being able to achieve our true nature and ability through our own physical manifestation of life. That is why everything that has the potential to become a part of our life existence has to experience the power I refer to as the *Ha'oba'cka'*, which becomes the energy and power of the woman's soul. Now let me get back to my main point; we were told that God created Himself, but no theologian can explain to me or even you what that power and energy was that God used in order to create Himself. And what was it called? Now again, that is the same power and energy I refer to as the Ha'oba'cka'. The Ha'oba'cka' is the same power that also created every human being that exists on earth, and it is that same power that gave the women their rights to be the true Gods of the universe because of the women's nature to create life. That, along with her compassionate character for life, is what gave the women the right to be God of the human creation, including the men that women created and raised out of their stomachs and from their breasts. We must recognize as men that women are more of a God to us than the actual God we refer to as the sprit and soul of all men.

The power I call the Ha'oba'cka' that creates life allows all women to be God, because of their nature and their ability to create life from the substances and essence of the woman's womb. That is why I say, "Beautiful is the mind, body, and spirit of the woman's souls." The soul of the woman is the key element that becomes the true force of life because within the woman's body, there is a transcending force that gives her the right to create life, and it is that right that also gives her the right to be the God of man, even if man feels that there is another God somewhere in the skies other than the woman. The only God man has is the woman. That is why everything that comes into existence that is a human being must first experience the mind, body, and soul of the woman's energy. It is the compassion and power of the woman that makes all men submissive to her power, even during the existence of life.

Could somebody answer this question for me: The energy that created the power that gave God the consciousness to create Himself as God, was it masculine or feminine power? How did God's consciousness come into existence in order for God to create Himself, and for what purpose and reason did God exist? I know it was not just to create man and give him domain over the birds of the air and animals, or even to justify what is good and evil through some theological philosophy. For example, to say that God created man is the same question as who created God in order for Him to create man? Or maybe, as some people would say, it does not matter. Rather, the power that created God is either masculine or feminine, at least He was created. Now if you were a person existing in life, you would appreciate the statement that I would say, and that is, "Beautiful are the souls of the women who give birth to the world's creation through the human experience of life. It is the woman's inner power that is able to transcend into the energy of life; as the woman's energy transcend into the human creation, it gives birth to every human being's soul, and it allows every human being to define their true purpose: to exist with a human body as the nature of a human being."

It is through the woman's soul that every human being experiences what their own life's existence and nature is; the woman's womb is the master of all the human creation, and the energy that created God is the same energy that is in the woman's womb, which I refer to as the power of the Ha'oba'cka'. We must remember that the only way we can experience life is through the woman's mind, body, and soul there is no other way that man himself can experiences life. Now the woman is able to give life from the process of energy and substance and then transform life into its own creation giving life its own nature of existence. Now this is what causes me to ask myself the question: What is life and how did life actually begin? Some of us would agree that all of life comes from the essence of its own creation, and it is that essence of life that comes from the woman's energy and soul. We must agree that all of the woman's energy is then transcended into the spiritualism of life, and it is that spiritualism of life that becomes the creation of our own existence in life.

Now the questions that come to mind again are what is life and what role does God play in our life. For example, is He a mere fiction of someone else's experience, or is God the true reality of man and woman? Now can any theologian answer that question for me, other than saying that it is God who created life and gave life its true meaning and being, or is it life that gave God His true meaning and being to exist as God because of the mere fact that energy is nothing more than a process of life. Now again we must remember that in order for something to exist as the nature of life's creation, something else had to exist that has created the thing that has already been in existence; this also refers to God having the ability to create Himself. If we do believe that God created Himself, something or someone had to create God; maybe God is not created as the reality of men but as the theory of man's thoughts. Now let me explain what I mean further, which is nothing more than a theology of man's ideology, not a true reality of man's creation and existence.

Now can any theologian define the elements of life without using God as his or her main source for defining what the elements are in life? Although most of the theologians would say that God is the main element of life, now I would say to them, how could God be the main element of life when in actuality, God was also created to become a part of our life, when in actuality, the same energy that created our life also created God. I do not want you to tell me as a theologian that God is life and that He is the reason for our life's existence and because God is responsible for the existence of life, then that is what makes God the element of life. What happens is most ministers are so busy pointing their fingers and depriving others of some of the same mistakes that they themselves are making in life and that is why they still cannot properly explain what life actually is to them. Most ministers use other people's mistakes to gain more control over them and project themselves to be in the image and likeness of God; and because most people are able to believe that God created Himself and the world, that is where the power of manipulation and control starts to influence people's mind and heart. When in actuality the person or people who do more of the creating of life and existence is the woman or women.

My response to that is, it was life that created God even if you say that God created Himself. Now the question I would also like to ask the theologian is life God's first experience of His existence? In other words, can the theologian define God without using someone else's experiences? Can a theologian define life through his or her own experience? Can the theologian even give life a true meaning based on what he or she has experienced without depending on someone else's information? Did the minister or preacher live life long enough or experience life enough that they can actually explain to others what is right and wrong or are they comfortable enjoying the power and pride that comes with being a preacher and minister, because it is that power and pride that made people look up to them as being God and not to the woman who created all of the preacher and ministers from her womb, and even God Himself.

I honestly would like to respond to the question: the theologian would say that he or she has no idea of what life is; many theologians have a false pretense about life in general. What most people do not know is, even in the midst of our life, we must recognize that faith is nothing but a deception that deters people from the actual truth of life and the actual truth of life is that the woman is the actual God of man, not a God who is a sprit in the skies. We must also remember that it is from the woman's womb that the same sprit we refer to as God is the same sprit that embraces the substance and matter of man that comes from the woman's womb.

Now from my perspective, life is nothing more than energy transcending into the substance and matter. As energy transcends into the substance of matter, it is at that point that life begins to take form, and as life begins to take its form, the consciousness of energy creates the nature of all of life's existence; maybe life was created first, and then the awareness of life became a consciousness of life that allowed us to become great survivors of life through the preparation of our own nature. Nature is the state that also prepares us for the reasons of why we actually exist. For example, even the fruits that we eat; there is a reason why it exist as a fruit, and that reason is to prepare us to eat it, because of its nature, as well as being a fruit and a food for the human's soul. The other question is why does creation have its own nature of existence? Why is it that when the male child comes out of his mother's womb he has to be given a nature that would allow him to conveniently embrace life? The reason that we are given a nature in life is simple: it is in the nature of our life that we give life its own meaning, being, and purpose for us to exist in life. Everything that has life has a reason and purpose to exist in life, and it is in that realm, our reason and purpose, that we find our true meaning and being in life that bring with it the power and energy of the woman's sprit and soul.

Now as man tries to define life, he is given a reason and purpose to find out what is his own power of life, and this, my friends, introduced me to a power that is in every one of us call the Ha'oba'cka', some people also refers to this power as God. But in this case, the power cannot be a God, here is why I cannot refer to this power as God because it was this same power that created God to be the God that He is today. So if energy created God, then God has now become submissive to the power and energy of life. That power and energy of life now transcends into matter, and that matter and energy is what created Him to be God, and that same power is the power that becomes the light of the woman's soul. Because within the woman's womb that created all life is the light that burns as every man's soul during his nine months of creation. That energy and power that created God into life is the same energy that embraces the inner chambers of the woman's mind, body, and soul.

Remember that light is the energy of all life, and it is that light that also transcends itself into the woman's soul, and it is that same light that keeps every human being connected to his or her spiritual world. The body is the place that actually helps embrace and create the spirit of man while being an occupant in the woman's womb; the energy of the woman's soul is the light of the world that becomes the energy of everyone's heartbeat. The energy that causes our heart to beat is the light of the soul. Now when man becomes aware of his power of life through his own consciousness, maybe that is when man is able to recognize who his true God is, and that is the woman. He himself must recognize that the most powerful force in life is found in the depths of his soul, and it is in the energy of man's soul that he can recognize that he is God, only to the convenience of himself, and no power is as powerful as one's own self, but man himself must also recognize that it is the woman who gives man the ability to exist as a God and as a human being. Also, it is the woman who gives man the ability to recognize his own power through the experiences of his own life. The experiences of our lives, whether good or bad, is nothing more than our path to knowledge; the realm of our knowledge is nothing more than wisdom, and our wisdom is the only knowledge and truth that actually teach people about what their life's existence is all about and help them find their meaning and being in life. People must recognize that the most important thing man can do is admit that the woman is God, and treat the woman as the God that she is.

Now that is why no man can comprehend the concept of God without first trying to understand who he is to himself, or, to simplify things: who am I? We as human beings must recognize that the spiritualism of man is that of man trying to define who he is through his walk with life, and it is in life that man himself acknowledges the fact that he is his own God, and his spiritualism is that of man being able to elevate himself by seeking who he is through the many obstacles that he faces in order to become the God of who he is—through his own power that lies within his mind, body, and soul. We must always remember that our spiritualism is nothing more than us being able to elevate ourselves into becoming our own God. Our life is more of a spiritual existence than a mere physical form of existence because whatever we perceive life to be, we can only understand it as being a vision of who we are, and that is when we transcends into being our spiritualism of existence. We analyze life through our consciousness of existence; whatever we learn, interpret, or understand life to be it is all mental; we learn through the mind's eye of our existence what our purpose and meaning is in life.

Trust me, that is why I would say the only God man has is himself, and it would always be himself; that is why it is also important that man recognizes that the woman is more of his God than the God that he has been told is some sprit in the heavens. We must always remember the sprit of man's soul is created—where? Think about it; it is in the inner chambers of the woman's womb. The womb of the woman is the spiritual essence of every man's life existence. Because that is where, before the human body was formed, the energy of that light we refer to as the soul was created, and it was created in the woman's womb. Think about it. That is why the woman is man's actual God than the sprit that man has been seeking for centuries to be his God. In the woman's womb, she holds the key to every man's sprit and soul and forms that sprit and soul into a human body, and when she transforms man into the creation of life, the essences of man is then given a nature to exist.

Now the theologian would say that God created Himself. I do not agree with them because I say that when you begin to become a part of nature's existence, it is because of the process of change. We must recognize energy that has the nature and the right to create change. For example, energy has the ability to seriously change the matter of life into something else that we refer to as the beginning of life. I think that God was created because in every force of energy that has the nature to create life, it is in that energy that life causes matter to change because of its magnetic ability to pull matter together to create what we refer to as *life*. We must remember that if every human being was created in the same likeness and image of God, then we all have the potential to be God. Only if we have the true mentality to become responsible for whom we are; this creates the first step into becoming your own God. Now as the power of the woman's energy brings us into to life in order for us to become a human being, it is our consciousness's effort that makes us seek ourselves to become our own God. This is when we begin to live life through our own nature, experiencing what life's true reality is; it is not a God in the skies, but a God on earth that we know as the woman; it sounds strange, but how could we believe in a God that we know nothing of? The only thing that we know of God is what we were told from someone else's experiences. The other question I have to ask you as a Christian is what are your true experiences with God? I do not mean that you go to church on Sunday and dress well. Tell me what is your true experience with God; I do not mean a God of what I have been feeling, but the God we worship as a God of faith.

We even experience the many obstacles we are faced within life and the good times we have in life. Some of us believe that in the physical manifestation of life, there is a divine power that is more powerful than the woman's energy that created all of us that most people refers to as the power of God. Now that same energy that created us from the woman's womb is the same energy that people refers to as God or Allah. Now how could God or Allah be a divine masculine being that is the first in all of the human creation, and still this God and Allah were never created from the womb of the woman? Let me be more explicit; in the beginning of life, the woman had to be first because it was the woman who had the power to split creation in order to create, within the energy of her womb, male and female. In order for the woman to split creation into male and female, she had to be the first and be the God of creation. Now if I am wrong, please correct me. I believe that the power that allows all women to be Gods is the power that lies in the inner chambers of the woman's womb, and that power or energy that lies in the woman's womb is what gives each woman the ability to become their own God, or the Allat and the God that people worship. For example, the woman, from the time that she was created, has the potential to be God; it is the woman's nature and, most of all, her conscience that complete her totality as God. The woman's womb is a world within itself that is not even explored by the people in society. The nature of man takes the woman's womb for granted because in the woman's womb is a world that exists with many separate universes that many people do not know about and that world is able to create life in its own reality. If man continues to look upon the woman as sexual object, man will always miss the beauty of the woman being his God and the spiritualism of who the woman actually is in life. We must keep in mind that this book focuses only on the spiritualism of the woman and not the sexuality of the woman; we already have too many books depriving the true existence of the woman, that is why it gives me great pleasure to write this book, *Women Are Gods*. From the hands of the women hearts, we can feel the love of the woman's soul transcending in how she actually cares for life and man.

Here is something that we should pay attention to: for example, when we discuss our position in life as it relates to the creation of God, life, and death, we must recognize that although women are the Gods of creation, it seems to me that there is a power that exists that is even more powerful than the women's power. Or could it be that because of the women's nature, to create life gives her the right to be God, and there is no power more powerful than the woman's power, and that is what makes her become the God of the human's creation. The power of the women's creation is more powerful than God's creation because she was the author and finisher of God's creation. It was the woman who created God. We must also remember that it is the woman who creates all forms of life from the inner chambers of her womb; it seems to me that the inner chambers of the woman's womb explains the story of heaven. What I mean by that is the forming of substance into matter and from matter into the form of life. This same power that creates all human life comes from the woman's womb is the same power that also created God from the same universe we live in that gives us a reason and purpose to exist in life. Here is why: it is the woman's energy of life that creates man in order to connect man directly to God, and all of this is done through the creation of life. It is the energy of life that created God and man, but it is the woman who transcends that energy to life in order to create man to become the reality of all life's existence.

If we were to say that energy created God, or even admit that God is the supreme energy of life, or even say that God is the only supreme power of powers, I would again like to ask the theologians, ministers, and rabbis: who actually created God? Then we ask ourselves: who created God? That question alone, as it pertains to the creation of God, makes the mind of many people become so limited and complacent that it is sometimes scary to many people as they try to define the existence of God.

The reason why someone would ask the question who created God is simple: most people cannot define life without first recognizing that God created life within this world. Also, most people cannot define life without the presence of God. When we discuses God and creation, we recognize that however powerful or omnipotent God is, He was also created out of the spiritualism of energy. Could it be that the existence of God and creation is nothing more than a mere fraction of someone's imagination that they implemented on the masses of people in order to give them some type of hope for the future that has no existence? And even when we die, because no one knows what life is until they become face-to-face with death, it is in death that we experience what the true essence of life is.

Our society has developed many theories on the concept of what supposed to be the only one God, still and yet, that one-God concept has created many religions in our society that these same people we call Christians would kill each other for trying to prove that the same God they all are worshiping favors one Christian group over the other because they want to prove to each other that their religion is the most true and is the most perfect religion in the world and that the same God that they believe or have faith in gave them the right to kill other people who do not believe the same way as Christians do. Why, if religions have become so competitive, how could a normal human being find his true God and self in the competitiveness of religion? Could it be that the woman is the true God of the human creation instead of some God in the skies? Again, could it be that the creation of all life comes from the woman and that it is the woman who is the God of all men? Could it be that man, in his state of masculinity, wanted to feel like he is God, but in our true reality of life, the true power of God is that of the woman. Why is it that men throughout the world feel comfortable in preventing the woman from liberating themselves? Men have hidden the true power of the women's femininity through their masculinity, by expressing that it is the masculinity of men that is a lot stronger and more knowledgeable than the feminine side of our human nature or way of life.

When in actuality, it is the woman's femininity that expresses the true divine inspiration of our existence. Now if there is one God, there should only be one religion. I have never know a Christian who had enough courage to ask their preacher why the world is so full of many religions, and we only have one God, and how do you know that the religion we practice is acceptable to the God in the skies? It is interesting, the many excuses they would find, trying to define that statement. The one thing that many people have done is assume that people who believe in God are honest and trustworthy people. Most Christians use their faith as an excuse to manipulate others who are not strong enough to make their own decisions in life. Sometimes a criminal in his or her own way of understanding life is more honest than any other Christian in the world. Many people are being foolish because we accept the truth as truth and do not search and ask ourselves how much of the truth is actually the truth.

If Christians were honest as they intended to be, they would have already asked themselves this question, and that is does God truly exist to the capacity as the theologians, preachers, evangelists, and rabbis say He does? Now if Christians were to ask themselves this question, "Does God exist?" and ponder on the answer, they might come to recognize that instead of asking this question, we could do a lot better by recognizing that we, with our own existence, are able to walk the path that led people to become their own God, all because of the woman's inspirational energy of life. The mere idea that allows us to recognized whether or not God exist already answers the question that God might not exist the way some people tells us He does.

Let me elaborate some more the mere idea that allows the consciousness of the mind to ask the question does

God exist or not. Could mean that He does not because it is in he idea of whether "God exist or not" could mean that He actually does not exist because man himself is trying so hard to prove that God does exist means that He might not. Many people do not have enough evidence in this world to prove that God does exist or not; we live more with the position that God does exist than with the idea that God does not exist because of how God is presented to us from the theologians' perspectives. Because we do not have anything that identifies us with God as it relates to the creation of life, it also seems to me that the same God that created me is the same God that created the God we worship. Think about it.

Think about it. God is a spirit, we are not; God knows everything, we as human beings do not; God made everything, including us, we did not. Still and yet we are told that God created everything; we did not. We see each other we never experience seeing God. The one thing that we do know is that all creation in life is definitely created by the woman, and God did not exist, because of a woman. Now look at this! God is too powerful to be created by the woman, but a woman created God's Son Jesus the Christ. Each son can identify with the spirit and soul of his mother. But not too many people can identify with the spirit and soul of God. The reason why that is so is because we never see Him. Some people would say we do not see the wind, but we do feel the wind. Now I would ask you, do you feel God? Think about it. We are told to believe in this God that we do not know exists, especially when it comes from the depth of the religious doctrine who expresses that God does exist, yet no one never physically sees Him.

The life that we live and experience only became a reality to mankind through the mind, body, and soul of the woman's own existence. If we truly think about it, we do not experience life through God's own experience but through the experience of the woman's own inspirational existence; most men might not want to admit that life in the physical manifestation exists because of the power and energy of the woman's mind, body, and soul. In other words, the woman is the true God of all men, and she would always be that, and nothing in this universe can erase that or replace her, not even God and His fabricated lies. God in His own nature does not have the power or courage to bring life into existence like the woman does! Think about it. Nor can we say that God gave women the privilege to bring life into existence because the mere presence of the woman's existence is what makes her the God of all men.

There is no God that is good enough to give men life as a woman could. I would always say that God and

His power is only a fabricated concept. The people who gave Christianity to the world are the same people who made God so masculine and powerful that I cannot experience his true divine love for mankind because of the wars, the hate, pain, and suffering that innocent people go through on a day-to-day basis. There are some people who have hell here on earth and not hell under the earth; you have some people who have heaven here on earth at the expense of causing other people to suffer, and through it all, it is up to me to make the right choices in life, or the bad choices in life. I can experience the love of a woman in many ways; you see a mother's love for her son is what I experience as a true form of love for mankind, but I can never experience God's love for me. Think about it. How can I, a human being, love a spirit, or that a sprit so powerful loves me when that same spirit can destroy me? Now is God a spiritual force that only has one purpose to exist, and that purpose to exist is to bring fear to men's heart in order to discipline people's behavior in society. Or was God created as means of purpose to bring fear to the hearts and consciousness of the masses of people. Or could it be that the more intense the fear of God is created from the Theologians perspective, the more humble people become about the religious doctrine of God. It seems to me the more people fear God from the Theologians perspective, the less questions people will ask the Theologians about the true existence of God's presence. If people do not fear God, the more questions and less control the Theologians have in controlling people's mind. That is why God never appears to the masses of people. We see and still experience the power and presence of the woman as God. I have never seen truthfully or experienced the presence of God. I have experienced emotional feelings of the words that pertains to God in the bible but not the existence of God. These words of the bible were congregated by the Theologians and other prophet's experience. The only God I experienced was the woman who I call my mother and she loves me from birth until now. And because of her love for me, she would also nail herself on the cross for me and all of her children. And that is why I say women are Gods. Because every woman will always make sacrifice for their children.

Why the Concept of God Was Created

Man, even in his ability to know about what is right and wrong, still does not have enough wisdom where he can live his life without worshiping a God. People, for some strange reason, feel that they need a God to worship in order to create peace within themselves. Somewhere deep in the subconscious of men's hearts lies a certain passion to worship a God or a particular God; sometimes, it does not matter whatever the cost is as long as man can admit that he is in a position to worship a God, and the God that man worships is supposed to bring him more happiness than the happiness man would find within his own self. I think that the thing that creates this passion for man to serve a God comes from man fearing the true reality of death. When you are poor and oppressed, you automatically assume that life is better some place else even if it is after death. I could not wait to find some type of happiness in the world, even if it means death, at least I can say that I have found some type of happiness within myself; we must also remember that death to occur as his reality. The only thing that man knows is the life that he is living in at the present time. Second, not knowing where you are going when you die is what creates in man the challenge for man to find peace within himself with a true God that is powerful and honest. Now the true way of life, we have no knowledge of. Sometimes, the courage to find a God has to do with the evil deeds man has done, and serving God is like man being able to repent all of his sins or pain and suffering that some men have caused others. So worshiping God allows that person to live more peaceful in life by knowing that he is going to heaven.

Remember, man does not fear life like he fears death. The question I would like to ask you is why do men fear death more than life? Here is why: Man is living now in the existence of life, so that gives man enough confidence not to fear life, but it is death that man, even within the strength and loneliness of his heart, fears; also, man has knowledge of his existence, as well as his environment while living in the physical realm of life so it does not makes sense for man to fear life. Now man in the physical manifestation of life fears death. The reason why man fears death is simple; it is because man does not know the true existence of life as it pertains to death, nor can man define the experience of death before it is his time to die. Man in the physical manifestation can see death even when it happens, but man has no true knowledge of what death is. Man can only experience death when it is time for him to die, and it is man trying to define or reason with his fear that he would try to prolong his life as long as he wants trying to prevent the cycle of death accrued as his reality.

The role that the theologians want man to fear about God is simple; it is to make man think that believing in a God would secure his life in heaven when he dies or give man some type of hope that they would be in a better place somewhere when he dies. One of man's biggest fears while he is living is not knowing when he is going die and whether he is going to hell or heaven when he dies. The one thing to remember is man's own fears are about his existence after he has experienced life. Whatever man does or tries to achieve in life, he would still entrap himself into his own fears. The reason is that men and women are afraid of elevating themselves to be their own divine God of self. I strongly believe that this is what allowed man to create the image and concept of God. Remove the true concept of God from the woman and replace it with the man concept, and you would have a divine creator becoming the God of all creation. The fear comes to man because of what he thinks evil is. Man has always been afraid of what he thinks fear is. Especially, those unknown fears that are dangerous and are secretly hidden in the subconscious of men's souls that causes him to be fearful in life. These fears end up becoming the fears of men's own entrapment of their own soul; without wisdom, man himself is entrapped in his own soul. So in order for man to pacify his own nature and have the courage to come face-to-face with his own fears, man had to create an omnipotent power called God, whom he does not know or cannot define even in his own physical realm. All of this was to remove from the women their power as the true divine image and power of God.

Now this God that man created was to become more powerful than anything man himself can comprehend and more complex than anything man himself can understand. Now why would a person believe in a God that is complex? Now think about it; if God appears complex to man, it is because of men trying to understand the complexities of this God's power that man would constantly try to have faith and worship it

as his God. It is also in the complexities of man trying
to define and understand God that he is being more
manipulated of the God concept. Now within this fear
that man hides, he even had to create something called
evil, and that evil had to become a part of us, just as much
as God is. Now the evil force is where man hides all of his
fears; whatever man is afraid to face, he relates it to being
evil; whatever man thinks about that is wrong, we say it
is evil. To me, whatever evil thoughts man has, it is his
own thoughts that he gathers from his own experiences
and images of life. Especially when man expresses his
evilness as an expression of hate toward each other. Think
about it! Could it be that man is afraid of his own fears
because he is evil? So maybe the evil or the fear that man
himself describes as Satan is nothing more than what
man himself actually is; maybe we are all spiritual beings
with good intentions that become and create evil desires
about ourselves, but through wisdom and knowledge,
we are able to think concretely enough not to allow our
emotions to become evil even when we are faced with
evilness, and maybe that is one of our purpose in life, to
battle and win over evil through knowledge and wisdom.
The more successful and pure that person becomes.
that person thoughts becomes. And that is what leads
to that person's success in life. Purity of the mind is a
virtue and character of them being their own God and
the inspiration as God of self.

If man is afraid of his own fears and uses God to determine and remove his own fears, how does man justify what is evil and what is good? In order for man to justify what is good, man must also be able to justify what is evil. If you notice, man can only justify what is good and evil through what he thinks is the knowledge of God, but in his own divine inspiration of what the knowledge of God is, man still does not have the mind and the power to know what God's actual truth is for Him. The concept of what is good and bad, man justifies what is God when it is something that he himself can accept, understand, and also make him feel good about who he is. Now the thing that man refers to as evil is anything that challenges man's own reality and makes him responsible for his own existence; it is also anything that is able to spark man's curiosity about what he thinks is the true knowledge of God and what he thinks life is. Man himself uses this position on good and evil to remove his original God from him, which, in this case, is the woman.

The woman is in the same physical manifestation as the man so that is why the woman was removed as the God of all men, although she is the one that created all men from substance and matter and then formed and molded man into the creation of life. The truth of the matter is that the God that man created had to be something that man himself cannot comprehend, or even talk to, or even understand; this same God is supposed to be the most perfect being in our existence; still and yet man is not as perfect as their God.

The question I have to ask is how perfect is this God that people talk about when it was this God that killed many people for not worshipping Him? This same God is more of a mystery to people than a reality to them. Still and yet we are to believe in this God, worship this God, and love this God yet we do not know if God does exist. Think about it. The only reason why we worship God is we feel that God is the most powerful force in the universe, as we were told; we were also told that He is that being that created the world and the people who exist in the world. The God that we were told of created the world; people worshiped Him out of being more of a mystery to them than worshiping God in faith and belief, because no one can defined faith or belief. The word *faith* and *belief* comes from the biblical perspective. For example, faith without work is dead; if you had enough faith as a mustard seed, from the Christians' perspective, you were told that you could move mountains.

How many people do you know go to church on Sundays and can actually move mountains because of their faith? Tell me what does all of this mean? Sometimes the most complicated thoughts that might seem true and honest, when it is explained in the simplest way, allow people to see the many lies it has suppressed in people's mind for years. The key to life is that simplicity within itself is able to reveal all truth. The woman, in some cases, especially when it comes to creation of life, does not get any recognition as it pertains to the creation of life. Now if the woman is able to create man from substance, matter, and then form him into creation of life, then she has to be man's God. The reason why man removes the woman from the Godhead is so she cannot be understood as well as comprehended, and her presence is among us. Also, to me, the woman is more of man's God than the God in the skies. She even feels our pain and suffering as human beings as we exist out of her womb, coming into the creation of life. The woman also comes to our aid as our mothers and our sisters, and also our wives, and as someone to love. The woman even gave man the privilege to begin the cycle of life, which is having her own children.

Now I know that the true answers and experiences of God can only be experienced as well as answered through the power and energy of the woman's soul. Here is why all life comes into existence through the power of the woman's soul. The soul of the woman is the energy that is able to bring life into existence. This is where man transcends into the creation of life; it is through the power of the woman's soul. It is the woman's soul that takes man in his state of substance and uses the energy that is able to create man and gives that energy a human body and places a soul into that same body and makes sure that the human body has enough intelligence to dictate that same woman who gives every man his own existence in life is man's original God. Man himself within the doctrines of Christianity has never placed the woman to be a part of the trinity. Some churches even admit that the woman is not able to teach or hold any responsible positions in the churches. This sounds more like man's ego than God's doctrine. God, who has created man, does not care who spreads the gospel as long as it is spread to the masses of people.

Again, who is this God in the heavens that we worship? And still and yet, we know nothing about Him, but again, most people, still and yet, place Him above us and everything that we do, either good or evil, we make Him responsible for it. The true Gods of men are the women who actually gave us life; many people would not admit that God is a woman, that God is a mother because she has already created and fashioned life after her likeness. Now the only way that any man can experience life in the masculine form is through the mind, body, and soul of the woman's existence; the woman is the force behind the creation of man. Let me please elaborate; if the woman did not create life in the physical manifestation of our existence, the concept and existence of God, life, and woman would not have been a reality that created man.

What we must recognize is does God really exist? Or is God nothing more than an imagination that someone created, or was God created in order to prevent people from recognizing their own inner power of life or to prevent the masses of people from recognizing that their God is the woman and not the one again in the skies. Why would someone want to prevent us from getting in touch with our inner power of life? We must also recognize that all the power and energy that brings life into existence comes from within our inner being of life; it is the power and energy of the woman's soul that transcend that power from the universe to become the spirit and soul of every man's creation. That is why I would say beautiful are the souls of the women who have created all men to become the prophets of God!

The Energy of the Woman
That Created Life

What is this energy that gives the woman the power to create life? Many people would say that the energy the woman has that created life comes from God. I could accept that if someone could explain to me where God came from? Or who actually created God? Many people argue the fact that God caused himself to come into existence. No one, if they are honest, could truly admit where God came from and how He was created, nor can they tell what type of substance, matter, and form created God and gave God a more divine purpose to exist other than being a human being. The question that always puzzled me is how did God, in the process of creating Himself, move energy from one place in the universe into the matter of life and transcend that energy into the creation of life, giving Him the power to become God of all creation, including the heavens and earth? How did God's consciousness of though got its inspirational spark to create Him, and what is God's purpose in order to create Himself?

Again, what energy of life form was able to pull substance and matter together in order to form life, or even God? If people think seriously about what it is, or who it is that they're supposed to have faith in, pray to, or even who created them from substance and matter, and form man with the consciousness of life to exist as a complete human being, it is the woman, not God. Think about it. Who created God? When you seriously think about who your God is, who you should believe in as your God, many people would come to this conclusion and that is does God truly exist as God? Now the other question is why does God truly exist, what is God's purpose and reason for His existence? God could not exist as God only for man to pray to Him, have faith in Him, believe in Him, and most of all, worship Him. There has to be more to God's existence. Maybe what is wrong with the image of God concept is the brush that the theologians painted God with to the world; maybe the theologians have not completed the true painting of God. Maybe the painting became so perfect that people could no longer recognize the imperfections of God in the painting. For example, some of the imperfections of the painting are that God becomes more powerful, more created, and that is not giving God the credit He deserves as God by mentioning that God is supposed to let man serve Him or just being man's creator. Maybe the theologians did have enough respect for the nature of the woman in order to admit to the world that it was the power of the woman's soul that actually created God. Maybe the truth of the matter is that God was created by the woman. The theologians came close admitting that Jesus Christ was born by the womb of a woman, but not by the sperm of a man or by man's sperm. Is God a human being because if we are made in the image and likes of God why is it that God did not use his sperm to create Jesus the Christ. Let think about why was Jesus from the theologian perspective accept the fact that Jesus was brought into existences by the woman's womb and not of man's ability, but God Himself was to good to be brought into existence by the woman's womb think about it? Is the theologians saying, that women can create life without man's sperm or could it be that women are the true creators and divine inspiration of life.

We all were created from something call the Ha'oba'cka'. The Ha'oba'cka' is an energy that transcends through the energy of the woman's spirit, and soul by first taking the elements of the universe and earth and then transforming those elements into the creation and existence of all human life. What then is life? Life is nothing more than energy transcending into the physical manifestation of our present existence; whether this present existence is an animal or human beings or plants or birds, we must remember that everything that comes into being is transformed from a feminine force that is willing and able to create life all over again, and that is what I refer to as the process of life's existence. That process of life is something called the oliverthorime. The *oliverthorime* is the energy that the woman uses to create all life that comes from the inner chamber of the woman's mind, body, and soul.

That energy that transcends life—we do not know what happens when that energy is transcending life because the energy of life is only created through the nature of what that form of existence is going to be. The truth of the matter is we do not know at what point and time that energy that transcends becomes an animal, plant, trees, birds, or even a human being. What is not told to us is that we are able to choose our own form of existence, substance and matter in order that we would better become who we are in our own form of existence. We choose to either be an animal or a human being. We also choose our family and the place where we want to be created. People are in more control of their existence and creation more than they are told from others; it is the choices we make in life that sometimes causes us more pain and suffering. Those choices sometimes lead most people to hate life than to love the life we all live in. This is when we actually start to understand what is good and evil. It is the right choices in life that makes most people appreciate the true essence of life. The only thing that brings people into the physical manifestation of life is the power and energy of the woman's soul. Could it be that they were a woman that created and formed God by giving God his own intelligence? Or as I would say, are women the God of our God's existence. Most theologians became honest when they say that Jesus the Christ was born of a woman, and so maybe the woman also created God? Now isn't this an interesting analogy about God, life, and death?

I believe that the only reason that people from the depths of their hearts have so much hate in their hearts for other people has something to do with how much knowledge they have of their God or the truth about who our own God is. The only way we can remove all of this hate and pain and suffering that comes with the passion we refer to as hate is when we recognize that the woman is a spiritual being that is able to transcend into being our

God, not only in her ability to give birth, but in her ability to be intelligent enough to care for life enough to preserve it as well as create it and not hate it or destroy it. The energy that created all life is what I refer as the Ha'oba'cka'. The Ha'oba'cka' is not a God; it is the energy that even created God Himself. It is a force that has used the gravity of the earth and the elements of the universe to transcend that energy into the spirit and soul of the woman in order that she can create man into the existence of life. That is why we must recognize that the woman is nothing more than the foundation and the liberator of all life.

Here is how the woman transforms man into the existence of life. We must first recognize that the woman is nothing more than a spiritual being as well as a force, especially of the human existence; that is why she is able to transcend life into its physical existence. That is done based on how we must first recognize that the woman is the spiritual force that is able to transform man into life while being in his mother's womb. The woman does this by first taking the elements and energy of the universe and the earth's gravity to create the motion that vibrate the first rhythm of the human heart in order to keep it beating for the duration of man's physical life.

The creation of life begins when the women first take the ultraviolet rays that come from the sun and transform those rays' energies into the spirit of man. The question one might ask is how does the sun's rays become the spirit of man or even become a part of life creation? The sun's rays are an energy that distributes itself as a force, which is able to transform into the physical existence of life. Now the energy of the sun's rays has a certain element in it that is able to create many changes of life, even in any form or matter that is able to create life. The ultraviolet rays of the sun are the energy that processes all life. It is in the energy of the sun's rays that allows matter and substances to change and transform into the many different elements such as animals, flowers, plants, and human beings as well. This is also the same way that God came into existence as a just spirit and not as a potential human being. Before the spirit and soul is transformed into a human being, it is able to recognize its own form of existence and its environment, as well as the nature and purpose of its own creation and existence.

Let me elaborate some more; if God came into existence as most Christians say He does, we know from their teaching that God is a spirit, and He has never shown Himself, or even His face, to man. He is known as a spirit and yet this same God has placed Himself in a position where He is able to communicate with man who is in their own physical manifestation of life. Now if God is a spirit and He wants to become a human being, God Himself would have to use the power and energy of the woman's soul in order to transcend into the creation of life. At this point, I would like to express how interesting it is that Jesus the Christ, in order to become God, or the Son of God, had to come into the physical manifestation of life in order to become a human being just to experience the temptation of what human beings have to go through in order to pass the test of faith and appreciate what it is like to become a human being tempted as well as being born into sin.

Now if God or Jesus the Christ had to experience the womb of the woman in order to come into existence, then the woman herself had to be God or more powerful than Jesus because she created Jesus the Christ from her womb. Now remember, God did not use the sperm of Joseph to bring Jesus the Christ into the physical manifestation of life, but He did use the mind, body, and soul of the woman. Now could it be that God knows that the woman has a certain power that He himself did not have, or even in our religious doctrines that the theologians try to ignore. Now think about it; as much as man believes that he is the most powerful and wisest being among creatures on the planet Earth, still man cannot create life without the woman.

I strongly believe that God knows somewhere that in the energy of nature, the woman is able to create life without God's help, and also without man's substances, and that the woman is more the true original God than God Himself is, or what people proclaim Him to be. Women are the original Gods, and God is nothing more than a spirit created by the many schools of theology. That is why we only have one God and so many religions, because people are trying to define God in their own terms and for their own benefit, and most of all what they think the true God is. Now the complexity comes to the masses of people because no one knows God well enough for them to actually define who God actually is; no one has seen or lived long enough to also define who God is. That is why I would say that the only God I know is the woman who gives life to all men.

Now think about this: God did not allow Jesus to come into existence by just creating Him as a complete human being, nor did God allow man to journey in the wilderness to find this child in the same way He allowed the Three Wise Men to do; when He wanted them to find baby Jesus they found Him. What is it about the woman that God had to use her in order for His Son to experience the physical manifestation of life? Could it be that God, in His own existence, was never a human being? What is it that God knows that man in today's society takes for granted or do not know, especially when it comes to the woman being more of a God than God

Himself actually is. Maybe what it is that is not told to the masses of people is that God knows, He is nothing more than the creation of the woman's existence.

Now the energy that becomes me or you is nothing more than life, and that life is nothing more than the consciousness of the woman's energy, and it is the woman's energy that is able to transform life, by allowing everyone of us to experience the physical manifestation of life. Now before that energy of life, that is either me or you, transcends into the woman's womb to become the physical manifestation of life, that energy has to have a consciousness of its own and should already know who it actually is. That consciousness of our energy is what allows us to choose who we are and what type of nature we are going to be, either male, female, animal, or even flowers. Now, that energy that is the consciousness of the human life becomes, also a magnetic force that draws all of the elements of the universe and earth together in order to create within us the human experience, or what some people refers to as the physical manifestation of life.

The matter and form of life comes from the DNA and RNA of the woman's mind, body, and soul, and it is that DNA and RNA that the woman embraces in her womb so that the energy is able to form the matter and form of the energy that creates the matter of life. The

DNA and ANA are most likely found in the woman's body fluids and that is what also helps shape and structure our bodies into what we now call our form of life. It is true that many people are told that life begins only on planet Earth, but for someone to say that life only begins on planet Earth, they limit the woman and the creation that causes us all to exist as human beings.

Now I also believe that we were told that life exists only on earth. People, there will be a time when we are going to find out that life exists outside of our solar system, and these people who exist outside of our solar system—they are more advanced than we are, and some of these people that are from outside of our solar system are able to live in love and peace without people from planet Earth coming into contact with them or not knowing who they are. That is why they do not want people on earth to know that there are other human beings that exist anywhere in the solar system, because people here on earth still have a lot of hate in their hearts; some people who have a peaceful heart that actually live here on earth have had the opportunity to meet the other people from the other universe. Please, people, do not take this lightly. Trust me, the people who live outside of our universe do live better, way better than we do here on earth. The reason that these people do live better is that they have reached something called perfect peace;

we have too much hate, and if some people get to know them, they would destroy their worlds.

If God created the universe with just human beings, it means that God limited Himself and became very selfish, and this is not an attribute of God, it is more of an attribute of man. It is better to teach the people the truth that life exists some place else just in case the wrong people or person came as Jesus the Christ, who lived only in heaven and on earth. The planets are running out of room, and we are coming to a point where we all have to accommodate each other's existence and way of life. Remember that most wars that are fought on our planet is fought to remove the population of people from that section of earth, or when the earth, for no reason, becomes overpopulated with people, the people are removed from the planet by creating war. When earth becomes overpopulated with the birth of people, that birth is removed because of war. The truth of the matter is we are coming to a point in our lives where we would begin to experience life forms other than the ones that we have been exposed to all our lives. The thing is we are to believe in, or someone might have told me, is that life begins only on earth, when in actuality, life begins outside of the universe and is brought into this universe through a transcending force that collaborates with our life existence in order to bring all the elements of the universe together that they might bring life into existence.

There is nothing magical about the existence of life. Because life is nothing more than a simple process or cycle of creation and existence, and it is the existence of man that becomes man's own reality. Now the question that comes to mind is who created the reality of all men's existence? The woman is the creator, she is the God of all men, she is the inspiration of it all, and she is the alpha and omega of it all. Now who created the woman? The woman has always been in existence; she was here way before God was created or even thought about coming into the existence of life. Here is why every force that is able to create life and reproduce life has to be a feminine force of life. Now in order for that life to create life, it had to exist first. Man is not able to reproduce anything, not even himself, so he is a force by himself; that force that causes man to be a force by himself is what allows man not to become a part of creation where he is able to reproduce. Again, if man existed as the first power in creating life, life would not be able to continue to exist; the nature of life would stand still or stop. That is why the nature of most men it seems it is to destroy, and cause many war in the world. It seems to me that most men do not recognize that the most beautiful creation in life is the nature of our existence, and that is where all of us come from, which is the energy of the woman's mind, body, and soul.

How We Were Created

Again, the one thing that I would like to stress from my perspective is that life began in the state of energy first and then it was transformed into the physical manifestation of life. While we were in the state of energy, we were able to consciously understand who we are; we were also a normal existence of people. This is what people refer to as the spiritualism of life; I refer to it as the consciousness of life, this is where we become who we are before we transcend into the physical creation of life. Now the state of energy is what people need in order to understand that it is also a form of life. We must remember that energy by itself is life, patiently waiting to be transcended into matter in order to create and fashion what we call life, and nothing can replace that energy, not even death. Death creates a different nature of life. Death cannot replace energy because energy is also a process of death. It is energy that is constantly existing even through the many creations of life that life itself has fashioned. Energy also does have its own nature and consciousness and experience. Whether we understand the true process of life or not, we must still understand that the energy of life, before we came into our physical existence, is what embraces itself into the woman's womb and has already existed as life. Now that energy, in order to become a part of the physical manifestation of life, has to become a part of the woman's mind, body, and soul.

That same life, in the state of energy before we came into our mother's womb in order to become a potential human being, is where we choose the people we want to be our parents, and now that is where our beginning and being start to exist. Even in the state of energy, before we are transformed into the physical existence of life, we know that we are as God existing in the state of energy that most people refer to as the soul. Now when that energy transformed itself into the substance, matter, and form of life, it becomes who we are in the physical manifestation of life. Now when that energy transformed itself into the physical manifestation of life, that energy lost all perspective of whom it was before it came into the solid state of energy. That solid state of energy is what we call the physical existence of life. We must now begin our process of life and death all over again in the physical world when we die. When we die, we start all over again, still not knowing who we are in the physical world.

Now in order for us to remember who we were in the spiritual world, or in the state of energy way before we transcended into our mother's womb, or the physical existence of life, we must first spend time with ourselves. The key to a good spiritual life is being able to know and completely understand who you are as a person, alone and separate from others. When we spend time with ourselves, we also get to understand why we are here, and that is what makes it easier for us to find our reason for living our lives in the physical manifestation. When we come into the physical manifestation of life from our mother's womb, it is important for us to know ourselves all over again, not actually in a state of meditation but because it is within our nature to know who we are as human beings. What we must pay attention to is the reason why most people are not happy is that they cannot face the fact that the reality of God's existence comes from the power that is within their own selves think about. We have more faith in someone's doctrine than our own true divine belief of us being our own God. We feel more comfortable admitting that our true reality of God is a being in the form of a sprit. The reason most people cannot get their life together is simple: people do not spend time with themselves. Most people spend time with others more than themselves. People are more external in their understanding and comprehension of life; they depend more on others to help them find their way in life than relying on themselves. Some people know more about other people than they know about themselves. That is what causes so much hate and confusion in the world. I have always said, "The more you are able to know about who you are, the easier it is for you to become successful in life."

As we were created into the physical manifestation of life, we now have a different nature than that in the spiritual world. In the physical world, we become children all over again, trying to learn more about who we are as a person and why we are here in the physical manifestation of life. What happens is when we mature from our childhood into becoming men; we now become dependent upon the woman's touch, feelings, and emotions. The woman now becomes the teacher of men's motions; the woman now becomes the God that all men ignore in their place of worship. The reason why I strongly believe that the woman is ignored in the theological doctrine as a divine God is simple: the woman is, in her nature, a physical being just like men are because the woman is as much a physical being as men are; it is the woman's physical existence that makes the theologians deny the woman her true existence as a divine God. Many of the theologians in their true form of existence deny anything that has the same physical characteristic as them cannot become a God. The one thing most men in society would not admit is that the woman is the most powerful force in existence today.

When it comes to trying to define God, we must remember that everyone's mind is a place that has enough knowledge where they can allow everyone to elevate themselves to become their own God. The concept of God to me is more mental than it is a way of life and worship. The woman is the true place of the man's creation and the inspiration of the man's own God.

Some people assume that women cannot be defined as a God. I think that we also believe that nothing that is in the physical manifestation of life can be defined as a God because the physical existence of life is nothing more than a lesser creation of God and angels. We believe that God cannot exist in the physical manifestation of life, so the woman cannot be God, but we do believe that God answers our prayers while we exist in the physical manifestation of life. So the woman being in the physical manifestation of life cannot live up to the expectations of God, or even be a God, still and yet we believe faithfully every story that is told to us by the theologians about Jesus being God living in the physical manifestation of life. This same God who is Jesus is the same God that people worship, and it is the God that Mother Mary brought into existence as Jesus the Christ.

Now this is very interesting because man takes more pride in worshiping a God that he knows nothing about; all man knows about this God is that he believes in is what we were told from others, like our parents, and grandparents, but still and yet, man still think that this God exists as his true divine inspiration of life when in actuality it is the woman who is actually man's God, who actually brought him from energy into the form of matter and, from matter, transformed him into a human being. We must remember that man's first experience of life, emotions, and love is first taught to him by his mother, who also becomes man's first God and teacher of all of his mature wisdom. Even in today's society, man still uses what he learned from his mother in order to help him decide on what to do in life. We must also remember that before Jesus was an adult, Mary who is Jesus the Christ's mother, was also his teacher and, I also believe, His God; here is why all children spend more time with their mothers than fathers.

The woman, during her pregnancy represents a powerful transcending form of life, and it all represents the power of the woman's existence. The woman's breasts becomes men's own means of survival; the men suck from her breast the gift that is the substance of life, and it is her substance that strengthen men's bodies while the men are in their mother's womb. Men also digest whatever is in her stomach for food during their nine months of gestation. The person that created the men from her womb is also the true God of every man. Just like the hands that raised men and rocked the cradle actually rules the world. But this is the same woman that we are told cannot become a teacher or sometimes a preachers, still and yet, she is the mother who created all men to live in harmony and peace with themselves. Who was it that taught God's prophet to become strong men, who gave all of God's prophets life and cared for them? It was the power and energy of the woman's souls, which now became the energy of each man's life. Because we now exist in the physical manifestation of life, that makes us recognize that the woman is our God. One of the things that limit us is the physical manifestation of life. Here is why: when we come into existence in the physical manifestation of life, this is our matter or form of existence. The only reason that you know who I am is because of my form, or, as some people would say, how I look; you are able touch me and feel me that is all matter or material. Before we were created in the physical manifestation of life from the womb of the woman we were nothing but energy; that energy is then transcended into the transformation of a human being. People must remember that they exist first in the form of energy, and that energy is then transformed into the state of matter. That created the form of our physical bodies limits us in many ways, even in our faith, as well as our belief that the woman is the God of all of humanity. The one thing that we must remember is we actually choose our parents in the physical manifestation of life. We choose our parents and family out of their own necessity for us; that is why when a child is born, it becomes a spiritual blessing for that family, because the child is placed here to protect and uplift the spiritualism of the family.

Our form of energy becomes life in the spiritual manifestation of life. The physical manifestation is nothing but matter being in the form of energy. Energy on the other hand is nothing more than spiritual because in that state of energy is where we as people, before we were created, were aware of our existence and purpose in life. OK! As the writer, I need you to stay focused on the idea of energy, matter, creation, and the woman. Here is why if people can understand the energy that is within themselves, that energy while in the physical manifestation of life, they would realize that the power and energy of their subconscious is what makes them their actual God of who they are; that is what we call the inner power of life. The inner power of life is the most humble way of life. People who understand their own inner power realize that their life becomes easier to live. The sun's ultraviolet rays is the power that transforms the energy of our soul into a changing force of matter that is nothing but life. There is a certain energy in the sun's rays that when it hits the substances of life, it gives the substances of life the energy it needs to creates its own nature of life existences. Please let me elaborate the sun's ultraviolet rays: as it shines upon matter, it is able to change that matter from it original state into a different state of existence, causing it to create life and giving life a reason to exist. The sun's rays exist because there is an element in it; the sun's ray that is able to produce life and cause life to change from one form to another form of life or mature into the same nature of life. The sun's rays are a force that changes life and causes life to exist in the physical manifestation of life.

The ultraviolet rays of the sun or, as some people would say, the temperature that makes up the sun, also becomes the energy of the woman's soul. The sun or the temperature of the sun is what people call the Sun of God and not the Son of God. Now that is why when we breathe, there is a hot sensation that comes from our breath, or even the air that we breathe. Now could that energy or heat that we breathe be God of the religious faith, or a part of the woman's transcending force of creation? The answer to that is no; here is why: if God needs energy to be God, then how could God exist as God; God cannot be God, God would have to be energy, but that same energy is found in the woman's womb. Now if God created Himself to become God and is more powerful than any force in the universe, and we do admit that God is so powerful that He is the only form of creation that can stand alone? What do I mean when I say that God can stand alone, has God been able to stand alone enough to create Himself from nothing to something? That is what people in the world have been taught. Now God is always independent; from the time that God become dependent on energy, He is no longer a God but a human being that was also created by the power and energy of the woman. Now if God, because of energy, exists, how could God become a powerful God? Now if God is a human being, why is it that theologians do not want us to know that God is a human being, why would they want us to worship God as a powerful sprit? In this case, I am not referring to Jesus the Christ who we know came in the sprit of being a man and not a woman, but God, who is all-knowing, still had to use the woman's womb as a main vehicle to create Jesus the Christ. Then if the woman is powerful enough to create Christ, why did the theologians left her out of the trinity and assumed that because of her monthly cycle, the woman is incompetent as well as unclean to become the leader of any church? Still and yet, you tell me that the blood of the animals during the Old Testament, that the sacrifice of the animals' blood, had to be pure enough for God to accept as a blessing toward Him, and the blood of the woman is as pure as any animal. The woman's blood is so pure that she was able to create all of God's profit in her womb for nine months and fed the men the same blood for food in order for them to live while in her womb for nine months, and as these boys become men and develop in their attitudes, they rejected the blood that gave them life in order to become a man of God and not of the woman as their God. Now the question is who is man's God? It has to be the woman. Could it be that the theologians are saying that the blood of a lamb or any animals is purer than the blood that the woman release every month and that same blood every man or prophet or even God, who is Jesus the Christ, had to eat while in his mother's womb in order to survive and become a man of God, or even become the Son of God? All of this had to happen in Mary's womb in order for Jesus to become God or the Son of God. Now are the theologians saying that the animals' blood is purer than the woman's? What is it about the power of the woman that the theologians or men in the religious faith are afraid of. The woman has always been a more powerful force in the universe, and as a human being, she does stand alone even in the creation and existence of life. The theologians do not want her to exercise her complete right as a person of divine essence. That is why I would always say that the beauty of life is the true energy of the woman's soul, and it is the energy of the woman's soul that makes her the God of all men.

The people who believe in the religious doctrine would admit that God is all-powerful as well as all-knowing, still and yet, they cannot tell you where God gets all of His knowledge and power from. Now maybe what the theologians are afraid of is when they tell people where God gets all of his knowledge from, people would become more powerful than the theologians, or maybe their knowledge may surpass what the theologians themselves congregated as God's true existence and knowledge. Now if God has power, where did God get his power from, because whoever gave God His power to become God, they themselves have to be God's God. That is why I believe that the God concept existed as nothing more than a theory and not a true reality of man's own existence.

Now let's say that God does exist; in order for energy to exist, or even transform into the creation of God, or even life, God Himself had to be created by a woman, because it is the woman who created us to become matter and a form of life's creation. The reason why I say that is God does exist and is transformed into the woman's soul. Let me elaborate more here. This is why I want the woman to be recognized as the true God, and God Himself could not be a God because God in the divine or physical life; God cannot be a male. On the other hand, the air that blows as the wind to cool the universe and earth off is also able to transform itself into becoming the soul of the woman and the sprit of the human body.

The dirt of Mother Earth represents the true structure of the human body. The waters that flow as the rivers of life also give life to the firmament of nature and also become the nourishment for man. Water is also used as the blood substance of human life. From the inner chambers of the woman's womb come all of the prophets that have denied her the right as the true God of the human existence. These prophets were first born as children, and it was the hands of the woman's mind that knew how to make these boys into becoming men, into becoming strong men with a lot of powerful knowledge and wisdom. That is why I would always say that it is the energy of the woman's spirit and soul that brought man from infinity into the realm of our own physical life existence as a living breathing soul.

That is why there is no man that can define his true existence and reality without first defining the mind, body, and soul of the woman's spiritual existence as the true God of the universe and earth. Until we are able to recognize that the women are the true Gods, as well as the true creators of life, we as human beings, and as a nation, would not make any progress toward love, peace, and serenity without first acknowledging that the woman is our true God.

Now the question I ask is who is God? Is God a sprit or is God a human being that was brought into existence through the woman we were told is Mary, or was God too perfect and omnipotent to be brought into existence by the beautiful womb of the woman, or was God Jesus the Christ who was brought into existence from the wonderful womb of the woman who, again, is God? God is the spirit that is embraced in the substance and matter that forms the mind, body, and soul of the woman's energy. It is the woman's transcending energy that makes her the true God of the universe and earth. The truth of the matter is that it is the mind, body, and soul of the women that has taken man into the inner chambers of her womb for nine months of man's life procreation cycle and made man into a strong human being.

That is why as much as men denies it, the truth of the matter is that women are Gods or, as I would say, women are the mothers who are Gods or, honestly speaking, women are the true Gods. Period. The power of the woman's strength is as strong as God's because the strength of the woman is God. Women are the true Gods of the universe, and her essence of life also blends in with the creation of life, and that is why the woman is able to give life its true meaning as life and being. Women are mothers who are God; it is the women who are Gods. God is the woman who is the true God of the human creation. It is the women's power that transcends into the power of the Ha'oba'cka'. The Ha'oba'cka' is the power that created all women to be the Gods of the human creation. The Ha'oba'cka' is a transcending power that has transformed, from the elements of the universe and earth, all women to be the true Gods of the human creation and existence.

The Spiritualism of the Universe and the Earth's Waves

Most people have been told that the universe is only there for people to enjoy. To me, on a spiritual level, the universe is there for people to communicate with and get a better understanding of life and themselves. For example, the trees that we see in the forest can communicate with every human being. The trees can give us the inspiration to live, and it is up to the individual to tap into their energy. We as people are very external. We were not taught to be internal. Internal means being able to come in touch with who we are as a person. The strength of who we are comes from how well we know ourselves from our inner being. Every man's success and failure comes not from God but from how well that person knows who he or she is as a human being or inner self. A lot of people are Christians, but a lot of Christians are not successful. Think about it. Our inner being is what makes us develop the integrity as being our own God. Our inner being is a certain type of energy that connects people or keeps people in tune with the spiritual world.

The tree, we already know, gives us our food to eat and purifies the oxygen that we breathe. For example, the universe only communicates with certain people about a lot of things, such as life and the way the universe and the planet Earth were created. This happened mostly to people who were in a state of meditation and purification of the human soul and mind. When people meditate, their energy stays in tune to the vibration of the universe's energy and earth's gravity. The universe does not communicate with a lot people because a lot of people have denied themselves the privilege to meditate and communicate with the alignment of the planets. Some people do not even know that the world and the universe have an energy force that vibrate in a wave that carries many signals that are capable of vibrating into the energy of universe and the earth's gravity. That same energy force that comes from the universe, the sun's rays, and earth is able to transcend itself into the beautiful womb of the woman in order that she can create the sprit and soul of every male. The energy that is in the universe and earth transcends as a process of creation into the woman's womb to create the soul of every man, along with the sun's ultraviolet rays; that is what we experiences as the energy of life within the woman's womb before the child's body is created.

Some people would say that the universe does not communicate with man or woman, that it is God that is the main communicator with man or woman. Every time people say that man or woman is able to communicate with God, why is it that God does not answer men or women back directly if God actually created the nature of man? The nature of man, I believe, is to see and experience God verbally communicating with man, or even appear before the people who pray to Him and believe in Him. No one can explain that question to me. If God does exist as God, then why is it that God never communicated with man in this day and age? Here is why. God might be too busy hiding his face from man and woman. God, being a spirit, cannot communicate to human being. If God decided not to communicate with human beings, at least God should be able to show his face to man and womankind. Why is it that God cannot appear to mankind in the physical manifestation of their life, why is it that the theologians treat the physical manifestation of life as a lesser form of creation than that of God and make God's creation a better creation than our physical existence? Then the theologians mentioned that no human being has the potential to be as perfect as any angel in the Godhead, still and yet Noah and Job were more obedient to God as a human being than Satan was to God. Satan was an angel of God! Now if you asked some of the theologians, why is that God never appeared to the masses of people or person? The theologian might say it is because God, being God, is capable of doing what He wants to do in order to achieve what He, God, wants done in this life. Now think about it.

The only way that God can communicate with other people is through energy.

"Mr. Grant, please explain to me what you mean, or what you are trying to say."

First of all, theologians teach that God is a sprit and not an energy. The reason why I think that theologians teach that God is a spirit is simple: theologians do not want people to realize that they can never experience

God, not even in the physical manifestation of one's existence. Many people are given a concept of God that sounds good, but how true is it? A lot of things in life sound good, how true is it? I love because it is the human thing to do, not because God wants me to believe in or to love people. Loving people is the human thing to do; the reality of that is when you are able to love a person more than they are able to love themselves. That is what would make me a better person, being able to love people; again, not because God wants me to but because I want to. The only thing that makes me a better person than someone else depend on my integrity. If you say that you believe in God and that the reason why you love people also is because you think that it is the human thing to do, then tell me why is that you hate people who are different than you are, or why do you think that because someone is different, that gives you the right to deprive them of their own human rights and interest in life? But you tell me that you believe in God. How much of God do we believe in?

Now let's assume that God existed in the sprit. If God existed in the sprit, and is also a spiritual being, a human being who is in the physical manifestation of life and is also a soulful being, then God can only communicate to men who are in their own spiritual essence of life existence.

"Mr. Grant, how can God communicate with man in his spiritual essence? God would have to use energy as a means of communication."

Because man and God are nothing more than a state of consciousness that transcends with energy; we are all a consciousness of energy. Now God would have to look at where that person's level of intelligence are, and where his spiritual awareness is, and then God would also have to transcend that energy directly into the waves of the universe and the waves that form the magnetic force of the earth's gravity. Now these waves would have to have a message in them as they travel in the state of energy for people to understand them. Most of the Christians refer to this consciousness of energy as their faith. Most people or Christian are told about faith, but the way faith works is never explained in the mind and hearts of people, so how can someone believe in something when what they believe in is not completely explained to them. So why believe in something that you know nothing of? So the majority of people give their life to the concept of faith and a belief in a God that they know nothing of.

As these waves travel, men and women might begin to interpret and comprehend these waves in the form of messages. This happens to us when we think about someone we love and they appear unexpectedly to us.

Our bodies are sources of energy that communicate with the message that comes through the vibration of the universe's energy and earth's gravity. People even interpreted the messages from the waves of the universe and earth, but lots of people do not recognize that they have the capabilities to communicate with the universe. That power that forms our energy is within their inner subconsciousness to interpret the messages that the universe and earth transcend for the human mind, sprit, and soul to interpret. Now there are some people who would say that the universe's energy and earth's gravity is an energy that comes directly from God.

What people do not know is that God uses the universe and the earth to bring messages to men and women. The human mind is an energy force within itself that translates and deciphers information and then sends it to the brain to be interpreted for a better understanding. As this information passes through the brain in the form of a wave, it is then brought to the consciousness of man to be interpreted as a message either from or of God. This is to tell people that God never wanted Christianity to separate the Christians from Mother Nature. Mother Nature, along with God, man, and womankind is connected through the power that transforms itself into the energy of life, and it is that energy of life that gives us a reason and purpose to live.

From the time that my mind began to comprehend this type of information about the life, energy, man, and womankind, I knew that my level of spiritualism has grown. The universe then explained something to me; it said I could communicate with you just like I have done to many people who are and want to be in tune with past, present, and future existence of life. Here is how the universe communicated with many people. I think that the universe always remembered that the earth is in a gravitational pull of energy so the universe uses that energy to communicate with some people through the waves of their brainpower that I referred to as a vibration of song. This message is then transcended into the human mind for them to understand and comprehend the message. That energy is what people call a magnetic pull of the earth's atmosphere, while the universe's energy pulls itself in the rotation of the earth's motion of gravity. All of this is what I call the power of the Ha'oba'cka' transcending itself into the energy that forms the sprit and soul of man and woman. The Ha'oba'cka' is what makes women the true Gods of the universe and planet Earth.

The Ha'oba'cka' mentions that the thoughts that you receive in the mind is transmitted and transferred in the form of many waves. Every wave is broken down into a single component of thought. That thought is then passed on through your mind and on its own frequency that interprets the messages. Now when these frequencies come together, they create and form many thoughts.

"Mr. Grant, whether or not you comprehended the thoughts that pass through your mind in the form of an electronic magnetic wave, these waves are the true vibration of the universe."

These waves are also how people are going to communicate with each other and the universe without using words. This process is what I call the power of mind transgression. Also, what people would definitely come to understand is how these waves are going to cause other people to communicate with the universe and the earth's gravity. These waves are the spiritualism of the human's vibration as well as the energy that transcends information to the human mind. These waves are used as the energy that will create the inner self that produces the spiritualism that is influenced by the universe's energy and your own human sprit and soul. These two energies, the universe's energy and the earth's gravity, will be your guide in everything that you do and achieve in this life. Now sit still and quiet for a few minutes and listen to the energy that causes your heart to beat in the same rhythm and harmony of the universe and earth. Listen to your spiritual energy, listen to the beat of your heart, listen to yourself, listen to your mind, listen to you getting in touch with your inner powers, and through it all, stay honest in your judgment at all times, and you would find your true self, and in doing so, you would realize that your only God in existence is—who? When a person finds their true self their would first recognized that the God of the universe and earth is the power and energy of the woman's sprit and soul.

What happens is you begin to experience again the vibration of the universe and planet Earth's energy that allowed me to begin to focus on the energy and sprit of the woman's soul. My inspiration and focus were to concentrate on the woman, not as a sexual object or for some type of sexual gratification or entertainment but to understand the woman from a spiritual perspective and how that spiritualism created a force that would project a positive image that is as powerful as God, and that image of the woman being is an image that we could relate to as being strong—even the people who are seekers of knowledge and wisdom, and not those who are seekers of religious worship, can identify with what I am saying

The Inspiration of the Woman

Also, to recognize the woman's inspiration is to first elevate the spiritualism of the woman's power. What have happen is some people have looked at the woman as mostly a sex object, and most women have come to believe that they are just that sex objects to most men, and that the woman has no inspirational significance to mankind at all and all they (women) can do is be in a submissive role of what society and religion have dictated for them to do, while I have come to experience that the woman's ability to mankind is far greater than just being a sex object. What I try to do is not to allow the women to be place in the role of being submissive in order to satisfy the gratification of men, but elevate her to be the God that she is of men. Now if any men felt the same way as I do they would first place the woman back on the pedestal as the God that she has always been.

As these thoughts about the woman began to transcend as a vibration in my mind, I began to feel a strong sense of pride and security that gave me the privileged to express in my thoughts the woman's inspiration and her spiritualism and still be able to define what the Ha'oba'ck4a' is. The Ha'oba'cka' in some cases is defined through the woman's power to create life from the energy of here own mind, body, and soul.

The Ha'oba'cka' discusses the beauty and soul of the women's existence. It is in the woman's womb that the energy of life exists and is then transcended into the force that brings all men from the spiritual world as nothing but energy into the physical manifestation of substance, matter, form, and then life. That is why I would always say that from the depth of life's own energy comes the true statement, and that is "beautiful are souls of all the women that allow all men the beautiful freedom of life. It is the women who have created all men from the inner chambers of her womb into the most powerful mighty men of existence."

As we continue to focus on the women's inspiration of life, which reflect the positive of the woman's spiritualism and beauty of her soul. The spiritualism of the woman's soul, I believe, is more of the authentic hands of God than what we refer to as God's authentic hands in the Bible. Because the woman's womb is where we as men were held comfortably and peacefully, night and day, for a period of ten months, which is the procreation of the human's existence of life, this is where all men become dependent upon the woman for the rest of their lives.

I also have emphasized in the book the Ha'oba'cka' the expressions that deals with the woman's power and spiritualism that reflect the woman's existence as God. Here is why: as the woman brings man into existence, through the process of energy, substance, matter, and in the form of a human being. We can best be sure to know that the energy that creates the spirit of man's life comes from the energy of the woman's soul. It was the soul and sprit of the woman that created man to be man and God to be God. That is why women are the Gods of the universe and planet Earth.

Now I know that people do have a strong belief in God, as well as respect. Now in regards to all this, there are some facts in life that people must face that brings us to more awareness of our reality. Now let me make this statement clear: I am not writing this book to be the gospel, but it is written to uphold its own weight in gold (God). The book *Women Are Gods* is not written to steal the faith of others or steal members from their congregation, it is a book written to satisfy the soul of mankind and womankind and give us a better look at life. This book was written in order to give people a clear understanding of what God and life is. I can personally explain to others about the God I believe in. It is a book written to inspire others about the beauty and spiritualism of the women's soul and her ability as a God.

If you are planning to leave your congregation, please do not blame the book for explaining something that you think your minister did not explain because I would say to you, change the church, but please do let nothing change your own faith in God; always change the church not your faith.

The *Women Are Gods* is written for people to look at life from a different perspective. Whatever that perspective is in life. In this case, it is the woman or women being the Gods of men and allowing men to respect women as the true God of their existence. I strongly believe that in this case, the book holds its value in weight as it develops into a powerfully written book that brings women from a submissive and oppressed role in life into being Gods.

Now the one thing that we must understand is that the biblical doctrine that placed women in a more submissive role still takes it roots from the many religious doctrine. It is the doctrine of religion that makes it imperative for women to be projected as being submissive and inferior to the men that they have created, but somehow in life, the man will always be submissive to the woman. The creator always makes her creation submissive to her.

I am not writing to degrade the faith of others or say to people, "Follow me as I follow Christ." I am not trying to become any people or person's Jesus the Christ because if I were to become your Christ, then I would look forward to you crucifying me. When a man or women say that there is your Christ to the masses of people, it is the masses of people that are going to crucify that person. Again, I am not your God or Christ because if I were to try to make you think that I am your God, you would definitely kill me for being your God or Christ. It is better for a person to become the Christ of their own life than to let someone else be their Christ. What I am trying to shed some light on is the spiritualism of the woman's energy is truly the God of men than the God we are told about as God.

We as men need to understand that there is nothing a man can do or achieve without first giving thanks to the woman of the earth. Whatever man want to become, or whatever man want, whatever man defined as his true existence, or whatever success he achieved in this life he owes all of it to the woman. That is why men all over the world and men in all cultures must first respect the woman. The man who respects the woman through the laws of return would definitely become successful. That is why man must first respect and worship the woman as his God. Even when man looks at what he defines as his own spiritualism, he can only recognize the true spiritualism of life as being the energy of the women's sprit and soul. It is the mind, body, and soul of the woman that creates and becomes man's true state of his spiritualism. Now men who are your true God? Trust me, it is the women or women of the universe.

The Fear of a Man

Let me use myself as an example instead of mentioning that it is the love of all men, in this case, that keeps women from recognizing that they are the true Gods of all men. Now as a man approaching this topic, I had to get rid of all my insecurities and reeducate myself about the true meaning of life and its true existence. I also had to travel deep into the subconscious of my mind in order to understand a deeper wisdom of knowledge, which I refer to as going across the mighty storms of the Nile river to find the knowledge and wisdom I needed that pertains to the idea that women are the true Gods of the universe. Actually, the truth of the matter is, as silent as it is kept, women are the true Gods of the universe. Because women even shed their blood for every male that have existed upon this earth, just like Jesus the Christ did when He died on the cross for the sins of men. Some of the theologians knew that in order for Jesus to be accepted by mankind as the true Son of God, He had to do something very miraculous; that would still be human enough to understand, but compassionate enough to be accepted by all human beings, whether or not they believe in God.

That is why some people say that the story of Jesus is the best story ever told to mankind. Do you know why people say that the story about Jesus is the best story ever told? It is simple: because people actually believe the story about Jesus. Some people would believe the story about Jesus more than they would their own life existence; in other words, people would deny themselves and accept Christ, whom they have not seen. If man cannot accept the fact that he is his own God, then he needs to accept the fact that his true power and wisdom comes from the woman who is his true God. Do you know that is why we judge each other is through the eyes of our religious preference? Now what happened to me is I had to mature beyond all of my insecurities, and most of my insecurities came from how society and religion portrayed the image of the woman to be and how women themselves portray the negativism of themselves from the many religious doctrines and the laws of society. What the egos of men are afraid of is it that women are the true Gods of the universe, and they should be worshiped as such, and it is the men who do not want to worship women as their Gods.

What brought most men to look at women in a negative perspective was very well influenced by the teachings of society and their love for religion. It was the dogma of religion that shaped the character of many men's mind and their relationship toward oppressing the woman. Trust me, everything that religion and society taught about women were in a negative, dominating, and controlling perspective; if they were a religion that gave the woman any authority in the church, that religion was considered weak in the eyes of God. Now remember that all of this negative information came from a negative perspective of life called Christianity. One of these negative perspectives was that men should always be in control wherever there is a woman present. These types of attitudes that shape men's character also created a submissive philosophy that comes from a negative theological perspective, as well as an academic perspective, on how women should be treated and how they should behave at whatever demands that men asked of them. As I began removing my insecurities about how a woman should be treated and respected, as well as how she should be submissive to men's authority. All of this is not true, about how a woman should be treated, or how women should be. Now the more I remove my fears, the more I began to experience the true power, spiritualism, love, and affection of who the woman truly is.

Many men have mentioned that women have broken their hearts. In passion and appreciation of love comes the true pain and suffering that comes with being in love. The same pain and suffering that men feel when they are in love is the same pain and suffering women feel when they are in love as well. Now the reason that love hurt most men is simple: it is the first lesson in life that men experience. Men also come to learn that he cannot control the emotion of love. Because love is something that is a personal expression that is full with nothing but emotions, and those emotions are feelings that cannot be controlled by the male ego; in fact, it is one of the most popular feelings that is able to challenge men's emotions, that allow men to recognize that there is a spiritual awareness to how we view the true essence of life. Nor is love something that depends on the male ego in order to survive its own existence. Love is an emotion that will exist longer than men will live their lives. When a woman breaks a man's heart, love itself becomes the first lesson where man can seriously become in touch with his inner self. Love also becomes the first learned emotion that men seriously identify with. That emotion also removes his entire ego and teaches man to develop a character of self-awareness and sensitivity.

When a man gets his heart broken, he begins to learn that love is controlled through emotions and feelings, and not just his ego. So it is through love that man learns that his ego cannot dominate or control that very act we call love. It is through his love that man even experiences the feelings that the emotions of love presently causes him, and the true strength of man is only evaluated through experiencing the most powerful gift of life we call love. Still and yet, no one knows what true love really is. Or does true love really exist? Love is like God; we all think we know what love is and who God is, but we still have not experienced the true essence and substance of what love and God is. The only way that people know what life is about is when we die, that is why we all have to die. We die to fully understand what God is and what love is and what life is. We live because we cannot define our true existence of what life is, what death is, and who God is. Death is the only wisdom of our true existence because through death, we have all the answer to what life is, death is; and before death, we now recognize that the most powerful force in the universe is the energy that the woman's spiritualism manifested to create man, and that is what makes women the true God of the human creation and the existence of all men.

✳ Now with all this in mind, remember that the man was supposed to be the strongest vessel in the world, or at least stronger than the woman, from the biblical perspective. Being a man automatically means having the ability to be stronger than most women emotionally and spiritually. Also it means being better and more intelligent than any woman. Now tell me, men. Is this true that because we are men, that makes us better, stronger, and more intelligent than women, both mentally and physically? This is the type of teaching that most men assume is the true gospel of God. So when we evaluate its teachings and try to be honest about what the Bible teaches about men and women, does our common sense agree with our true wisdom or do we substitute our common sense and intelligence for faith or a belief in a God we know nothing about. Men must realize that this is not true. There are a lot of women that are more intelligent than men, stronger, and most of all, better. I know that intelligence comes with how much experience and knowledge one has of a subject or a thing.

The truth of the matter is that women are the most powerful vessel on this planet we call Mother Earth, trust me, not men. Even when we evaluate life from the physical manifestation of its existence and move into the spiritual realm of the women's existence, we can still experience those women still becoming even more powerful than men. That is why I make a reference to the idea that women are Gods; I know that this statement is more of the truth than to say that because I'm a man, I'm stronger and better than a woman and that all women should be submissive to me; it sounds good, but how good is the truth if it is not right? Why is it that most men believe that women should be submissive to all of them, but men cannot believe that women are their Gods? What I have always done is search for the light that reflects the truth in life; most people who search for the truth know that the truth allows us to better evaluate our lives about what is right and wrong about life and to try to correct what the wrong might be in order to make it right. The one thing that we must remember is the truth is never told to us, what we have most of the time is the mere fabrication of a lie that people in society wants us to believe is really the actual truth of our life existence.

When I talk about the strength and power of the women, there is a story that people mention that deals with the man and woman being tempted in the Garden of Eden. It was that same God that I am supposed to believe in that had the audacity to say because of one women's sin, all women had to suffer labor pains. What happened in this situation was men also ate the fruits, and men had to till the earth because they to have sinned. It would be interesting if men had to receive labor pains like women do when their child is born. When God, who is omnipotent, mentions that He is going to make women suffer because man ate the apple, I would have to start looking at what type of a God I would be serving and having faith in and worshiping, because if God had to give birth to an eight- or nine-pound baby, He would also be in labor pains, and that would have nothing to do with someone sinning; it is more physical, because anyone who would be giving birth to any child that is even five pounds would still be in pain because they are giving life to a child. Think about it.

Now if God's only worry was about man or woman eating an apple, and God is contributing the eating of an apple to sin, then God who is all-powerful and omnipotent is seriously acting like a possessive man who wants to control the minds of the masses of people. Remember, it was God who said to man and woman to be fruitful and to multiply. Now think about it. Do you think that God, who is all-powerful, would want to burden women with the idea that because of their birth of every child, they would have to suffer a painful birth while giving life to their child? I would like to know if this did apply to God's mother when she also created Him to be God. Now did Mary have labor pains when she brought Jesus the Christ into the world? Now if Jesus's mother had pains, then we all know that Jesus was born into sin, so if Jesus was born into sin, then that made Jesus the Christ a sinner just like men are, so when Jesus dies, He should also go to hell or be judged like a human being.

Please let me use the apple in the Garden of Eden as an example to prove my point about the woman's true power and strength. That same power, strength, and bravery that the woman display in the Garden of Eden was misinterpreted by God and man. The lesson that took place in the Garden of Eden strongly relates to the doctrine, and faith in God. It is the woman's power, strength, intelligence, and bravery that make the woman a true God of her existence. Many people are under the impression that it was the woman's fault that caused the first sin in the world that accrued between man, woman, and God. Now stay with me on this topic by first understanding that the man is to be the stronger vessel and is also stronger than the woman.

In the biblical story of Adam and Eve, many said it was the woman, Eve, that caused the first sin in the world. It is interesting to know and find out women who are the weaker vessel; and within the weakness of woman's ability, she was still able to find room to cause the first sin. Now when I ask most men who are Christians, how did the woman, who is the weaker vessel, Eve, manipulate the man, Adam, who is considered to be the stronger vessel, to eat the forbidden apple if she was the weaker vessel? How could a woman such as Eve be able to manipulate Adam, the man who is the stronger vessel, causing Adam to sin? It seems to me that God who is all-knowing is misjudging the same woman's power that He is supposed to create in the woman. Anyway, what God called the weakness and sin of the woman became the most powerful act that God might have overlooked when He judged the woman as being weak or being a sinner.

Here is why the woman is God: she was able to make God take man out of being helpless and dependent upon God and made man responsible for his sins. Now to me that sounds like a strong woman, wanting her man to become responsible or a mother wanting her son to become a responsible man in life. Although man did not have the power to challenge God on any level, it was Eve's sin that gave man the courage to face God, even if man wanted to or not. It was in Eve's sin that man came into his own understanding of his self. In other words, man knew what it was like to sin, and with all of us both male and female, we all sin, even the ministers, preachers, rabbis, and evangelists; everybody's sins, no one is excused from the freewill of sin, not even me. I also sin.

Man has to have the ability to know life and its existence for himself, and in some cases, this is done through sin; some of the positive lessons we learn come from the many sins we experience. The only way that man can know what life is, as well as his God, is all about through the inspiration of sin. I do not care how powerful God is; if God was in the physical manifestation of man, He to would also be a sinner because everything that is in the physical manifestation of life is all subjected to sin. If God is in the spiritual world, then it is wrong for God to judge man in the physical world, especially if man does not understand what right and wrong is, like Adam and Eve did. I have a question. Why is it that because man wants to know what is right and wrong, it becomes a sin in the eyes of God? It seems to me that religion tells people that they should not have knowledge of what is right and wrong, but instead, they should have faith, hope, belief, and prayer. So does that mean that the more knowledge I have, the more of a sinner I am? To me that seem more of man's way of teachings than a God that is omnipotent. Any God that is omnipotent is not worried about whether people are smarter than He is. That is why the laws of the Ha'oba'cka' let men or women know that whatever decisions men or women make, they should be held accountable for their actions. This is where I say that man's first lesson of self-responsibility and independency came from the inspiration of the woman's wisdom that challenges man to become his own God.

The idea that man bit the fruit and ate it from the hands of the woman became the first independent process of self-enlightenment. This enlightenment of self made man and woman become their own God. The woman gave life and independence to man through what the theologians call the sins of Adam and Eve. It was because of the apple that man recognized what was right and wrong, and God had to appreciate the idea that man and woman wanted to know what was right and wrong. Now God should be happy that man knew what was right and wrong because it gave God more of a reason to judge man through His compassion than to assume that man should be judged even if man did not know what was right and wrong.

What people overlooked is that if God did not want man to know what was right and wrong. Why did God, who is all-knowing, it seems, made it imperative to bring pain to the woman while she is procreating and giving birth to the men who are His prophet? I think that God committed the first sin because he did not want man to come into his own enlightenment of what is right and wrong. Man should be able to understand life well enough not to be responsible to any God, and God should be considerate to man and let man live life without him intervene in man's life. God should give man that state of ultimate freedom. God, to me, seems to be the first one who committed the first sin. So when God had children, He should be able to give birth to a child and have pains while giving birth to his son or daughter. God, it seems to me, is a very selfish, arrogant, and dominating God and demands a lot from people. What God does not realize is that the woman did God a favor by allowing God to experience what it is like for man to live in sin when he knows and experiences what is right and wrong. The power of sin is not to destroy a person but to better help people grow in their lives; sin is nothing more than a progress where man can better understand who he is as a person separate from others.

The woman, Eve, through the inspiration of life, made God recognize that man should be given the opportunity to do wrong and be judged while doing wrong instead of creating a garden that became a vacuum of man's life, isolating him. Man, being in this world with sin, can only experience sin by living in it and committing sin. In other words, sin teaches us not to fall in love with sin or commit sin because it will cause you to die. Now again, who is God, the woman? The woman, Eve, even proves to man that she is more powerful than the God they serve. Here, man knows that he was not to eat the fruit, but instead, the woman still made man eat it. So it was the power of the woman's spirit and soul that challenged God in the Garden of Eden, and the woman became successful.

This book focuses on the woman's strength and integrity and how she has, and still, is influencing men. The one thing men need to understand is if the woman is the weaker vessel, how did she influence Adam to eat the apple. If man wanted to be the leader and dominating force in the universe and earth over the woman, he must first have enough knowledge and wisdom to know what to do as a leader in order to become the dominant force over the woman. The truth of the matter is women are truer and stronger vessels than men are because they are able to cause him to commit the so-called sin of the earth. The power of the woman is what makes man fall short of the most powerful and precious force in the universe, which some people refers to as God's grace.

If the woman makes man fall from one of the most powerful force in the universe, which is God's grace, then the woman in all creation has to be the stronger vessel of the two. When God said He was going to bring pain to the woman during childbirth, it seemed that God was jealous of the woman, proving that she was stronger than God's grace. The woman proved that when she made man eat the apple that she was more powerful than God. Now it seems to me that women who, from the Christian doctrine, were the third person to be created, she ended up being more powerful than God and man, who were created way before her. Now if God is going to get mad, frustrated, and angry about a woman and man eating a fruit, and in that fruit man can recognize what was good and evil, I need to ask God what he was hiding from man and woman. Maybe God is just a man, or more of a man than a God, who is omnipotent.

Who now is the strongest vessel? The woman who made man fall is stronger. Men, you are blaming women for the mistakes they have made instead of being responsible to yourselves for the sins you have committed when you ate the apple. It is always easier to blame someone else than to accept the fact that you might be wrong. If man thinks that he is stronger and smarter than a woman, then man is saying that he is smarter than his God, the woman. My question again goes back to the idea that maybe man also is guilty of not teaching the woman the knowledge she needed to prevent her from causing man to sin. Now if man had the knowledge and did not teach the woman of the knowledge that is of good and evil, why would the woman be blamed by God for committing a sin, when the man, Adam, did not give her, Eve, the knowledge she needed in order to prevent her from committing the sin against God.

* I would approach the sin of Adam and Eve in this manner and that is recognizing that the first sin was caused by man by not sharing information with his wife, Eve. Why is it that even in today's society, men do not want to share information with the women; even in today's society, men hide knowledge from the women. Most men who are married hide information from their wife. Most men who are successful in their marriage are the ones that share information with their wives. The men who always fail in life and blame it on the women are the ones who withhold information from their wives. When ministers preach on the Adam and Eve story they have a tendency to blame the woman for the sins of the world. Why do the preacher, and ministers do this when we as men were born from the depths of the woman's womb who in turn work very hard to first bring all men into existence through their own pain and suffering of life.

We must remember it was the man who actuality bit the apple, and so it is the man that should be responsible for biting the damn apple and the sin of the world. Now I, as a man, cannot appreciate anyone mentioning that women are the primary factor for committing sins. I do not want you to say that my mother is a sinner when in actuality it was the men that was using and controlling the world on the bite of an apple and blaming the women for that same sin. Many women do believe that they are sinners because Eve ate the apple. To me, that is man's way of oppressing the woman in the name of some God that we know that do not exist. Always remember that if God Himself had to push a baby out of his womb that was nine or ten months old, tell me, He to would also have labor pains. Now would God say that He sins and that is why He has labor pains, or is it because it would be the size of God's womb bringing birth to His child and His sins. If God was pushing eight or nine month baby out of his womb, he would be in pain also.

In order for me to understand the powers of this world and experience the woman as God, I must first cleanse myself of all of these ignorant fears and false pretenses that were obstacles placed in front of me as a man to control the minds of the women. I had to totally remove from the chamber of my inner soul all of the biases I have built up about women over the years, and reeducate myself. I now know that the power and energy of the women's soul is the authentic hands that have created me from her womb, and in her womb is where I struggle for my life with much of her help and support.

1 Peter 3:1,5

I also was led to believe that women should also be submissive to all of men's authority. Approaching and writing this book gives me a new inspiration on life as it refers to the power and energy of the women's soul. This allowed me to flush out all my negativism assumptions that I may have felt and learned as a child maturing to manhood about the true significance of a woman's life.

All of these ideas or ideologies were nothing more than theories coming from an insecure society that has denied the woman her rightful place in life as the God, that she is in her existence and is Mother Earth. As a man, I now have the opportunity to view women for who they are and respect the silent mood that created their true powers, not as a woman, but as a God. I also feel privileged to be able to tap into the woman's spiritual energy and bring it to light in this book we call *Women Are Gods*, and it is this energy that exist in the woman's soul that I refer to as the Ha'oba'cka'. The Ha'oba'cka' is what makes women the true Gods of the universe.

This is how I also know that I was inspired to write this book I call *Women Are Gods* because as I was writing this book, this book became more of my teacher than a book to me. I would sit for hours and minutes thinking about certain thoughts that transcended themselves through me from the spiritual world of my own existence about what I

idol – pretender, imposter
Hebrews 11:1 (message bible)

should be writing about in this book. I think that it is time people take a deeper look at religion in order to embrace what the truth is about women being their God.

Now what I still do not know is why me? Why was I chosen for this book? What caused me to be the one who completed this book in order for me to become a mature individual? Maybe when others read it, they too would become a nurtured individual as well. I was told that I was not the only male called to achieve this task. Many men were called; I had the courage and willpower to challenge the information I was receiving from the energy of the Ha'oba'cka'.

This information came to me without me being inspirited by any research. I was able to breathe in the cosmic air of the universe that connected me to the energy of my sprit. Here is how that happens: everyone has already experienced that energy that transcended itself into my human body, and my mind focused that energy into the transformation of the human mind. It was the human mind that helped me stay focused on the information that inspired my heart in order for me to become the author of the book called Women Are Gods. I will discuss this more in the book as you read.

What is Love?

2 Peter 3:13-15

As I search the world looking for peace, I found one thing that could solve the wars in the world today, and that is love. Many people do not appreciate love. Although love is something that we appreciate, it can bring true peace to the world as well as heal it from the pain and suffering we go through on a day-to-day basis. What this world needs is the essence and substance of what true love is.

Galatians 2:20

What is true love? True love is the ability to respect someone's personal space and build friends and enjoy the relationships that you develop with others. Now that

(#1)

The fatherly concern of God for humankind —

1 John 3:1-3

sounds like a good definition, but the truth of the matter is no one knows what true love is. Many people wrestled with the idea of what is true love but to actually define love with our actions and emotions, that is where all of the complexities lie about love. We mentioned it to make it seem that it is one of the most poetic and romantic sense of feeling still and yet no one can define what the truth is about love. If we cannot define something most of the times, how can we express it to each other?

In some cases, people would say that love is also a sacrifice of someone else's time, that they have contributed to helping others that were in need. What most people need to do in this world is to be more considerate and compassionate about other people's emotions and feelings. When people say that they love you, ask them what love means to them or how they can prove that they love you. I think what people call love is nothing more than a comfortable zone that people create with each other. The reason why I think that people cannot define love is no one knows what love is. We think more of what love represents than what we really know what love is. What people think is love is nothing more than a form of emotions that become one's security and comfort. We also share that emotion we call love with those people we live with in order to create a certain form of inner peace with ourselves. *Psalm 51:6*

People should not take advantage of others who express the virtues of love and who actually allow themselves to embrace the love that others have expressed toward them. Love is an emotion that is able to elevate both men and women on any level of their lives. Most men need that emotional expression of love, as women do. Many people might need to come out of that vacuum that they have created because they have been hurt. It is that vacuum of isolation that causes so much hate in the hearts of many other people and also toward each other. I think what I thought was true love is what I actually experienced coming from a woman; it was the first woman that defined my existence through what she was told is true love.

People must realize that human beings have one of most beautiful emotions in life, and that is the ability to express what they think is love or what we define is a love experience. We as human beings or people of the human race have such a beautiful destiny of love that we hide in the depth of our hearts. Even love can become very painful to the hearts of men and women because of so much pain and hurt that people have experienced through expressing it. It is love that has prevented people from knowing each other and caring for each other. Love is a good sense of expression because when it is expressed and received from people, it gives a person a sense of security, pride, appreciation, and love for life.

What people need to do is bring more of what they think is love to the surface of their consciousness instead of people bringing their negative feelings into the surface of their consciousness where they are responsible to express and act upon that same hate that dwells in their hearts. Also the negative emotions that people have been born with or learned, produces the passion of hate, and from the passion of hate, people judge each other. The passion of hate also feels a sense of obligation to hurt others; all hate come from people wanting to be more superior to others. Hate is first observed in the conscious mind where the energy that is the passion of that hate becomes our own reality of life that sometimes causes us to be violent. It was the hate of men that caused women not to have their rightful place in the universe as God. Even in the beauty of love, they breed a beauty of hate. The way we feel, the things that we were taught in our lives, are built on nothing but hate and how love is defined.

Most people who understand the pain and suffering that comes as an expression of love, especially when someone tries not to let others know that they are truly expressing love to them or someone else. The thing with love is it is a powerful emotion that sometimes weakens the souls of men and woman, and it is within that weakness of love that is what causes other people to hurt the ones who they are expressing love to. The world is searching for something, and that something is not God. People have been fooled by the many people who represented God. The reason why people have been fooled about religion is that the people who are preaching and teaching about the existence of God cannot even live up to God's so-called expectations of what He wants of them. It is true we do need to learn how to express that positive emotional energy called love. The energy that most men first learn to express as love comes from the expression of their mothers. The women that are the mothers of men are the first people who taught men how to love and gave them the knowledge and wisdom they needed to survive in life through love;, the egos of men are what destroy the true love of their mothers.

With love, we can begin to appreciate each other for who we are and not what people want us to be. Love is the only emotion that can change the passion of hate. Love is the only emotion that is the cure for all of mankind's hate, wars, and destructions. People have to search deep in their subconscious an energy that is translated into a powerful energy of love, that we have learned to tap into because people are constantly being polluted with the passion that causes so much hate from others and the subtle laws that dictate how society treats certain people. People need to define what love is because love is a very much indefinable emotion that is full with illusions and have no real understanding of what reality is.

The energy of love is first experienced as the power that we feel in the procreation stages of our mother's womb. If people were to express love toward each other, everyone in our social environment would benefit from it and begin to live in peace and harmony with each other. The question that comes to mind is why is it that we do not express love among each other? We as human beings have been created with a heart, a mind, a spirit, and a soul, but we cannot find within our hearts the power to heal the world of all of its pain and suffering in order to bring man and woman into a happier state of existence. Love would make us all happy enough to enjoy life and recognize the beauty and harmony that exist in life. Some people go through this life without ever experiencing what love is, and then they died. The world to me is like a dull, gloomy day, where nothing means nothing, because there is no one there to express enough love that would bring the gift of love into its own meaning and being.

When we try to define the reality of love, it seems that love came out of someone else's theory of who God actually is so the concept of God has become a hidden substitute to replace the emotion we call love, and we do

that because we were told we give God all of our love, but
still and yet we do not know what love is. Love by itself
could be defined as nothing, especially when it comes
from the heart and is expressed as an emotion of love.
Just think about it; if we exercise love, and it is just an
emotion, then, and only then, would love become nothing
to understand but an emotion. Now when we look at
God, the people who developed God as a substitute for
love gave God a character and a reason to exist. Now
the character of God was to become a reality to man,
just like man is a reality to himself. Now the character
of God became a reality to man when in actuality, how
could God exist if no one has ever seen Him before? The
theory that developed the concept of God gave people a
need to believe in God, to have faith in God, as well as
to love God. Still and yet God it seems have no real ties
to the reality of man; God to me seems to be all theory
to man and not a divine omnipotent being of love.

꙳ The people who developed God for the masses of
people to believe in also gave God a part of man's essences,
making God a reality to man, but still and yet, the reality
of God is to be better than man, but man cannot reach the
potential of the God that was created by the theologians
for the masses of people to worship. Still and yet, this God
was to be the major presence of man's existence. Now the
woman who created man is a true reality of man because

it was the woman who created man from substance and matter and then formed man into the creation of his own existence, which is a human being. There is something in the ego of man that allows man to search for something that he cannot find or comprehend to be his God. Second, this same God was also given the image to be more powerful than anything in the world. Also, this same God that man has faith in cannot be comprehended by the masses of people but still and yet, the masses of people are to also believe that this same God does exist and will save them from their sins and give them a happy place afterward that we now call heaven. Religion is like a product that is put into market for people to purchase. Some people would say that to believe in God is to have a personal relationship with God, but even in the essence of God being personal to us, we still miss something, and the thing that we miss is our personal relationship only becomes who we are to ourselves or, may I say, to yourself. Our thought magnifies the existence of a God, but it is still up to you to learn how to relate to your own pain, suffering, and happiness.

No one else knows your pain and suffering but you; think about it. How else do you know your pain? This is when you want to believe that there is a God that can heal you; trust me, it is more of your state of mind that heals you. Again, the only God men have is the woman who created them and yourself. Now think seriously about this one: who is your God? It is the woman.

Think about what you are faced with when it comes to believing in God; for example, people cannot relate to God or even comprehend where God is or who God is; God does not exist to man but man have so much images of God, and still and yet, (they do not know God.) It seems to me that God was more created by man instead of God being some omnipotent power that created man, instead of God being an actual part of man's original existence. What I believed happened was the theologians gave people a theory and concept of God and developed within that theory and concept a truth that would give people faith, hope, and belief in this divine God that does not exist or could not be comprehended. And in that need for something, that need developed a purpose for people to love and appreciate God, and that is where the theologians began to develop their theory and character of God. God's character became a true reality of man's creation. The creation of God also fulfills and accommodated the fears, the loneliness, the love, the life, and the faith people were taught to believe in when it comes to God.

Mr. Grant, what do you mean when you say that people created God in order to have something to love and worship? In other words, (God is a mythology) and not a reality of man's existence; most people who worshiped, worshiped God more as a mythology than God actually being a reality to them. God is thought of by many people, or a group of people, as someone who wanted to control the masses of people through a theory that the theologians created called God. This thought was to create some type of faith and belief, as well as hope, and most of all, that power had to be expressed to the masses of people as an omnipotent power. That power that we use as the integrity of God can never exist as a part of man's reality or even the nature of man nor can man be able to comprehend His true existence as God.

Still and yet that same power had to be become the present existence of man. The people who experience God in the flesh know that God never existed, especially the way religion seriously says He does. Most of the time, people use their own imagination to create the image of who God is to them. Do you know that God becomes more of people's imagination than He is a part of they true existence, faith, hope, belief, and life. The truth of the matter is that maybe each of us is our own God, existing in our own reality of life, and the only God that we can define is based on who we are as a person.

Do you know what is interesting about the theory of God? The people who believe in God never see him or experience the reality of his own existence and presence.) They are depending on other people's information and experiences in order to define God. No preacher in our society has seen God, ask them. Most of them would have an emotional experience about something physical, and the people who believed in God would say that it is an inspiration from God. Now ask God if He loves the people who worship him, and God would say, "I turn my back on mankind just to experience how mankind is going to lead themselves into their own state of destruction." Go ahead, ask God whether or not he loves mankind, and God would say no. As time progress, people would definitely stop believing in God and start realizing that there is a stronger essence of life that comes from within the energy of the woman's womb. That is the God that is within each and every one of us, and it is that God in us that makes us who we are today. That God within us was first created by the woman's energy and then transformed into substance and matter and then formed all of mankind into the beings that they are today. The God that is in us is the God that is more powerful than the physical manifestation of who we are. The God that the woman created in us is even more powerful than any other God in Christianity or any God that other religions created for people to have faith in, believe in.

What has happened? People view the God of Christianity as being the most powerful God that existed on earth. To some people, this is true because many people have not spent time educating themselves about the knowledge of other religious doctrine. So people only experience God through Christianity or any religious doctrine. Why is it that people do not want you to know about the God that is within you? The truth of the matter is the true Gods are the women who created every man that is in existence today. What the theologians say is that the God of religion is so powerful that He was even able to create you and me, and still and yet, we cannot comprehend his existence or had the opportunity to speak to Him because God is too important to speak and answer to the people he created. The reason why the woman is the God of the universe is because from the inner chambers of the women's womb there exists a powerful force that transcends into the transformation of every human life; it is the woman that makes nature and energy become a true reality for people to exist in. The existence of all life comes from the energy of the women's womb, and it is the soul of the woman that is the transcending force of life's procreation. That transcending force of life's procreation is the sprit and soul of the woman that is passed on to every human being that exists on this planet we call Mother Earth. It is the woman's energy that transcends and procreates the inner peace that becomes the power and energy that is man's God, or the God of man; this is all done from the inner chambers of the woman's womb, and the power that creates the energy in the women's womb is the spirit and soul of every man's existence.

Now as men and women, we must learn how to get back in touch with the God that our mothers created in us during our procreation development of life in order for us to reach our full potential as a human being. That is why I do believe that the most powerful and independent God, man, and woman have is the God that is our mother's energy that also exists within us *(The seed of Christ)* during our procreation stages in life. The God in us is the most powerful energy we have in order to develop who we are as individuals in this world today. That God that is in us is the most powerful God in the universe and earth, and the power of the human mind, which I *(abundance of the heart, the mouth speaks)* call mind transgression, is one of the most powerful force in the human body. Because the human mind (mind transgression) is able to communicate as well as control the vibration of the universe's energy and earth's gravity, this is the power that brings man and woman back to the power and energy I call the Ha'oba'cka'. The Ha'oba'cka' is the power that creates the energy that transcends itself into the women's womb to create the mind, body, and soul of man and woman from the elements of the universe's and planet Earth's gravity.

In order for people to reach their own inner peace, they have to (stop depending on a God) and start being *this belief will result in death* their own God. I believe that people feel a need to be dependent on something, whether it is a God or something as powerful as God. Still and yet people do *death statements* not have enough confidence and faith to believe that they themselves are their own God. The truth of the matter is in reality, we are our own Gods. Remember, if you are a Christian, you must first love yourself in order for you to love God, and also for God to love you. I know that our mothers have love us even when we are bad. The question I always ask is why would you love a God you never see or experience and disrespect the one that has always loved you from birth, which is your mother. To (love something without seeing it or experiencing it, that within itself is a state of ignorance, to love something you never experience or see enough of in order to believe or have faith in.) Our mother has carried us for ten months *Nope is the norm* and has always been close to us, more than God, but we reject her as our God, and that is why the world is falling apart. The only way that the world can correct itself is when men are able to accept the fact that women are their God. The idea of the God concept from the Christian perspective is to put fear in man and try to make God appealing and convincing enough for man to believe that there is a God. We believe in God based on someone else's opinion not because it is actually the right and faithful thing to do. What is your opinion about who God is, or you do not have enough self-confidence to make your opinion count about who God is? Well let me tell you, it is the woman. The women in today's society, from the Christian perspective, believe that God created them because of how we were taught as children in school; and coming into adulthood, and were taught not to believe that the woman created God, instead of God creating the man. We must remember that she is the creator and God of all men.

Think about it, could you define who God is without someone else's opinions or idea? The people that actually believe in God can actually define the existence of God or can strongly accept the fact that God either exists or not. Now the God that we believe in is the same God that sends His only begotten Son, Jesus the Christ, to be killed on a cross for the remission of the world sins just to prove what? That man or woman would and should not sin or that they should be forgiven of their sins. That in itself is not true because people are still sinning, innocent people are still dying, and wars are still going on based on other people's sins, so why did Jesus waste his time and God's by dying on a cross? What did Jesus die for on the cross in the first place? I can admit that my mother loves me, I cannot admit whether God loves me or not because I do not know if God actually exists or not; (society would indoctrinate my mind with the idea that God does exist and is all-powerful.) Now I know that I have experienced the true love of my mother, as my God.

Religion is good if you are a person that wants to be loved by a God or wants to believe that there is some force in this universe and earth that is more powerful than you are or because you feel lonely on this planet we call Mother Earth, and you are now looking for some kind of love to compensate your loneliness. Most people who want to be loved or feel loved lean toward religion with the mind-set that God will always love them unconditionally for who there are. When in actuality, these same people do not know who God really is, but they express an emotion of love for this thing we call a spirit that is God. People, we have a better chance of loving ourselves than loving a God we know nothing about. The only God I know about is the woman, who is the mother of all men.

Because I can experience her love, her touch, and most of all, her emotions, and if I need help I know my mother is always there to help me, not the God of religion. I would never experience God through the religious doctrine that

the theologians have taught the world to believe in. Why
is it that you cannot believe in God through the religious
doctrine? Here is why: most people experience God's
faith based on someone else's experiences. How many of
what we know of God is our own knowledge of Him?
Seriously, think about it; what we know of God is not our
own knowledge but from someone else's experience. Now
the other perspective is God is in the spiritual realm of
our existence, so that is why man and woman would not
experience God's presence. To experience God's presence
not true, miracles were done to authentic Gods word/religion.
is to say that dead people die and come back to life again.
The reason why people do not see people after they die
is because death is a reality only to the people that are
dead and not to those that are living. Death and God
cannot break into our solar system to reexist into our
own dimensional form of existence. The only Gods that
are in our existence that created us are the women. We
must remember that life and death only meet when they
are transcending into a different form of nature, existing
into the realms of life.

humans are emotional + love is part of it.

The thing that becomes very interesting to me is how
people live their lives trying to think about what other
people think about them when in actuality, people should
never care who love them, they should just live their life
according to the natural conditions of life, which are beauty,
serenity, and silent meditation of life. Second, people should

never express an emotion if that emotion does not know to whom it is being directed or being expressed; to love God is a misdirection of emotional feelings because people do not know who God is. Now think about it, (what does God look like) who is God? At least everyone knows what their mother looks like, who their mother is, and most of all, what she is to them. (People have faith in God because of the mystery that surrounds God)

"Mr. Grant, what do you mean when you say 'the mystery that surrounds God'?"

People have faith in God because they do not know who God is and because they never experienced this God's true presence in the flesh. For example, even if the emotional feelings of love is being expressed toward God. (People, how do we know that God does exist?)

this the day the Lord has made, so let us rejoice + be glad in it. Psalms 118:24

Please don't tell me that God exists because He created the heavens and the earth. Is that enough to define who this true power is that we call God? What happens if the same person that created the heavens and the earth also created God, and the person that created God is everyone's God? If you want to believe that God existed, tell me, people, that God existed because you spoke to Him directly or He can call me up on the phone. Please do not tell me that God exists because the Bible told us so. It is time for people to *this is like questioning God Himself, you can do it through prayer but the Holy spirit always brings you back to trusting in God + having faith in what he wants,*

question the authority of the Bible and the information *has, + continues to do in your life.*

that is in the Bible. Especially the religious information

that shapes and creates the integrity and character that

forms the sprit of God for people to believe in and worship

also. The scriptures even say it is all right to test every

spirit to prove if it is of God. When I test the sprit of my

mother, I understand the integrity and character of that

woman I call my mother; I do not understand the integrity

and character of God because I have never really spoken

to him, and I do not know what God looks like, I never

felt the energy of God. I have always seen the energy of

my mother even when she was working hard to provide a

way of life for my sisters and me.

held what is read out to scripture to prove if its from God or not.

lack of prayer life. lack of communication to his word.

We are commanded to love one another because we are able to see the other person. We cannot claim to love God who we don't see and hate the ones we see every day.

God's love. Agape.

When we talk about love, our love should be expressed

toward each other, because we understand each other. We

should express that true emotion that we call love to each

other; it is imperative that every one of us uses love to

create a better world and make people feel comfortable

with each other. If you are a person that expresses love to

people, remember that if people do not reciprocate that

love back, then do not feel rejected or feel that you are a

lost cause in this world—people hate each other because of

someone's skin color, body size, or sexual preferences.

The word says what you have done + according your.

Some people in this world reject love; the love we

express toward each other is more of an imaginary love

than a true expression of what true love really is. (No one knows what love is!) Always remember that. I believe that most people live in a mystical world when it comes to understanding what love is. The thing with love is no one knows what love is until they get their heart broken. The thing we must recognize is that love and God are emotions that society creates to make people comfortable with, it has nothing to do with experiencing what the truth of life actually is. So what happens is so many people end up living in a world of an illusion than the real world that is presented to them. That is why life itself, for some people, are so complex and difficult for other people to live and appreciate the beauty of the world. The truth of the matter is the love we feel from people is a sensation of emotions not love. What we call love is nothing more than a sense of appreciation for each other that makes us feel secure with that person or persons we are around.

People do not understand or appreciate what true love is. That is why people who always express love are the ones that get hurt in the end. The reason why people are getting hurt is we do not know nor do we understand what love is. Those people who know what true love is will tell you it is not the way society dictated true love to be. True love is a process that has the ability to first allow a person to love themselves even in the midst of what their own shortcomings are in life.

[handwritten marginalia in left margin, partially legible: "There is no other reason we have over God. He sent His only son to die on the cross to let us live... Him so we can't be forgiven. So if he forgives... that we... continue to... will do. We too must to... reach or approach to... God."]

This love that we express should even be extended into people's own shortcomings. Love is being able to appreciate someone even when you recognize and know his or her flaws in life. Love is not an emotion that will entertain you all the time to be happy, love should best be expressed in the midst of when people do not understand or appreciate it all the time. Love is being able to appreciate it even in its disappointing and sad times that love itself causes. Love is an emotion that is beautiful as well as ~~it is~~ destructive. Still and yet people cannot love those people who hate them, especially when you are able to understand the reason why people would hate you.

The one thing that brought love into existence is love comes from knowing a person by looking at them physically. The reason people love their mothers is because they know their mother, they feel the beautiful presence of their mother, they sense their mother's smell; all of this is what creates the love a person has for their mother, wife, girl, friend, or a husband has for his wife and children, son has for his mother, boyfriend has for his girlfriend. We must get to know the physical person as well as the personality of the person in order to fall in love with someone. Now when Christians ask me if I love God, I tell them I do not know God well enough to love Him, He might know me well enough to love

[handwritten at bottom: "He ~~died~~ dead for your existence"]

commandment

me, and it is His duty as God to love because He knows
me. Now God could also know me well enough to hate
me, now if God hates me, then God would not be a
God that expresses the emotions of love or would He be
a God that causes people to die and burns them in the
fire of hell.

*life, you live + you die, how you die is up to you
the bible is the word map to life. ignore it then you
will die according to the letter statement.*

Now who is that God? Again, people only know God
through other people's experience, like God's prophets
and the many stories that have supposedly taken place
that people experienced and wrote down. The question I
always ask is who is God, what is God? When I evaluate
the question, the only answer I can come up with is that
all the women are Gods, especially the mothers who
created all men from the inner chambers of their souls. All
mothers are Gods, or mothers are women who are Gods.
Love is an energy that is a transcending force that women
or mothers have that is the energy that created all men
from the authentic hands of the woman's womb. Now
who is your God? In this case, it has to be the women.

I wonder if the author ever prays?

What I always ask people is why do you want God to
love you? People, your life is not built around God loving
you, your life is built around you first loving yourself.
God is not going to stop a car from hitting you or a bullet
from killing you; if you want to avoid a bullet from killing
you, you have to love yourself enough in order to get

If I've never been about me!

*God keeps you out of these damning situations +
God forbid something happens, God gets His glory*

→ out of the situation by the seed in the person
the accident happens to. The person changes + demonstrates attributes of God.

God love everyone, no matter what condition you are in.

out of the way of the bullet. God cannot use anyone to

benefit his glory if they have not first loved themselves.

I cannot worry about people loving me because some

people do not love themselves. There are people who

enjoy being stressed out, frustrated, and angry, wanting

people to pity them and feel sorry for them, and most

of all, there are some people that when they are talking,

they always say, "I am in pain." These people who talk

constantly about being in pain, they want people to pity

them. The reason why people always complain is this is

how these people view life and themselves in life; some

people think that they have to be in pain to feel good, or

it makes God love them better than other people who are

not suffering. Where does the attitude of feeling sorry for

yourself come from? Where does the attitude of people

always in pain come from? It is a philosophical school

of theology that first developed out of Jesus the Christ's

suffering on the cross for the sins of the world. (In order

now for a person to be like Jesus the Christ, he or she

has to suffer, be in pain, live in very bad conditions like

Christ did when he was a baby being born from His

mother's womb.)

Faith is the word tells you Christ loves you.

What people need to do is stop warring whether or

not people love them or whether God even loves them.

People must first learn to love themselves and realize that

it should be people's primary goal in life, and that it is

you who have to love who you are. Loving yourself first is not being stuck-up or selfish, in order for you to know what love is, you must first love yourself. The minds that have developed through the doctrine of the Christian church come from the Christian school of theology. (What people need to do with their lives is just move on with their own lives and try to become independent enough to depend on themselves to be their own God.)

Don't rely on self, debtermented

In the process of just moving on with your life and always trying to make a positive impact in other people's lives, as well as your own life, don't feel that God wants you to love every person that you come in contact with, because He does not. God Himself does not love everyone, or maybe God understands mankind enough to know that you cannot love everyone, but we must respect everyone's individuality. People, when you love someone, you always want to be with them and make sure that they are secure, you treat them right just because you love them, and most of all, you try to enjoy their company. Now a mother's love is one of the most powerful loves in this universe and the earth. Yes, a mother's love is more powerful than God's love because a mother loves her son, even if that son is a criminal or even a cripple. The love of a mother is a strong, true expression of love, and she is always there for her family. A mother loves even when she knows the faults and flaws of her children, the mother would still love him and would still do anything for him. In essence, the mother's love is one of the strongest emotions in the world.

Do you know what is interesting about God? God's love is not as strong as a woman's love. A woman's love is more powerful than God's love. Here is why! Because for everybody that God hates or disobeys God, what does God do to them? God placed them in hell; if I am not mistaken, hell is a place that is full of burning fire. Why would God be so evil as to place someone in a place of fire just to experience their skin melting in the fire while it is burning? To me that sounds more like man's theory than God's owns theory of what sin is. Because when man sins, couldn't God, who is all-knowing, handle man's sinning a lot better than just burning him up in a leak of fire? To me, again, this does not sound like the authentic wisdom of God. Because man has sinned, is that really a good thing for a God to do to mankind, and that is just to burn man in a lake of fire, of man being able to sin. That is not a godly thing to do; I am a human being, and I know that is not right, still and yet, people feel that it is right for God to do it because He is God. Just to let you know, a woman who is a mother would never place her son in hell. Most of the time she takes him out of hell and put him in heaven, with her appreciation and power to understand love, she always save man from hell.

Even when he has sinned; now that is what you call the power of God and love.

As a matter of fact, a mothers have always been the one who had taken her son out of hell and liberated her son to become a better human being in life; most men have understood this type of lifestyle because most men would still be in hell if it was not for the woman. Although the egos of men would not allow them to admit all of woman's power and strength, we might not want to admit it, but it is the truth comes from the woman. Even, when the people in the churches turned their backs on some of the men, it was always the mothers or the women who made the contribution to place that man back on the right path. I know that because I have been there before, and it was the love of the woman that rescued me.

they do not have power to rescue, the Love that God has for you. He sends the Holy spirit down to reside in you & gives you strength to overcome any situation.

If God created what is good and evil, and it is up to man to make their choices in life, then whatever choice man makes, God should be satisfied with it. If God created good and evil, then God is responsible for man's actions of what is good and evil. People, we must make *a choice* God responsible for the choices He created in our lives. So why would God condemn man for doing evil deeds? Now in this case, the woman did not create what is good and bad. We have a tendency to blame the woman for *and she was. She did not follow God's direction.*

causing the first sin. Now if that is the case, how come
God does not have labor pains? How come God is not in
hell if He is not the doer but the creator of good and evil?
I do believe that the creator should be more responsible
for what he created as being evil than the people who
are committing the act of being evil. Why does man
accept the fact that God created evil for man to do and
made it imperative to punish man when he does evil. We
as human beings accept the idea that God can do evil,
such as burning people in hell and causing the floods
upon the earth, only because He is God. Should it be
that because we are human beings, God should have no
problems interfering with man's concerns and existence?

free will

Now should it be that because man, being human,
does not have the omnipotent wisdom as God, should
man be judged on the same level as God's divine wisdom?
But think about it, does that make it right for God to do
these things toward man? The problem with Christianity
is when you question with wisdom its foundation on how
it was built and the wisdom behind it, nothing makes
any sense. For example, or maybe you were taught like I
was, not to question God but accept everything that is of
God and everything that God does. When I do look at
this same example, everything that I say that God does is
evil toward man for some reason; it seems to be nothing
more than man's own ways of controlling the masses of

people through some type of theological message but making people feel that there is a power higher and more powerful than man, and that power is God.

Now why is it wrong for people to exercise their own freewill when God created the situation for people to have their own freewill of life. For example, if God is all-loving, why did God find it fit to inflict pain and suffering upon the woman because she ate the apple. Every child that is born of their mother's womb, the mother bears the pain of the universe and the earth that comes directly from the hands of the woman being the creator of all life. Why does God cause this type of pain on the woman because she just ate an apple? What type of a God causes such a burden on women to have children, and He did mention be fruitful and multiply. I would like to know how would God answer this question that He created, and that some women do have children without having labor pains. Now if women are able to give birth to children without having labor pains, then God who is all-knowing is a liar, because some mothers do have children without having labor pains; that is when the woman would say that she spit the baby out of her womb.

People, it was not because of the woman, Eve, who ate the apple, that she was cursed; it was because the woman was able to recognize what is Good and evil. This brings us back to the idea that knowledge is a powerful tool to have, and it is good that all women educate themselves a lot more than what society dictates of them. The woman is the first to exercise her freewill that God created for her to exercise, and as the woman exercises her freewill, maybe God got jealous and cursed the woman, afflicting her with labor pains.

Now here is a question to ask Christians, did God curse Mary for having Jesus the Christ? Now did God still love Eve although she ate that fruit? People do not place curse on people for the duration of their lives. Yes, our mother's curses at us, but our mother never places a curse on us. Now if you were my mother or I was your son, trust me, I would have made you curse a lot; that was I being a child. God does not love his enemies, so God told mankind to love his enemies. If He did like his enemies, Satan would still be in heaven. Remember, God cast Satan out of heaven; God did not turn the other cheek when Satan wanted to take over heaven. God fought against Satan and defeated Satan because if God were to turn the other cheek, God would have been in hell, and Satan would have still been in heaven.

No one loves their enemies, not even God, and that is why I am going to love people that love me. Now do I love people that God wants me to love including my enemies? No, because what God demanded of me might not be the right thing for me to do because I have to know what to do with my life. Now if what I am doing collaborates with what God wants of me to do, then I guess I am a better Christian than most people thought I am. I have to be the God of my life and not live my life the way God told me to live it. I cannot love my enemies because God wanted me to love my enemies; I have to love people who love me. Now for someone to love their enemies they have to be hypocritical person to love someone that is willing to kill you. Now even if you make an attempt to love people because you want them to love you—that is also hypocritical. People should always express love to each other because you feel like exercising that compassion of love to others, especially those that love you. Now being able to express love, that is the right thing to do because it is in our nature to be love as well as express love only to those people who love us.

The reason why people cannot express love is simple. How many people know what love is or what the expression of true love is? Some people all of their life will never experience what true love is because they are either hurt or afraid to express their love. Now most women are able to express love from the time that her child comes out of his mother's womb; the woman, in some cases, has already experience the pain and suffering that come with the integrity of love. Love is a beautiful thing, and no person or people should be denied the privilege of love. One thing for sure, many mothers never denied their children their true love. Love is one emotion that people would never experience. What I think would happen is no one would be able to define what true love really means like the woman can, but everyone knows what kindness is. People can only appreciate each other through what we experience and what we are told about what love truly is.

The Inner Chambers of the Soul

The one thing about the life we live as human beings is that in all the obstacles we face, we have to use our spiritualism to create a positive force to overcome them. This is why we have to realize that we have a strong power that the woman has created in every man in order for him to learn and overcome all of his obstacles he is face within this life. What we gathered from the inspiration of our souls allowed us to grow both spiritually and mentally. It also brings us more in tune with who we are and our inner self and strengthens our knowledge of who we are from the depths of our inner self. We can only reach this state of knowledge through the power of mind transgression and my own transmedisoul. Transmedisoul is having the understanding to bring one's own ability into perfect harmony with themselves in order for them to better have the ability to help understand one's own self. The state of transmedisoul is what I refer to as the perfect state of one's meditation, and this is where we find our own tranquility of our own inner peace. People, you would be impressed if you spent some quiet time with yourself, either in the house without anyone being home—no radio, no music. The power of who we are is best defined in the quietness of our soul. We can best define who we are as our own individual because we must first remember how to separate ourselves from others in order for us to have and understand that great power that the woman created within our sprit and soul.

When we separated ourselves from the others we recognize that there is an energy that is more powerful than our physical existence that has always existed within us, and it is that energy that best defines who we are even when we were in our mother's womb. The key to our physical life existence here on Mother Earth is to become knowledgeable enough through the insight of our wisdom to elevate ourselves into becoming our own God. I believe that the most important sin in the world, or the most important sin that God would never forgive man for, is man not being able to elevate himself into becoming his own God. We as human beings call on God for everything; God needs a break, and that is why I do believe that man must elevate himself into becoming his own God, which is our final level of spiritualism. People, remember that the only sin man can commit is not being able to seek enough knowledge in order to elevate oneself to become his or her own divine God. Man must also recognize that the most powerful force in the world is the woman, who is also his God. When one is able to elevate oneself to become their own God, this is the only way we can actually define who we are as a person, and understand the God within ourselves. This is done because it is the divine right of mankind, at one time in his existence, to elevate himself to be his own divine God and to have a complete understanding of who he is as a person. It is in the separation of oneself, being apart from others, that he or she becomes their own divine God and creator of themselves.

When people try to seek out life for their own spiritualism, they are saying it is time to seek a better way of life through experiencing their inner self. What actually happens when we seek for our inner peace is like experiencing the eyes of your soul opening up to a new perspective toward life and knowledge. People can only achieve this by first being able to wrestle with their subconsciousness and fears. As people wrestle with their own subconsciousness and fears, they begin to come into a new perspective in life, knowing who they are as individuals and, most of all, why we are here on earth. The one thing that we must recognize is it is the concept of God, life, and death that gives us our first true reflection of who we are, only in that realm of theory. But the true realm of our life is to know ourselves apart from other individuals only in the true state of reality. We as human beings should never let people define who we are. To know yourself apart from others is to recognize the responsibility of your existence and to realize that when you know who you are, you become more powerful than what people expect of you. For example, you might have a best friend or family member who might expect you to be in a certain position in life; as soon as you try to go beyond your friends and family's expectation, that is when the jealousy and hate starts to come from them. If you do not separate from others in order to understand who you are, you would use their expectations of you and that would prevent you from making progress and becoming successful in life. When you start to search your soul, it will let you know that you can go further than what people's expectations of you are in life. They key to all this is that no man would ever have inner peace if he does not accept the fact that the woman is his God. No man can find God without first trying to find himself as an individual.

Some of those fears that men hide have to do with not recognizing that our true God on earth is the women's mind, body, and soul. The more we get rid of our fears that are hidden in our subconsciousness, the brighter the light of our souls will appear and will begin to reflect who we are. As it begins to shine and glow, we can now realize that the beauty and inspiration of life will begin to unfold within who we are. This is when we can begin to realize that we are the truth and the light of our own life. This will also help us recognize that we are not the truth or the light of anyone else's life, just the light of our own life. We can never be the light and the truth of someone else's life because the nature of all of us creates within us a different perspective and focus in life. The power of knowing how to achieve in life first begins with knowing who you are in life and not what people know or think about you. To elevate oneself is to go beyond the realms of what people think of you especially if it's negative. You must take people's negatism and turn it into becoming your path to success. And continue to take the path of being your own God. When a person or people use their negatism towards you especially when you are on your own path to success. The negatism that people plays towards you, if you continue your path to achieve in your positive path to success. It is in your reflection of your positiveness that impacts the negatism that people plays before you. Do you know that through your power and positiveness without you recognizing or knowing or even having anything to do with it. Your positiveness causes them more pain and suffering that they instill towards you while you were achieving your success. Sometimes, it reciprocates back causing that person or people pain and suffering because of their jealousy towards you and it sometimes leads to their death.

Now this is when we can realize that the light that reflect the glow of our subconsciousness had now became brighter, something like a lantern upon a dark hill waiting to be shown to the world. The more we removed our fears that prevented us from recognizing who our true God is on this planet we call Mother Earth. The more we are able to penetrate the thickness of our own inner subconscious of our soul's eyes—now this is when we have to face our own subconscious fears and accept our present realities toward our own life and the true existence of our life. The power and energy that created us from the universe and planet Earth's gravity allowed us to become a man or woman woven into the web of our mother's womb, to be created as a person with a mind, body, soul, and spirit. This is done through the process of what I call Ha'o da'ne. Human beings, whether dead or alive, will always become a part of the process called the Ha'o da'ne. The Ha'o da'ne is changing something into something else that gives that thing a different nature as well as a value of life or in life. The Ha'o da'ne is the spirit or soul transcending into the substance, matter, and form, and as that energy transforms itself into the substance, matter, and form, it creates a different nature of the thing or things that the cycle of life is transforming into the existence of our life.

As the energy and spirit of man becomes woven into the web of the woman's womb to become a human being with a spiritual essence and insight, we must always remember that we were created because of the woman's energy of life. The woman's energy created you and me from the substance, matter, and form of her womb. Now this is the process the women uses in order for us to be procreated as men in our own existence of who we are and what we are and what we are to do as human beings. That man that the woman created was I being procreated from my mother's womb. For example, after I realized this as a man, I was able to face my fears head-on and remove all of my fears from the subconscious of my mind.

"Mr. Grant, how did you remove your fear?"

I had to remove my fears by first facing them. Then I had to recognize that the same energy that created me as a human being came from the woman's spirit and soul of her womb, and it was in the energy of our mother's womb that life was given to us all. It was in the woman's womb that the gravity of Mother Earth held me close together in the arms of my mother's womb for me to begin my procreation cycle. All of this happened as the energy of my mother's breath from her umbilical cord developed my spirit that is now embraced into my own human body as matter transforming into my physical existence of life.

That is why I can say that it was the woman that created me from the energy of the universe and the elements of Mother Earth. The reason that man was created from the women was to become only an instrument of nature's procreation cycle, and it is in the state of nature's procreation cycle that man's purpose and reason would be completely defined as his ability and to give the gift of life. When the the spirit and vibration of the universe influenced me to write this book, it seemed like everything came to me in a vision. I could not believe the impact this vision had on me and how it focused my mind on the topic of women being the Gods of the universe and planet Earth. This experience was different; it was like the power of the universe taking the energy of my mind, especially the part of my mind that produces the waves that cause my mind to think about the subject matter that women are Gods of the universe and planet Earth.

These waves were broken up into frequencies, and these frequencies had many messages in them that needed to be translated through the power of mind transgression. These messages came to my mind in frequency. This frequency that exists comes from the energy of the universe and the elements of the planet Earth's gravity. My mind had to comprehend all of these frequencies and translate the messages from each frequency into a written book called the Ha'oba'cka' and give it the name *Women Are Gods*.

I could now feel the inner chamber of my soul vibrating in harmony and rhythm with the universe's power and the earth's gravity; when the power of the universe and the gravity of the earth collaborated together, they created a magnetic current that held the solid matter of man's substance and formed together to help create his physical body. I could now feel my spirit begin to vibrate as it elevated from one chamber into another chamber of higher knowledge and wisdom.

Some people in this case are chosen by the universe to ignore the higher order of things, especially the knowledge and wisdom of life. This happens when men and women are in the state of energy, being transformed into the cycle of procreation to become a human being. This is what I call the power and energy of the inner chamber of the human spirit and soul. As the inner chambers of the soul and spirit begin to elevate itself in the higher consciousness of life, through knowledge and wisdom it begins to raise the curiosity of the mind's power, and it is the mind's power that becomes focused through the energy that creates the current that causes a person to elevate himself in the perfect state of mind transgression.

The process of mind transgression is to allow someone the ability to take complete control of whatever one is focusing on or wants to execute. In other words, the power of mind transgression is to allow people to better understand and control their life through the power of their mind transgression. Even when people talk or try to define what spiritualism is, they are making references to a certain process of life that they themselves want to embrace, as well as change the way that they are going about how to view their life and the people who are now around them. The power of mind transgression is being able to have a thought and not act upon that thought; also mind transgression is being able to act upon what you want to do and achieve the things you want to do. People can even use mind transgression as a tool to change the dimension and shape of something into something else. This is what I call the power of mind transgression.

"Mr. Grant, can you give us another definition to define what mind transgression actually is?"

Yes! Mind transgression is being able to us the energy of the mind's waves to elevate people or yourself to a different level of understanding through the use of energy; that energy is the process of the creation of life's own existence. This will be discussed in the later chapters. Now that energy that become the waves of our mind is the same energy of life that created all men from the woman's womb, and that same power transcends into what I call the power of man and woman's spiritualism, and it is that same energy that starts to become the light of men and women's spirit and soul.

Now when we begin to use the power of our minds to create the process of mind transgression, we begin to feel a certain vibration that is in the inner chambers of our souls. As we begin to progress on a different level of life, this is when we would begin to feel our body becoming more in tune with the earth's atmosphere. As our souls begin to develop, it brings us closer into a new spiritual world of our life's own existence, and it is that spiritual world that gives us our new self-awareness about life and enlightenment.

My self-awareness and enlightenment were enough to elevate myself on a different plane of life's existence and bring me to having a better understanding of life and our own existence. This process of life caused me, James Grant, the individual, to grow and mature into something called the power, energy, and spirit of the Ha'oba'cka'.

These are the letters that are used to create the word that I mentioned call the Ha'oba'cka'. I was told that the word itself has been inspired by the energy that surrounded our life. The word *Ha'oba'cka'* is one of the most powerful words in the universe. That power that helped created the Ha'oba'cka' is what blossoms in the fullness of all of men's spirits and souls through the inspiration of how we live our own life. These words are only sacred to the people who know them through the inspirational message of the Ha'oba'cka'. When people remove themselves from many of the religious doctrine and learn of their true inner self and peace, they can truly learn how to communicate with the powers that exist in our universe and the planet we call Mother Earth. That alone is evidence enough to let you know that the concept of God is very limited as it relates to the existence and form of all human life. People only experience the limitation and control that religions have when they begin to elevate themselves and try to grow in search of their inner peace and self-knowledge.

Now that powerful force that makes people God is a part of the Ha'oba'cka's power and energy. The power and energy of the Ha'oba'cka' is supposed to be my life and the destiny and future of my own achievements in this life. One of the thoughts that has transcended through me was to be touched with the power and energy that created me. Through the power of the Ha'oba'cka', I am able to produce the energy that I needed to focus and concentrate on in order for me to better use the process of mind transgression. What mind transgression does for many people, and for you as well, is to keep you constantly staying in touch, as well as in tune, with the power and energy that gave me the ability to become in tune with the same power and energy that created me while I was in my mother's womb. It was this power and energy from the Ha'oba'cka' that created me to be or not to be my own God of my own existence and my own life. Why do I have to depend on some God that people told me is a spirit? If God is a spirit and I have a spirit, then what makes God different than me? Because the energy that created God also created me. That being the case, I have to be my own God and salvation.

Now it is time for people to learn to be their own Gods and stop depending on someone that you do not know exists to be your own God. I was told as a young man that some God that created me never created me to be my own God, instead, this God created me to be constantly submissive to Him. My mother, who actually is my God, created me to be my own God, and I should not place any other God before me or her in order to be my God, not even the God of the heavens could be my God. The power that created God is the same power that created me and you to be the Gods of the universe and planet Earth also. You see, God did not create the power that created me, the woman created the power that created me and you, and in our mother's womb is where all men receive the gift of all life.

The questions that comes to mind is where I am going on this path of spiritualism? The spiritualism of this path was for me to define the power that created me to be my own God instead of God creating the power that created me to be me, and that me is me being just a human being. Here is how I was traveling on that path to a new enlightenment. How I was traveling, I did not know. The one thing that I know is that I had to travel the destiny of that path in order to grow and progress into my next stage of life as I mature and continue to grow in the walls of my own inner self of spiritualism.

If you are a person that wants to receive the power of the Ha'oba'cka', you have to be a person that have desired to know the truth about this things we call life instead of constantly living our life on the basis of faith, hope, belief, and prayer. If you want to know through the power of life's wisdom what the truth is about our own existence, then the Ha'oba'cka' is the power people need to get more involved with. Trust me, neither faith, hope, prayer, nor belief fit into the scope of the picture. What really fit in the frame of the picture was to have the ability to know, and knowing is where all knowledge and wisdom comes from, and that is what gives us a better way of life.

The people who are in the state of knowing and want to know—I was told that I had to be in a state of knowing. Also remember that in the state of knowing, there is a seed of wisdom that blossoms like the flowers of spring, ready to procreate the beauty of life back into the world of people's subconscious, to give birth to a new life and a new season of wisdom and knowledge. Spring is the true season of life because in spring, everything that has the essence of life blossoms into its own complete nature of life. I receive the true knowledge and wisdom of life's spiritual essence from the power of the Ha'oba'cka', and it is in this wisdom of power and life that my spiritualism elevated itself, because of the true knowledge of who I am. The knowledge of self is the foundation of it all, where you find your true self as your own God and we are to be inspired as Gods of the universe and earth, both knowing all things including the secrets of the universe and earth.

I would definitely like to make this clear, I am not a prophet, rabbi, preacher; I'm not Jesus the Christ. I am just Tabitha Grant's son. I am a human being that knows what my meaning and being actually is in this life. Each man and woman exists with a true meaning and being in life; the one thing that man has to do is search from the depths of his subconscious mind, and this brings about his true meaning and being in this life. Men can only find their true meaning and being in life through the spiritual light that burns within the human subconscious as either their spirit and soul of every man and woman. The most difficult thing in both men and women's lives is to define what our true meaning and being is in life. We are here to praise ourselves, enjoy life, as well as find out what our true meaning and being is in life. The reason people never reach this understanding is we are too busy observing ourselves through the negative things that exist in life and not in the positive things in life.

Now what makes life simple to live, even in our own existence, is when people can define their true existence, completely understanding who they are from the energy that has created them from their mother's womb. We must realize that the Ha'oba'cka' is a life force that has transcended itself into the transformation of our true existence; the energy of the Ha'oba'cka' is what makes us the God of our own existence, and that is how we can find out who we actually are in our own existence as a human being. All of who we are comes from the authentic hands of our mother's womb. The energy that comes from my mother's womb is the same energy that gave me my existence in the physical manifestation of who I am as a person. The spiritual side of every human being is the one that has been traveling the path of righteousness where I am to come into my own meaning and being from my spiritual existence. When people come into their own meaning and being, they reach the highest potential of life and self, which is to be their own God. The creation of woman's soul is what makes all men become their own spiritual beings.

"Mr. Grant, how does religion destroy the individual?"

Religion destroys the individual by making him think that there is a God in the universe and planet Earth. Religion takes people away from themselves and makes them worship a God that does not exist; the only God that exists is the one that gave you comfort in life, which, again, is the care and love our mothers have for every man. While religion is taking people away from themselves as being their own God. Now the hurt and pain that comes with religion comes because people sometimes are not capable of knowing that they are their own God and that they should be worshiping and serving no other God but the woman. This is what religion does, it takes the individual away and out of himself or herself. Religion not only takes the individual away from themselves but religion also allows the individual to deny themselves as their true God and makes him or her subservient to a God that is supposed to be the spirit and soul of man. People still do not know whether He is a spirit or a man. I would like somebody to tell me who this God is. The only thing that people know about God is that He is millions of miles away in the skies. The same God we know as a spirit has said that He already left man to suffer and saw man lead himself into his own destruction. That is some God for man to worship.

Walk Only in Your Righteous Path and No One Else's

I don't want to walk in the path of Jesus, Buddhist, Muhammad, or any of the other people who we refer to as so-called prophets. I do not even want to be referred to as a prophet. Here is why. People have more respect for other people who can convince them that they are prophets, that is someone who is called by some divine Godhead, whether that is God, Buddhist, Muhammad, or Allah, than someone like me who is only inspired by the knowledge and wisdom that my mother brought me into this world with. A lot of people in this society suffer from a lack of emotional happiness; it is sad but it's true. People are easy to manipulate through their own sense of emotions. A person's emotions sometimes weaken their sense of judgment through the concept of fear, and that is what people use to manipulate others. That is why it is easy for the theologian to give the people in this society a God-fearing theory about life, God, and death that they themselves have not even experienced. Think about how much of this God theory. Do you believe in all of it, some of it? What is acceptable to you, or do you pick and choose? Still and yet this same God that you yourself have never experienced or even seen is going to take you to heaven and forgive you of your sins. When in actuality, the only God you have seen is your mother who gave birth to you, cared for you, and for some instances, still cares for you. People, think about it!

What is happening is many people would say I am prophet; I was called by God, Buddhist, Muhammad, and Allah just to convince you that they are better to you than you are to yourself. Now anytime that you place someone above yourself, you are giving them complete control over your life, you no longer control your own life and destiny. No one should ever have that much power over your life. Think about it. Always remember that you are who you are because of who you are, not what people want you to be. Whatever you want to be in life, you can only achieve it because you want to achieve it, and that at that time, it is what you want to do for yourself. Let us be true in our judgment. The truth about life is it has nothing to do with how strong your faith is in God, Buddhist, and Muhammad, or even Allah but how much faith you have in yourself. These teachings about God and a divine creation are what these so-called prophets do teach you because they want to control your mind; the only time that you are control is when you believe in others as your God or prophet(s) instead of yourself. Now if we believe that we are our own prophet, these theologians would not be able to control the people's minds through their knowledge of theology and not God. The truth of the matter is you are what you are only to yourself because you choose to be that way to yourself. Whatever you want to do in life, you can achieve it only through your own inspiration and determination in life. No God is going to give you the determination or inspiration you need to become successful in life. In this case, it is all about you and your success and what you need to do in order to achieve your success; do not leave it up to anyone to help you achieve your success. When people know that you are serious about what you are doing, then and only then would you experience the help of others.

Some people would give these so-called prophets their land, life savings, homes, sometimes all of their assets, whatever that might be. There is nothing wrong with helping people who are honestly trying to support you through the inspiration of knowledge and life, especially when it means that you are about to become better in your wisdom and spiritualism. The only people we can refer to as prophets and God are the women who created all men to be the so-called prophets of the world that people are worshiping. What I would like to explain to people is these men are more advanced in their spiritualism and awareness than I'm in mine. These men already walked the path of their own righteousness and was successful in achieving who they really are as a person separate from other people in the world, and these are the people who have already walked in their own spiritualism and gave birth to their own meaning and being in life, and they have reached a level of a divine omnipotence that makes them their own God of their own lives.

These men became spiritually aware of themselves and, most of all, who they are. As these men became aware of themselves, they follow their own path in life, and that is what I have to do, and you and me also have to walk our own path, trying to seek who we are separate from the other people. That is why I have to also walk in my own shoes and create my own path and destiny in life. Most of people's confusion in life is because they either have someone's perspective in life or they are trying to live in someone else's image in life, and that is what adds to people's loneliness and causes them a lack of happiness.

What happens is we have a tendency to look at other people's achievements as our own achievements in life, and we feel that their achievements are inspired by God more than ours. When we do not spend time on becoming successful, we become more impressed with people's success than ours. So what we do in turn is worship them like they are our own Gods than we are ourselves. When people do that, they are actually benefiting from someone else's achievements. People should never use the fame or popularity of other people to live their own life through because in our life, we have our own destiny in life, and we have to also walk our own path in life. People have to first appreciate themselves, love and cherish who they are, in order for them to live in their own shadows, as well as know who they are. I can only live my life and my achievements through myself and my own life's destiny, I cannot perfect who I am through someone else's life. I have to live my own life through my own inspiration. I have to perfect who I am through my own life because in every man and woman's heart, there are lots of room for them to perfect themselves, so why not try to achieve that perfection that is in you and me by being who we are? The reason why we are here on earth is to recognize that even in our human existence, we are to use the wisdom that our mothers gave us to elevate ourselves into becoming our own God, creating our own divine interest in life and not forgetting the women who are the Gods of all men.

"Mr. Grant, what do you think lead these men that people call prophets to their spiritual advancement?"

Any man that knows who he is would always be successful in anything that he does or wants to do or achieve in life. The key to life is to know who you are and your inner self through the wisdom that life has bestowed upon that person or people. When people understand who they are, then, and only then, would they become successful. True success comes when a person or people have embraced the inner chambers of their soul through the knowledge and wisdom that the universe and earth have bestowed upon them. Knowledge comes from the experiences we have in life, and that is what creates the wisdom that exists in every one of us; every man's wisdom is based on what he experiences in life, and the one thing that gives us life is the woman. Knowledge, on the other hand, is information one gathers from the many experiences that people have experienced in life. The experiences of life also develop the strength of the inner self by giving the inner self enough wisdom to better judge any given situation that arises in life. The inner self is like a bright burning light that becomes the life force and energy of the human creation. That life force and energy is what I refer to as the core of the human soul and spirit that can also exist without the physical manifestation of our human bodies. That is what I call the power and energy of the Ha'oba'cka'.

Many people who were profound leaders develop their qualities as a leader through their own character and integrity; it has nothing to do with someone being chosen by some miraculous divine inspiration, it has to do with how well you know who you are and your integrity and character in life; the strength of success depends on how well you are disciplining yourself in order that you might achieve your goals in life. All of these leaders had one thing in common: they recognized who they were through the brighter light that glowed within the inner chambers of their soul, or the human soul. These leaders also recognized that at a particular time in our existence as human beings, we needed to correct the hate, pain, and suffering that people experienced as well as existed in the hearts and minds of people, and the hate, pain, and suffering that caused people to destroy each other. Most of the prophets chose not to stop even if that means that they were going to die for what they believed in. That light sends a spark that becomes a bright light of everyone's spiritualism; it also gives them the inspiration to fight for what they believed in. That light is the energy that is in the inner chamber of every human being's inner soul; that energy is the true essence and substance of everyone's energy and power. That light even transcends into our own life force that is found in the chambers of the woman's womb, where she created all men to be human beings.

The spark that becomes the power and energy of life is also the bright light of the human's souls; that is where we can feel the power of who we are, burning in the desire and compassion for us to become who we are as a person. That same light is what people mistake to be the true power of God in their soul, some people even refer to it as physically seeing God after they died and came back to what they referred to as life. That same light is the light that we experienced when we say that we died and came back.

"Mr. Grant, what do you mean when you say we see that same light when we die?"

That is the light when we die. The soul of our eyes does not experience what is going on in the physical realm of our existence. So, in turn, our eyes reflect what is going on in our human body, which we now experience as the light of our soul. Now this is the same light that is found in the inner chambers of our mother's womb;

that same light is also on the ultrasounds that the doctors take while we are in the process of becoming a potential human being in our mother's womb.

That same brighter light is the light that blossoms into the understanding of the power and energy of the human mind, body, and soul. It is that same power and energy that transcends into the transformation of what we call the human experience and existence. The creation of the human existence comes from a transcending force of energy that created every human life on this planet that we call Mother Earth. These men became martyrs because they had a certain truth that challenged the integrity and character of the political and economic system. They had a truth that caused them to be killed, or, may I say, Jesus had a certain truth that made Him a martyr, and the same people He loved are the same ones that actually killed Him. The power structure did not accept Jesus's teachings because it conflicted with the way they controlled the massive amount of people in that society.

So the power structure of society killed Him (Jesus). The people of society accepted his teachings because He brought them into the perfect knowledge and wisdom of themselves. The knowledge and wisdom of self is an awareness of who you actually are. Knowing yourself is what causes that bright light to become important in your soul. Because the persons who recognizes that light is within the subconscious of that person's heart, soul, and spirit are those people who are ready for spiritual advancement. But remember that all prophets, all Gods, all come from the authentic hands of the women's womb, including Jesus the Christ. Now ask Jesus the Christ who is his father and He would say God, but who actually created Jesus the Christ? It was his mother, Mary, who brought Jesus from energy force, into the light force, and into a human soul and spirit. The woman embraced Jesus's soul from the time He was energy and from energy to substance and from substance into matter, and then the woman took Jesus from substances, transformed him into matter, and then from matter into the form of Jesus the Christ who then became Jesus, the man.

In order for people to find their true spiritualism, we must realize that we can only learn from others who have the knowledge to give us that wisdom we need as well as teach us about our spiritualism, but the true reality of one being able to find our true spiritualism comes from that person who is walking their own path. That is why I can never walk in the same path as someone else and plus wear their own shoes nor can I believe in the existence of someone else being my God when in actuality, they have not spent enough time with me to know who I am. That is why my first God would always be my mother; I can now become my own God through the knowledge and wisdom I had to search my path for.

We as people need to stop being fooled by others who project themselves to be role models if we want to reach our own spiritualism. What people call role models are just that, role models, something rolled up to be a model that you and I are supposed to worship. Role models, they are nothing more than people who are playing a role or are all rolled up like dough in an act to impress people in society and accommodate the egos of others. What happens to most people that play the role of role models for their audience is that when they let people know that they are nothing more than human beings like them, especially when it comes to making the same mistakes that ordinary people like me and you make every day, it damages the character of the person or people acting as a role model, and society looks upon the role model now with the eyes of shame and hate, and then most of all, they are disrespected by their fans or the people whom the role models have been playing their roles for.

It is only when people realize that role models are as human as they are that people in society get upset and find excuses in their character to develop the many reasons that produce hate and shame toward their role model. Some people feel that they need to be led in order to be happy, while others become their own leaders. Some people feel that ministers are more of a God than God Himself being God toward all men. Some people even want to be led by the preacher in order to feel that they are accomplishing their own satisfaction in life. What people need to realize is that the preachers themselves are sometimes more imperfect than the members of their church. What happens is people give more credit to the preacher and the minister than to themselves. No man should treat another man better than he would treat himself. This happens more with people who are preachers and ministers because people who are just members of churches think that the ministers and preacher are the closest things to God. The truth of the matter is there is no preacher, rabbi, or minister as closer to God than any of their members. Ministers and preachers make people believe that they are closer to God than anyone else and that in order to get to God, you have to go through the preacher and minister instead of Jesus the Christ. Some people think that the ministers and preachers are God, and they treat the ministers and preachers like they are God. For some of the preachers and ministers, their members fantasize about them even when they pray to the ministers as if they are God.

It seems that some men and women prefer to be in a state of constantly praying to God for whatever they want than taking the responsibility to change their own circumstances. Some people who pray would go to the minister to get his or her approval for everything instead of having confidence in themselves to get their own approval about what people want done. People who are trying to reach a more perfect and relaxed state of spiritualism must realize that because a man is a minister, preacher, or rabbi does not mean that he or she knows what is best for you. What the power of spiritualism and Ha'oba'cka' does is allow you to connect with your inner soul; the inner soul is the resting place where the energy of the soul allows men to communicate with their own spiritualism and gives them the courage to become successful in life.

Anytime people give others that much control over their lives, they have allowed themselves to become manipulated, and now that is when people begin to control that person's or people's lives. People have so much confidence in preachers, ministers, and theologians that they have placed the preacher in their marriages and family life by giving the preacher first priority in their lives because people make the preacher and minister their own role models. That is very bad thing to do, and that is to place someone in your home situation. If the preacher is a man, what you are doing is letting the preacher be the man of your household, and the next thing that the preacher does is break up the relation, and sometimes it leads to having sex with the wife or the husband. Keep the preacher and minister from your house, learn how to solve your own problem. Now advice is OK when it is given with love and understanding. Remember, keep the preacher out of your life and learn to solve your own problem yourselves, be understanding to each other's needs and wants because role models are just that a thing rolled up to be a model, and always remember that models are not the original thing, that they represent a model that is a fake of something else.

The reason why most people's marriages are not successful is simple: they have a tendency to entertain too many people's decisions in their marriages. What makes you think that what they are saying to you is better or more profound than what you know for yourself? People must take time and try to work out their problems; if you have respect for each other, that is enough to allow anyone to have enough confidence to make whatever decisions they need in order to work things out for the better. I am not saying that you do not need support in life; I strongly believe that we all need some type of support in order to continue to travel and walk in the same path and righteousness we need but sometimes, we must recognize that a friend is better than a preacher or minister. Especially if you are married and you are looking for answers. But be very careful on who you choose to be your own supportive friend. This is why I say that the strength of it all comes from the woman, most of the time in the relationship, whatever the woman says is right and true to the situation that the man is facing.

What people need to do is constantly be in control of their lives, enough to be their own God of their life, because you are either lazy or afraid to face your own problems in life, so that is when you allow others to think for you. People need to stop complaining to God, and start doing things for themselves that would allow them not to always depend on God. People need to stop allowing their lives to be that of a burden to God because God is not listening to human beings' problems. If He did, people in today's society would not have any problems today. We as people have the knowledge to elevate oneself to be our own God, we as human beings have the same power to work things out ourselves; we need to stop thinking that we are helpless. You are your own role model, no one else. I cannot even be my own role model, I can only love and appreciate me because if I show no interest in who I am, people or God is not going to love me, what people or God would do is become critical of you.

The True Essence of God and Faith

When you pray and your prayers are not answered, the preacher always says "Have faith." But when the preacher asks you to have faith, ask him or her what should you have faith in, who you should have faith in? In other words, what you should have faith in and what the hell is faith.

"Please explain to me what faith is."

Now faith is something that breeds something called hope. What is hope? *Hope* is something that we are expecting to happen. Now when that something does not happen, what happens now to hope? Hope is now placed in the state of nothingness.

Now what about faith is something that you cannot see or experience, but look at how faith is defined: *faith* is defined as a thing that people cannot see or believe in. So if you cannot believe in something that you cannot see or experience, why would you want to have faith in it? Think about it. So why have faith when we all have the ability to know for ourselves what we need to know. What we need to know is based on research and listening. Because knowing is knowledge, and knowledge brings about wisdom, and wisdom brings about the true divine respect. It is in this state of wisdom that faith serves no other purpose but to create a lot of hope that leads to nothingness.

In other words, do not let your ministers, preacher, or even rabbis be your role model; be your own person and create your own image in life. Please do not give people that much power to dominate your life as well as control it, allow yourself the freedom to grow mentally and spiritually because that is what life is about. For example, some people might be able to identify with me on this statement, you might have friends or family that still do and say the same things that they have been talking about for many years. They have grown mentally, still discussing the things over and over. Always remember that your life is your life, and that is actually what life is. You and me in the physical manifestation of our existence are nothing but energy that transcended from the woman's womb into the creation of our physical life. That is why I would always say that the true Gods are the women because they are the creators of life and the existence of all life, nothing, including Jesus, comes into life without first the power and energy of the woman's spirit and soul.

When people realize that role models are as equal as they are in the human creation and are capable of making just as much mistakes, or even more, these people who hold role models in high expectations end up losing much respect for their role models. Even sometimes the love that the people have for their role models that they have very high expectation for, most of those people we refers to as role models. These very people even die just like you and me; there is no difference between the role models and you. Anytime you place someone in a higher position that you are, that is when you start putting out the light that shines in the dark room of your soul. Now always remember that we must respect authority because authority has its own nature of reasoning. Every time we realize that an athlete or someone that we look up to as a role model is as human as we are, we end up hating him or her, and we even lose respect for them.

That is why society gives us a God that is more powerful than you and me, still and yet, we cannot touch Him or comprehend His existence, yet you are to believe in Him, to put Him as your God. If we realize that God is as human as we are, we would not worship God as being God the all-powerful because He would become to us as being human as we are, just like the woman who is our mother. Now if God were to become a human being just like us, in the same physical existence as we are in, people would have no fear of God, most people would assume that the God in the Bible is not as powerful as the theologians teach. Again, we worshiped God out of fear and not out of faith. When people realized that God who was Jesus was in the physical existence of life, people crucified him because God being Jesus was a normal person that was not a mystery to the masses of people.

"Mr. Grant, why do people lose interest in an athlete when they find out that he or she is as human just like they are?"

People always admired the talents of other people that they can look up to. It is in some people's nature to admire the best things in life and look up to people who are talented because those people remind us of what we want to be like, we admire those people because we want to be like them instead of being ourselves. When we begin to look within our souls to start to develop our own talents that people can also admire from us, we cannot live our life in other people's shadows. The reason why God does not appear to man is simple: God is a human being just like you, and we would sacrifice our life for Him because we believe in him and make him our God. God is a man just like you and me; He eats and drinks just like you and me.

When an athlete feels like he or she has made mistakes, they are letting you know that they are also human beings just like you and me. What happens if we were to realize that God is a human being that have, and is capable, and still is making the same mistakes that all the human beings are making, would you still have faith in God, would you still worship Him every Sunday or would you say that God is as equal as you are so you cannot worship God as all-powerful anymore? Just like we are, would we now get upset and be mad at God because he is a human being like we are, or would we still have the same respect for Him as we do now? If we say that we would still worship God as the all-powerful God, why is it that we would not worship the women as our most powerful God who actually created man from her womb?

The reason that most men do not respect the women as God is simple, the women have taken the mystery of God from man because man does not relate to women as God because women are in the same physical manifestation as men, so anything to do with a divine God has no physical manifestation like men have. God can only be a spiritual being that exists as a spiritual being separate from the physical manifestation of life. Think about it! We as human beings hold high expectations for God, would we still worship God as God, or would we stop worshiping Him anymore, because we find out that God is capable of making the same mistakes as human beings? Because God who is Jesus, or Jesus who is God's son, was brought into our solar system from the inner chambers of the woman's womb, who was Jesus the Christ, God being created in the womb of a woman. This woman was a human being, and that makes God a human being and Jesus a human being.

I strongly believe that people have the ability to be as powerful as the God they believe in. Here is why. Men or women have the potential to be God because we also believe in God and you are what you believe you are, and that means a God. If man was created in the image and likeness of God, why do we look different from each other, and also, why do we have so many different blood types instead of one? We were all created from one source of energy, including God; God was created from energy just like men and women were. Image, in this case, might not mean physical appearance but a transcending force of energy that is being transformed into a human being from the inner chambers of the woman's womb.

The woman who is our God is as human as the men she created. Now the reason that the woman is not respected as the God that she is supposed to be is that she is as human as the men she created. Now we would believe in the God in the skies as being more of our God than the woman who is our true God. The mistake, I believe, that we make is we believe that a supernatural power is our own God and not the woman. Always remember that it is the theologians that created the theory of God, making God more supernatural than He really is. God is so powerful that we cannot appreciate or understand His power, God is so powerful that He does let mankind see Him in the physical manifestation of his true existence. Still and yet we have faith in the God the theologians created for us to believe in when we should have more faith in the women who created us from energy, substance, and matter.

The Elements of the Human Creation

Now we must admit that the power that transcends as the energy of man is the force that creates man's spirit and embraces that spirit by placing it into the human body of every man and woman as a life force. All of this again is achieved as a transcending force in our mother's womb. What we need to understand is energy by itself is nothing more than energy, but energy that embraces the ultraviolet rays of the sun is also able to absorb the participles of our universe and the earth's atmosphere in order to create the human body. This happens because of the magnetism and gravity that occurs in our solar system that creates the energy of life's existence, as the gravity and energy that existed, as it holds the matter together in order to form what we call the human body in our mother's womb.

It is the materials of our atmosphere, along with the earth's gravity and power of the universe, that magnetically draw all of the materials together in order to form the human existence and allow the human body to experience what the energy of life is all about. To be honest, I believe that even if God did not create man, or even if God did not exist as the God of our divine creator, the process for man's existence would still exist as long as man is able to respect the woman as his God; then and only then would man still exist as a human being? I did mention in the beginning of the book that people could talk to the universe. The universe within itself is an energy, and that energy is also transcended into our mother's womb as the energy that causes our hearts to beat in rhythm with the universe's energy, and it is from our heart that the energy that is our soul begins to slow down, and as it slows down, the matter that is the energy begin to create matter; the weight that is caused by the matter is what starts forming the human body. I know it sounds crazy, but here is how the air we breathe is nothing more than a cosmic force of energy that comes from different solar systems. That cosmic energy, as we breathe in the cosmic air, our body breaks it down in the signs of many waves; these waves translate what is going on in the universe with men and women through their own brainwaves.

Here is something that some people do not have knowledge of, and that is that human existence is of a spiritual existence, one that is created from a divine God. Some people must realize that there is more truth in the spiritual world of man being created as a form of energy in the woman's womb than by some God who created man from the nature of life. The energy of our life is what connects us to the spiritual world. Now our brainwaves are what connect us to the energy of the universe. Now the energy from the universe that also creates the waves connects with the brainwaves we have in our head. As these waves connect the universe, this gives us information that we have to decipher, and this is how some people become revealers of the hidden truth.

The hidden truth is nothing more than the reality of life's existence and how it relates to the nature of man from the wisdom of the woman. Those people who become what I call revealers of the hidden truths, I am speaking of the human body receiving messages from outside of our planet; as this energy comes into the earth's solar system, it is able to receive information from outside the earth's solar system because we breathe in the comic air or energy. This is when people are able to predict things that are going to happen in this lifetime before it truly happens. It also sends a message about what is going to happen before it happens to the energy that is embraced into the human soul and spirit.

This happens because the human body is already a transmitter and a receiver of cosmic information. People can only receive this comic information during the process of mind transgression because this is where the silent mood of life's serenity becomes a silent room of energy waiting to be explored by the human mind, body, and soul. That is why people come up with some strange ideas that later affect us or changes our teachings and philosophy. People even receive information from the gravity of the earth and the energy of the universe because they are receiving information from the universe and the earth's gravity. This is when people mention that they are in tune to the universe. People's brainwaves are the interpreter of the universe's wave and the energy of earth's gravity.

The Substance and
Essence of the Ha'oba'cka'

The substance and essence of the Ha'oba'cka' is to reclaim the true nature and existence of the woman's spiritualism. The spiritualism of the women consist of her soul, her power of her energy that have been her transcending force to procreate all men from her womb. The credit and popularity of the women's power or of the women being a powerful source of the human creation has been removed, and she has been stripped of her pride through many religious doctrines that have became a part of the educational institution that, even now, teaches our children to believe in. The reason the woman has been stripped of her pride is simple: we are living in a world that developed many religious doctrines that are very much degrading to the existence of the women, and now it is time to give back to the woman her rightful place and position in life as the true God of the universe and planet Earth. To remove the woman as the Godhead of the male existence is like taking away God from the existence of what we recognize to be our life.

I believe that is why the world is in the chaos that it is in. For example, the killings, wars, and most of all, the hate that exist around people, especially the women—how could a man hate or remove or not even recognize the woman as the true God of his existence. Remember, people, it took a lot of hate in the hearts of men to remove the woman as being the true God that they are. Because men have not given the women her rightful place as their God, and they also removed the women permanently as his God; it created in the minds of the men that removing the women from being their Gods created more chaos in the world. Men in society have replaced their true God, who is the woman, with some external God that does not exist to the capacity as the theologians say God does. If God did exist as the theologians say He does, why does God has so much ISM, CISM, theory, and theology that have created so many religions in the world and still and yet, we have one God we know nothing of, and the God we all know of, most men do not want to respect her as God.

These religions in the world have brought man outside of himself from being in tune into the inner chamber of his own spirit and soul into believing in a God that man himself has no knowledge of as being his God. The only knowledge man has of this God is what he was told by others, who were also told by others. The truth of the matter is no one knows who God actually is. The divine omnipotence of man and woman is found within the inner self, which is actually their spirit as well as their own God of existence. The God that we believe in is actually the transcending energy that comes from the energy of our mother's womb. We can only become who we are based on how well we know who we are as a person separate from others. The energy that makes us who we are is what people refer to as the spirit of God. Now that spirit of God is actually their own life energy that was created in them from the authentic hands of the woman.

Now people who believe in a Christian God theory cannot, with all of its divine omnipotence, admit that they do not understand or is able to comprehend the true teaching and existence of who God actually is and the true significance of God's true existence. What we have done is taken the concept of God from it true state, which is the woman, and placed God some place where he cannot be reached for men to comprehend. We as men cannot even comprehend with our minds, which is actually God's true existence. We cannot reach or hug Him with our hands; we cannot even love God with our hearts. How can man love God with their hearts when they have not experienced what it is to love. We cannot see God with our eyes. How much of God do we recognize that is even in the image and likeness of ourselves? The truth of the matter is we do not know. The question I ask is who is that God? That has caused men to rape the women of their identity as the true God of men. What is in the power of the name God or being able to comprehend the idea that the woman is the true God of man's life? I strongly believe that it is time to replace that reality of God with the truth concerning the women as man's true God and produce the facts that the woman is our true God.

The most interesting time I had in writing this book was how people responded to me based on my belief about this book. My belief in the book is about women being Gods and the power of the woman's inspiration and spiritualism. Here are some of the responses from people. First, many people believed that since I had such a strong and positive influence from women, that I never experienced anything positive coming from a man. Let me clarify; I have always had men in my life doing and achieving positive things. What I had to deal with was the truth about who our God is and its relation to the existence of all men and women. If we were to remove our traditional teachings, we could recognize that God has to be a woman and not a man. Women, I believe, by nature, are more spiritual than men because of how she is gifted with a respect for life and how she takes good care of life. The woman, if we are true, must admit that she takes good care of life like a God who knows how to take care of life, and this could be one of the reason that could add to God being a woman. Some of the men that I spoke to about the Ha'oba'cka' thinks that I am so naive to even think that women are Gods but still and yet, I am not naive to think that God is masculine. Still and yet, when I refer to their mothers as being a God, they accept the idea that women are Gods, as well as being very hesitant about the statement that women are Gods.

Now in most cases, men do not treat their wives and girlfriends with as much care and love as they do with their mothers. Most men do not give women the same respect as they would their mothers because if you as a man can love and respect your mother as a woman, then with every woman you meet, you should extend that same courtesy to all women; even our values as men are not the same on how we treat women. The question I would like to ask is why do most men treat the women they love with less respect than their mothers? This is because we view the woman as one thing only, and that is that she is nothing more than a sexual object. Most men do not appreciate or even understand that the women have more of a responsibility to life than just being a sexual object. The woman is a spiritual being; she is actually a human being that is a spiritual being that has a divine essence to be the God of all men through the inspiration of our life. Think about it! Women also have a spiritual connection to the reality of all of men existing, even in today's society.

The one thing that men need to do is respect all women regardless if they deserve respect or not. For example, most women cannot comprehend the idea that they are a powerful God or are spiritual and omnipotent beings like the God of the Bible. Because society has conditioned their minds to believe, and that is that the only God in existence is God of the skies, so the life conditions that they live is only how they feel and the behavior only of what they expect of themselves. Those women that do not respect themselves are the women that have adapted to the teachings of society, especially those teachings that portray as well as stigmatize the women as not being Gods. There are a lot of women who would assume that my ideas are wrong; most women cannot wrestle with the idea that they are Gods because most women are so submissive, as well as controlled and influenced by society's ways of teaching that these are the women that are cough up in the theologians' concept of who God is. These women became submissive because the theological doctrine states that they should be. Most women prefer to remove themselves from being the true God of the human creation. Now when I told my friends who are men that their wife and girlfriend have the potential to be a God, most them said, "No, women do not have that potential to be God." Now when I asked them could their mother be a God? Because she was able to transcend the power of creation from her womb in order to create life. Then when their wives or girlfriends give birth to their children, that is when the women get the same respect as their mothers as being God. Most men would admit their mothers are Gods; most men, for whatever reason, do not respect their wives or girlfriends as their God as they would their mothers.

If words could cut, I would be cut up into a millions different pieces and be cast along the Nile, still waiting for the hands of a woman to sow or bring me back to life because I know that I cannot exist unless it is through the creation of the women's mind, body, and soul. That is what many men cannot comprehend the fact that women are the true Gods of the universe and planet Earth because men cannot separate their true emotions from the true reality of life, which is, again, separating the spiritual emotions from the physical emotions we have as human beings. The problem is that I believe that men who have the idea that women are Gods are trying to understand God in the physical manifestation of life. For example, the women sometimes have more intelligence than; she breathes the same air as men and eats the same foods as men, and she gives birth to men, so why is it that the woman cannot be the God of all men and women? Why is it that men would take time to believe and have faith in a God they never eat with or even experience or see with their physical eye?

What I have come to realize is knowledge produces the wisdom man needs to remove all of his fears that prevent him from experiencing his true insecurities about life. That is why I would say that women are the Gods of the universe. Men must remove their egos from the religious doctrines because it is the egos of men that have first created their own insecurities about life. The fear that created the egos of men is that of women being the ultimate Gods of the universe. When men remove their egos and fears, they experience the beauty and harmony of life for what it truly is; and in that beauty and harmony of life, man even experiences women as being the true God that they are. Then let me ask the question of what is life? Life is allowing women to be the Gods that they actually are, and that is done through the energy of nature.

The world is truly ruled by men, but it is the women that control the four corners of the world and keep it in tune with the beauty of nature. Here is why, because it is in the power and energy of the women's soul that control the population of men that exist in this world we call Mother Earth. This is one of the reasons why women are the Gods of the universe and planet Earth, because through the woman, the population of life existence of men is controlled through the process of procreation. Also remember that it is the power of the woman's energy that brings man into existence.

Now is the time for all men to recognize the power and energy of the women, which is what made women their own God. Also, men need to recognize that there is more to a woman than just being a mother. There are more qualities to a woman than just being submissive to the authority of their husband, or any man that she created. There is more to a woman than always being dominated and passive in order to be a good woman or wife to a man. Always remember, people, who respect the women as their God, that that belief is the key to the nature of the universe. Men need to experience and see the strength and spiritualism of the women's mind, body, and soul. Men need to experience women as the God that they are. You see, it was the egos of men that have concealed the women's integrity and prevented the woman from becoming the true God that she is. Let us give the woman back her freedom as the true God of the universe and the earth.

The wars that are caused in the world are nothing more than a reflection of men's egos. The egos of men also are reflected in the many passions of hate that accrued in this world today and yesterday. Again, could it be that the reason why there are so many wars and hate in this world is because of the masculine force and personality of men. Maybe if men were to understand the silence of the women spiritualism and the warm feeling of serenity that surrounds the woman, that might remove the harsh emotional feelings that occurred in the world and its realities of the many passionate hate and wars in the world today. The mentality behind wars and hate is to have the ability to control the many people in the world. Now some men interpret strength, power, and security through the wars and hate that they created, while some interpret it as plain death to people or a nation of people that is affected by these war and hate.

So that is what contributes to a world that is populated with a lot of hate and wars, and that in itself leaves no room for sensitivity, appreciation, and love, which are some of the emotions and attributes for people who actually need a world of joy, happiness, and most of all, peace. If you do not believe me, look at the condition this world is in today, and it is going to get worst. We need to focus our emotions on the sensitivity of life, where the spiritualism of life's energy flows into the streams of developing both man and woman, or on wanting them to become a better person or people for us to appreciate and love.

The world needs to be more sensitive to the harsh conditions of its own reality before we, as men, destroy Mother Earth and her children. We as a nation of people cannot let men rule the world with their egos; we want men to rule the world with love and intelligence. If that is the case, because the egos of men produces to much hate and, most of all, much bloodshed, look at the condition our world is in today; it is all because of the male's ego.

After I have expressed my opinions on the conditions of the world, with all of its hate, war, and bloodshed, and of course, now, even when I gather the idea that women are Gods. Do you know that some people had the audacity to even go to the extreme of saying that I am gay?

It seems to me that when a man gives women the credit they deserve, many people assume that man is either gay or has an extra-sensitive emotion about himself. I hope they meet. Being happy in my own ability produces such a masterpiece about the spiritualism of the woman's soul. Just because I am a man that have brought the true attributes of women being Gods to light doesn't mean I have to be gay. Again, that is just the egos of men feeding on the ability to dominate because they do not have the ability to appreciate that level or school of thought.

The strength of a man does not always have to be forceful, as well as dominating, to be respected as the strength of a man; it could sometimes be as shallow as the oceans and sometimes be as smooth as the waves in the silence after the storm. The strength of the man does not always have to cause rough waves and uncontrollable storms. Some people strongly believe that because I have taken a look at the spiritualism of the woman, I'm gay. There has to be some soft spot somewhere in my life for me to look at women in a divine state and from a more divine perspective. I have no time to criticize the women who have the same nature as my mother, and this is the time that I need to thank my mother—who died in July of 2007, which is the same month as my birthday—for the strength that she has placed in. That has made me the man I am today. There are many literary pieces of literature on the market that have won many prizes, but the literature has degraded women. Even if it is written from a woman's perspective, even if it is written from a man's perspective; it is still degrading to the woman.

I cannot write that type of literature because there is no man or woman who is perfect, even in their own eyes but let us now elevate each other to be the Gods that we are, especially if we are taking complete responsibility of ourselves. People must realize that writing has a stronger impact on people's subconscious, and positive literature does not sell. What I am writing is for us as people to have a better understanding about the life we live through and the spiritualism of our existence, so we can take complete responsibility for who we are as a person. Positive literature can still change or, as some people would say, heal the world of its pain, and suffering. I am writing about the spiritualism of the women's spirit and soul and the power and energy that created all men from the hands of the woman's womb. This power and energy is what created the Gods and Allah of our universe and earth, and it is that energy that I call the power and energy of the Ha'oba'cka'.

Men, you need to take a look at yourself again; behind every good and perfect man, there is a better woman. It could be his wife, mother, daughter or even his sister.

Men, wake up, we are the cause of the planet shifting into damnation because our egos are becoming more destructive toward Mother Nature. Even if you take the women out of the churches, what you would have on Sunday mornings are just the ministers preaching to the pews. The ministers would have a congregation of empty pews. Women have always been the strength of any organization, such as the churches, family structure, and even in the White House. That is why women are the Gods of the universe and planet Earth.

The perception of people did not stop there; it continued. Some even took it a step further by expressing that I am using the spiritualism of the women as a God as an excuse to come out of the closet and freely express my homosexual tendency in life, that I am acting out what has been concealed in me for many years. This happens all the time because I took it upon myself to express the women's spiritualism and her manifestation as a God. Most of these statements that I have mentioned appeared on a T-shirt I did for the Million Woman March; that is still available for sale as we speak, which you can also order at the end of the book.

Society always dictates people on what they want them to know about the truth, and most of the time, what people think is the truth is actually a false pretense and not the actual truth. So what happens is that people have been brought up in a world that is influenced by a God who is masculine and not feminine, but the thing that kills me about this God is how he makes women suffer during child birth. The birth concept through the theology of God is He still knows with all His divine authenticity that women during childbirth should suffer while giving birth to their children who is Jesus the Christ or God. The one thing that I do not understand is why did God make my mother's and your mother's birth painful instead of my mother's and your mother's experience of childbirth being happy and joyful.

God himself never had the audacity to let women bring life into this world without suffering. Women who have children should enjoy having children; they should be happy, looking forward to bringing life into this world. God, with his great idea, destroyed the happiness of bringing life into this world by allowing women to suffer. To me, this is not a God who loves but a God who controls the power and freewill of people, especially the woman's. During birth, women should be allowed to have a sensation of love that comes with giving birth to a child.

That joy of love should be a feeling that women have when they are in the process of having children, because the life of a child is the gift to this world. So why should someone give the gift of life and be in so much pain, all because of God's anger of the woman eating the apple from the tree? And because of the situation in the Garden of Eden, it gives man the right to oppress the woman in God's eyes? What type of a God would want man to oppress the very women that brought him into this planet and give him life? Women are the ones who bring life into this world, why is your God of religion allowing her to suffer as she begins to give birth? What was God thinking when He made it painful for women to give birth? Life in itself is beautiful, and bringing life into this world should even be better. The giving of life should be even more beautiful than anything else in life. Why would God allow the woman to suffer? How does God allow pain and suffering to become a part of life's beauty? Again, what was God thinking? The reason why God allowed women to suffer is that God really does not know what is right for human beings; human being must know what is right for themselves because God is not a human being, as some theologians already admit to. Trust me, even God does not know what is right for you and me; we already have to know what is the right thing for yourself, you and your partner, wife, or husbands.

Women who bring life into this world should be so happy that God should allow them to have a sensation of many organism as a substitute for the pain the women suffers because she is bringing life into this world. The woman should never have to suffer when giving birth to her children. I believe that the pain of bringing life into this world has nothing to do with God cursing the woman. Because if you look at the womb verses the child, now if God was forcing a baby out of His womb, He would be in pain also because His tissue would be torn because of the pressure of forcing something out of a small hole like Gods womb.

This is a simple analogy. Look at the size of a ten- or nine-pound child coming headfirst from his mother's womb that is painful. Now, God, tell me the pain the women feel during child labor—is it because the head of the child is too big to be forced through the woman's womb or is it because you, God, decided because she ate a damn apple and so she should be in pain for eating an apple; for every child that she brings into this world, the woman has to suffer in this world. I would like to ask the theologians this question: was Mary in pain when she procreated Jesus the Christ? If Mary was in pain, then why should other women have to suffer if Mary did not suffer for having Jesus the Christ. Now if Mary, was in pain when she had Jesus, then Jesus was a sinner also.

If one woman suffers during child birth, then that should also include Mary because it seems that Mary never suffered while giving birth to Jesus the Christ. We must also remember that Jesus the Christ is also the Son of God; that is what the theologians teach the Christians. These stories of Adam and Eve are stories that the theologians use to paint an image that women in the world would never become a strong and positive image for the people in the church to admire. Always remember that the reason that these images are created is to paint pictures in the minds of people in order to develop images that people would remember although they never experienced what it is these images represents in life. Now all of this is what people would use to control the mind of the masses through the authentic words of God; these same stories that the churches have explained to the world in order to control the minds of the masses are the same stories that are going to destroy the foundation of the damn churches because people are going into a whole new set of information that is being developed into an enlightened stage of wisdom and knowledge. People are no longer depending on faith, hope, and belief to be the ultimate source of evidence to prove that the theory of God is true; what people might recognize is that the theory of God is nothing more than a theology. Men in theology or religion need to give the woman back her credit as a God, because if the woman starts to recognize the truth about God, the women would realize that they are the true Gods of the universe and men.

So any person who goes beyond the physical realm of our existence, and into the spiritual world, already knows that the spiritual world is control by men. It seems that men are the ones that are controlling how God is defined and is being interpreted to the masses of people in the physical world. So anyone who expressed that life existed in the spiritual realm of our existence had to come from the woman's soul and her spirit. We must remember that what we are told as the truth is nothing more than a fabricated lie of who God is. I believe that if people allow themselves the time to reach what they think is the truth, most of what we believe as the truth would be more of a lie than the truth.

A Path to the Inspiration of Life

Let me mention something about what many of the Christians have said about me because I had the courage to say that women are Gods and should be respected as such. I thought that would be one of the easiest things to mention about the women being the Gods that they are because the women are mothers who create all men, including Jesus the Christ, from the energy of her womb. I also believe that in the creation of life, women do not need men to begin the birth process because the same liquid or substance that man has is the same liquid and substance the women have also in her body. So if we were to view the true essence of life as a man, we might recognize that women do not need men for procreation. Think about it! When a woman is in a sexual mood, her body can produce the same substances as men to create life. That is why the woman's body is able to procreate life from the inside and not from the outside. The inside of the woman's body has a transcending energy that is able to create life. The woman's body is the true hands and essence of the human creation. What the man is used for in the cycle of procreation could be more of a little to less. Maybe we as men are also taught to believe that we play a more major role in the procreation process than we do, or maybe we as men also control the information about the procreation cycle so we mention that we as men are determine whether the child is going to be a male or female, maybe that is not true.

It has always been a mystery to me how Jesus did not need the sperm of a male to be procreated into Mary's womb. I believe that is how Jesus the Christ was born into this world and became the prophet that He is today, and that was directly from the energy of the women's womb and not from the substance of man. Why is it easy for us to accept the fact that Jesus the Christ was born from the woman's womb without any support from the man, but you do not believe me when I say that women can give birth without the support of a man's sperm?

Always remember that there are a lot of things people tell us that is not the truth, but a lie is sometimes more believable to the masses of people than the truth itself. Most people who know what I am talking about might have experienced the fact that most people believe a lie more than they would the truth. Most people in society are living their life more in a lie than the truth; that causes us to create the lies.

One thing in life that I have always done is to try not to accept what people tell me but to search for the truth in life for myself. I have always enjoyed being supportive to people and hearing their opinions because I believe that that is the human thing do and not because I want to impress people or want praise from people, it is because it is our nature to want to know the truth about our existence, God, and death. Many people have taken this to mean that I am weak or naive because of the care and love I have for people in general. I have even placed people before myself sometimes because I know that they need what I may have or what I can do for them at that time; there is nothing wrong with that because that is what being human is all about. Somehow, many people have interpreted my actions as being weak; it seems to me that there is no strength in being good and doing good. Now I have come to recognize that I can only be me, and that is to continue to help and support people but also to become more careful with my actions because that is what my inner truth is all about, and that is me being me and being supportive to others.

I have even wiped the tears from many people eyes because of the pain that people have suffered and are still suffering today. Christians even talk about compassion; some of the Christians do not have the integrity to be a person of compassion or even feel compassionate about other people's feelings and emotion because they are trying more to prove to people that they are the most perfect person in the world, more perfect than anyone else who is not a Christian. I know and have experienced what compassion is because I have exercised the acts of compassion toward other people. I gave compassion to the world that exists around me. I have fed the world around me, especially when the world was hungry. Christians, I have done all of this without wanting to step into heaven, without trying to make sure if God sees what I am doing; I gave love where love was needed, and is still needed, not because God say it was good to do so but because someone needed my love at that time I gave of myself. Or if someone needed to be felt or even want to be touched, I would even touch them.

I have come to better understand the beauty of life without expecting heaven to be my window of reward in the end. I have a question for some Christians and that is would they still believe in God if heaven was not promised to them? I know some Christians make the devil jealous because they have more of the devil in them than the devil has in him. Most of these Christians do a good job at fooling people, but remember that there is no one who is perfect, not even me; that I do know, but I am not going to make you believe that I am better than you are. If you are a person that goes to church, maybe what you should ask yourself, if you want to ask me something, how the church could lose someone like me, or young men and women like myself. What has happened is the church has never been challenged outside of God, or about God being a woman. That I have known about maybe not until now.

The People's Misconception

Why is it that when a man begins to look at a woman as a spiritual being, especially the woman who is able to transcend life into the existence of the physical world, we look at that man as being a homosexual or someone who is out of touch with reality? Now when man goes off to war and kills thousands of people, mothers and babies, he becomes a hero and a man with a strong masculine integrity, giving birth to a new life in a revolutionary sense. Think about it. Because of my position that I took as a man saying that women are human beings that are Gods to all men, I am weak and sensitive, weak and sensitive enough about life to become a homosexual. You know that is why most men end up not giving most women the respect they need as just human beings, so how could men even respect women as their Gods? Most men feel that respecting and loving a woman with as much compassion as she deserves and needs and wants is a sign of being emotionally weak and not that of being strong. One of the virtues about being a spiritual being is you have to be sensitive and compassionate to life and the truth that creates life for all of us because to destroy life is to destroy a part of your own life.

For example, the war hero is highly praised, but as time progresses, his life now dwindles in his own pain and suffering, especially the pain and suffering that he caused other people. Time heals, as well as cause, a lot of wounds; what happens is everyone loves the pride that the hero gave them, but it is the hero that suffers the most as time prolongs his life and the spiritual man reaches old age gracefully. Trust me, it takes more strength to be a spiritual being than to become a hero of violence because our environment is populated with violence. Being sensitive and compassionate about life does not make you weak; it gives you the strength to become a more of a divine inspirer, strong enough to better understand what is true about life and stand up to the principles of life whether people think that you are either right or wrong. The spiritual man knows that whatever people think about you, you still have to stay focused on developing who you are as an individual in the spiritual realm of our physical life.

Why would most men mention that I have to be a homosexual because I recognize that there is some truth that is not explained to the masses of people? Now about me being a homosexual, let me tell you something. This statement about me being a homosexual came from some Christians that I know because I mentioned that God is a woman instead of being a man. Let me explain this; I am not a homosexual nor am I bisexual. Now this is where people or some Christians become very judgmental toward me, but that is all right. When people say this to me, I have to laugh because a lot of the homosexualities that I have experienced have come from the churches, and still is in the church. I do not have the power to determine what is right and wrong. I have always said that this it is not only the Catholic church; there are a lot of other churches also. The whole church world needs to thank the Catholic church for taking the controversy away from them, but all of that is going to come out in time. People in the church know this, from the members to the musician to the pulpit: you have them in this category, even the preacher, minister, and evangelist, and you know what I am talking about, but most Christians are busy being perfect and faking who they are that they hate to open up their eyes to the truth that exists around them; the truth about the woman being God.

If you think that I am lying, then next time you go to church, look around you, observe your environment, and you would experience what I am telling you. There are some people in church that are trying to do their best; this seriously excludes them. I am talking about the Christians that are pretenders. What some Christians need to understand is that from the time that people were in the Garden of Eden, sin existed. Although man and women both have a right to make a choice, they choose the wrong path to walk in sometimes. Because we all commit sin, we recognize that sin is not a punishment; sin is a process that we learn, so we can mature into becoming a better person to ourselves and for ourselves; and if you do have faith in God, then you to can become a better Christian of God. Do not let people tell you God is going to punish you; as long as you learn from your sins, God is not going to punish you but will reward you with more praises and a longer life.

Some people choose homosexuality; those who cannot make up their mind choose bisexuality. I cannot decide for you what you should do as a person. I cannot decide for you who you should go to bed with. Still and yet, out of one topic comes a statement about my sexuality. People, let's face reality; I was told that the person who edited the Bible, King James, was a homosexual. I was told that Jesus travelled with twelve men who, out of many, were homosexuals; some people have mentioned that Jesus might be a homosexual, I was told some of the forty-six councilmen that helped edited the King James Version of the Bible were gay. I was told that some of the popes were homosexual. Now because of all this, look at the hate and misconceptions that have occurred here about people being homosexuals. It is wrong for people to hate each other because of what they believe in or write about, but still and yet, these people who are Christians are still loving the lie they blame others for as a sin. Still and yet they have a lot of hate in their hearts for other people. Hate sometimes occurs from the ignorance of people or what people think is right. The idea that what people think is right, either religiously, politically, or socially, is because men never sat down to get to know each other or talk things out among each other, and that is what created so much hate in the world today; we are too busy wanting others to be like us, and those that choose not to be like us, we hate them. I find that most of these people are religious.

Now think about it; there is only one commandment I live by, and that is treat others the way you like and want to be treated—with respect and love. Before you judge people, get to know them; in knowing them, you learn who they are, what they are. When you know who they are, then you have a right to make a conscious decision about whether you love them or not. For example, if you, or your children, were being raped by someone that broke in to your home, trust me, you will kill that person. The commandments mention that people should not kill; trust me, under certain circumstances, you will kill anyone that tried to take your life or your family's.

Here is why it is your nature to kill whether you agree to it or not, and people would kill based on the circumstances that they are faced with. People live based on the emotions of their nature, but it is the discipline of our spiritualism that allows people to make the right choice in life, whether to take someone else's life or not. We must remember that when we talk about homosexuality, we could be referring to someone in our family. When it becomes a part of our family, do we become distressed or do we now get to know the person? The example that I am trying to let people know is whether you are a Christian or not, do not judge others because of their actions because you do not know what people's circumstances are, because the person that you judge might become a child or grandchild of your own, and now the window of life is no longer viewed as judgment with punishment because we want God to punish the homosexuals with brimstone and fire. We must be careful because the people that we want God to punish might become our sons or daughters. Or someone in our family that we love might become a homosexual; when that happens, we now say that it is a behavior that needs to be understood. We need to have an open mind because we have to now come home to the behavior of a relative being a homosexual.

For example, do not judge people with AIDS, do not judge people that are crippled, do not judge people that are homosexuals, and most of all, do not judge people because of their skin color. We as a people have to share this planet we call Mother Earth. Tell me, do you hate a child based on what you think is right or wrong? to be honest with you, no one knows what is right and wrong, not even God. That is why He flooded the world at one period in time and then turned around and said He was sorry about flooding the world. People, we live this life to accommodate each other, and as long as we are living here on earth, we should enjoy each other's lives together. For example, a person would say, "I would never kill anyone, not me." But based on your life's conditions, trust me, you would kill anyone that threatened your life's security and your family's as well.

Again, just vision a child that is five years old, a son or daughter, trying to hurt or even kill you or your family.

The question comes to mind, would you actually kill someone who threatened your family although they are five years old? Only you can answer that question when you are placed in that situation. Again, what people need to do is realize that in this world, we all have to live in the essence and beauty of love, so why should we create circumstances that produce emotions of hate? We must start to love each other and learn to elevate ourselves from the hands of our own oppression by reaching into the depths of our souls and spirits to get the energy that created life on this planet we call Mother Earth and begin to produce the love we all need to become better people in life.

Many people have degraded homosexuals through their writings because lots of people know it is wrong for someone to be a homosexual, but I even become wrong in my judgment when I say that the act of homosexuality is wrong when in reality, I do not care if it is wrong or not because it does not concern me. The one thing that I do know is it is not an act that is capable of producing a physical child from birth, and from that perspective, I can make a better assessment about life based on that idea that homosexuality does not create children. Here is something to think about: if the American society was to remove people that are gay from the population of the masses, our society would have no talent, poetry, athletes, our sons and daughters, and most of all, no damn preacher, no damn minister, organist, pianos players, especially those in the church. The Bible would have never been written if it were not for homosexuals.

Remember, Christians, you brought the subject up about me being a homosexual; I am justifying your statement. I know you did not think that I was going to let you mention this to me, about me being a homosexual, and if you did not think I was going to respond to your statement, you are a damn fool. You can scare people with your God-fearing religion but not me; I have seen you for who you are and not what you want to be. There are some Christians who try to give God a good name—I love you, and you know that I love you—but for the others, stop playing with your God because you are a sinner beyond the comprehension of your own God.

I think on his note, people should wake up. I would challenge you on anything you mention about me. What I have noticed is that you, Christians, feel so righteous when talking to people about their misfortunes; with your righteous attitude, you are worse than I am and a whole lot of people you try to judge. What Christians need to do is study more about the God they believe in and talk less about people and express the love that you preach and talk about to the world. I know most Christians cannot accept the truth unless it makes you feel comfortable and relaxed. I am direct and straightforward, trust me. The truth is the truth however you say it, toss it, flip it, grow it, or even protect it. However you approach it, that is what makes the truth an honest statement of reality. What I need to ask you Christians is who are you and what are you. I already know who I am and what I represent, and if God comes back today, I would go to heaven, and most of the righteous Christians would be in hell thinking about what they did to make them go to hell.

Spiritual Mood of Serenity

Feeling, creating a mood of serenity to reach that inner peace, is even sometimes mistranslated as being feminine or having a soft side. What people do not realize is that is the peak of our spiritualism is setting and creating a mood to use the process of mind transgression to get to know our true spirit and soul. When a person says that he or she is getting in touch with their feminine side, this person is basically saying that there is a feminine side to the energy that creates our spiritualism. Again, think about it; that is why the energy of the woman is what makes them the true God of all men.

Although many people who experience the religious doctrine recognize that God is in a masculine form. Now those previous religions, during their sacrament of things, the foundation that was laid for all religions of the past God was feminine. It is amazing how people equate feminism with spiritualism; this tells me that people recognize that they have a spiritual side in them that have transcended as an energy force that seriously connect them into the spiritual world. When I mention *spiritual world*, I mean a state where the energy of the human soul exists in harmony with itself; there is no matter, just a state of consciousness of energy. As matter dies, or the physical body dies, the soul, because of its state of energy, exists as life that is transcending as one remembers its physical existence of life. That energy that creates the spiritualism of who we are comes from the inner chambers of the woman's spirit and soul. When people use feminine emotions to describe the spiritualism of an individual or themselves. When a person mentions that spiritualism is a feminine side of reality and a person is admitting that there exists an energy that keeps them in tune to the spiritual world that their soul comes from. Also, it lets me know that when a person such as a Christian calls spiritualism a feminine sense, it let me know how far removed we are from reality and ourselves.

Let me mention this, people. Christianity, in due time, is going to take more of a look at meditating and start teaching a lot more on the topics of spiritualism in order to survive as a religious movement. And oh, I forgot, those churches who do not want to let homosexuals worship in their churches trust they would have to allow homosexual to worshiping in them. Here is why. One, they are already worshiping in the churches. Second, because the hidden agenda of the church, the doctrine of the church, which we refer to as the King James Version of the Bible, was edited and written by some of the people who were homosexuals. How are you going to worship something that is the inspiration of God that was influenced by the same homosexuals that you hate and do not want to come into your churches or even be friends with your churches? It is a damn shame! God himself knows that homosexuals have contributed to lot of society's improvements and advancements. People cannot go around hating people because they do not live up to their expectation. Again, the churches have to let the homosexuals worship with them; trust me, I know.

I have not written or degraded people based on their sexual preferences because I was even told that if people think that they should remove homosexuals from the earth, we would never be able to benefit from the talent in the world. I love people based on who their are, what they represent as a person, and how they define love to be, and also based on one thing, and that is love and how a person reflects their integrity about this thing we call life and love. No man or woman is perfect; I myself am not perfect. What I do not like about some people is how they use the concept of imperfection as an excuse to continually do wrong by judging people as well as justifying that what they are doing that is wrong. Could this be right because these people who judge do not know any better, or are they trying to be more perfect than what they really are? What I do as an individual is learning from my imperfection, as well as using my imperfection to perfect myself, and that alone is what makes me and helps me to strive to be perfect because Jesus the Christ came to save the world of its sins, but this does not mean that the world stops sinning; it might mean that the world has gotten worse because most people in the world have become very judgmental.

"Did Jesus the Christ come to save the world of it sins? Then that means that I can sin all the time because God will forgive me through the shedding of Jesus the Christ's blood."

No, from my perspective, our sins are forgiven based on how much knowledge we have of that sin we committed. The other thing about sinning is it only becomes wrong when the person does not learn from their sins and continues to dwell in their sin. Now the forgiveness of sins comes when that person has matured from experience of the wrong that the sin has caused them to do. Sinning is a process where a man or a woman mature in. I have reached the conclusion that I have outgrown the sins I have committed, and I do no longer have a need for that sin because I now have enough knowledge to surpass that act that have always kept me in sin. Now the forgiveness of God toward people comes through the grace of God because when that person or people have matured from one level of sinning to another level of sinning, that is when the forgiveness of God begins to take place. Sometimes, when we sin, the reward of sinning is not always punishment but a form of progress that we have to mature in; the act of it is not to be handled with the idea of pacifying people, but it can also be a learning experience that makes us stronger.

When I was young man, I have always respected the love that was told to me about the omnipotent power of God and the love God gave to this world. I, at one time in my life, tried to give that much of myself, but the more I gave of myself to people, the more I left room for people to take advantage of me. I gave so much that I myself tried giving God back that same love He shared with the world in order to try and compensate God, but God's love would always be greater than mine. Now as one progress into the realms of life, I had to search for what the truth actually is. I did have the determination to search for the truth. Now as I search for the truth, the path of the truth took me out of the church. What I have come to understand in searching for the truth is that the truth is not found in the edifice of the church but in the edifice of the human soul, which also includes the person's mind, body, and spirit.

Now let me get back to my point about how the churches have degraded the women through their religious doctrine. Men have to give women back their rightful position as the Gods on this planet we call Mother Earth, as well as even treat them as Gods and stop mentioning that women are weak. Women are not weak; women are very strong because it was the woman who was also the mother of all of God's prophets. Also, we should stop creating negative names for women. I would like to know what is the image that the churches paint of the woman. Tell me, what is the image of the woman? Most of the time most people who are religious are not able to comprehend the spiritualism of the woman outside of their own religious doctrine. What most Christian people need to do is to stop being religious and to start being honest and truthful toward themselves. People, please be truthful to the cause of our life existence because that is what makes life more comfortable for others to enjoy and love.

The Spiritualism of Life

The only time that Christians are able to understand the power of spiritualism is if it is coming from a religious perspective; most people do not have enough confidence within themselves to recognize that the way we define God is based on a mental image of who God is, so to try to define our own spiritualism through God who is only an image and illusion of who you are. The only way that we can define *spiritualism* is by first understanding that it comes from within. People, I believe that if you do not know your inner self, or even if you do not know or understand your inner fears, then do not expect to know your inner peace or God through your own spiritualism. The key to life is knowing who you are and understanding what you want to do in life. I believe that each person's spiritualism is best defined through the way people live their lives.

I do not care how God-fearing you are or how religious you are; if you do not know yourself, you would never find the ultimate peace that is within you or that you need to understand. What most churches should do is to start preparing people to find the joy and power of their inner peace and stop trying to define inner peace through the so-called power of God. I believe that the only way people can define peace is by the path we choose to walk in life. The inner peace is the water flow of man and woman's mental state of serenity and meditation. To find inner peace is to know what true spiritualism is. The serenity of inner peace is well represented in the spirit and soul of the human being. Inner peace is recognizing that we are our own Gods, and it is in our inner chamber of our soul and spirit where the energy of life brings us closer to being the Gods we want to be in life. Remember that the God that come from my development of my inner peace represents, and would always be, me, the individual; it is in the inner peace of my existence that I actually find out who I am as the God of myself.

People who believe in a religious faith assume that religion is the only faith men and women have ever had, and that the only way to become a spiritual person is by doing good things and through some type religious faith. If people want to define their spiritualism, they have to go into the inner chamber of their soul and unlock the doors to their subconscious and begin to walk the path that leads to that individual spiritualism. People cannot find true spiritualism in a belief or a concept that some God exist in the skies and that He is willing to help you or me on a day-to-day basis. Trust me, God does not have time to be with people on a day-to-day basis. People, you have to help yourselves. The thing that people do not let others know is that from the time that man recognize the woman as his God. From the time that men come fourth from the woman's womb life become ours in the physical and spiritual world. In actuality, you have to help your own damn self in order that you or me would not become a burden to others, such as friends and family. We cannot let the conditions and circumstances of life take control over our own lives and spiritualism; we have to learn how to elevate ourselves to become our own God of our survival through the many life experiences and mistakes we make. You and I have to be stronger that we have to take complete responsibility for ourselves. The truth of the matter is all life and all truth is best understood through the experience of the inner chambers of the woman's womb, and men should be able to comprehend the existence of God through the woman's existences, because if it was not for the woman, there would not be any men living that would be able to dispute or even even prove that the woman's existence is being God. Men would not be able also to prove that God himself also existed. It is the power of the woman that allow man these privileges to exist and question the existence of God, even if man condemn her existence as the woman being God.

When we define *spiritualism*, we must recognize that it is not a feeling or an emotion; it has something to do with knowing, and knowing creates knowledge, and it is in realm of our knowledge that creates a humble integrity in a man or woman. Spiritualism helps one to elevate themselves to becoming their own God. The key to life is being your own God and to stop placing the burden on a supreme God. People have always asked the question why are we here on planet Earth. What is it that is not told to us? It is the reason why we are here, and that is to first become our own Gods.

"Mr. Grant, what do you mean by this statement that we are here to be our own Gods?"

First, when we were in a state of energy, we were Gods; we were not people. And yes, this is not our only existence; we did exist before as Gods in the state of energy, and then we were transformed into existing from our mother's womb as human beings in life.

The Power of the Human Energy and its Existence of Life

We then become challenged by becoming a human being. What I mean by being challenged is that being a human being means being limited in our own physical existence. We are not able to travel when we want to or move through the elements of the universe when we want to. Now before we were created in the inner chambers of the woman's womb, we existed as just a form of energy. Being in the state of energy, we were able to transcend and transform into different dimensions and things. One of those transcending forces is feeling the pain and hurt of getting your heart broken or being tortured, and most of all, feeling the passion, intimacy, love, and the passion of hate. We never experienced these things as Gods in the state of energy. Being in the form of a human being, we now experience these things that hurt us and cause lots of pain and suffering to us as human being. We also experience the passion of sexual love. Sexual love is the true physicalness of our own emotional love.

When we become physically manifested in the human body, we are now being challenged because of our physical existence. We must learn through all of these negative circumstances in life that we must still find room, without any excuses, to elevate ourselves back to being a God in the physical manifestation of our life's existence; and when that happens, we can elevate ourselves back into our original state of being in a state of energy. This happens through what we call death, and it is at that state of death and energy that men and women become Gods of the universe and earth. The energy of life is for all human beings to experience death; death itself is a different form of life that adopts a totally different nature of existence. The reason we remember dreams is that dreams bring us back into our original state of existence where we become conscious of who we are, before our soul was placed in our human body. For example, our highest state of existence, in the physical manifestation, to me, is being able to dream and remember what your dreams are. This should let you know that life exists beyond the physical realm of how we were taught life to be.

What people in religious faith do not understand is that the concept of knowledge that comes with one's spiritual awareness is what surpasses the education of this world and any religious doctrine that is given to mankind. One of the things that I have come to understand is the knowledge that is given to people in the Christian doctrine sounds good but in reality, it does not apply to the life of mankind. Here is why; if it did, all men would be saved; that is why God is recognized as being masculine. The closest thing we have to God is Mary who was the one that gave birth to Jesus the Christ. When someone is given the knowledge that produces wisdom, they learn how to depend on themselves. The one thing that I have come to recognize is that the people who have wisdom even recognize that God needs a break from people continually complaining about life and their problems in life and begging for some kind of assistance. Most people that have faith in God do not pray to God when things are going good in their life. God, to some Christians, is only good when they're in a position of suffering. The knowledge that produces wisdom within a person is a powerful force of energy that makes them responsible to walk in the path of the Ha'oba'cka'. The energy of the Ha'oba'cka' is more powerful than any school of religious theory or doctrine can ever produce, through the thought of mind, which you would never find at any university or college.

People must understand that the only way to receive eternal life is not through a religious belief but through knowing that when you die, you go back into your original state as being a God. Here is my definition of *eternal life*. *Eternal life* is a process of nature's way of complementing life with death. Death on the other hand is another way to say that I have evolved into a different realm of life's existence and experience, and now I am returning to being my own God in a solid state of energy that is able to leave my body. Still and yet no man can experiences life or death unless he transgresses through the mind, body, and soul of the woman.

Although some religious people do believe that the only way to receive eternal life is through Jesus the Christ. What most Christians do not know is that eternal life is offered to everyone because everyone goes back into their own state of energy and existence after death. Also, death is where we all first existed as the energy of life, way before we became into our original form as a human being; we only become a human being based on how the woman has created all men in her womb. We must now understand the importance of being open-minded because our physical existence is what creates our consciousness and awareness in the physical manifestation of our life and existence.

I have come to appreciate the idea that man cannot think about being a God if he has not understood the true power, energy, and force that have created him in the woman's womb. Also, it is the spirit and soul of the woman's womb that have breathed the breath of life into man's body. That force and energy comes from the inner chambers of the woman's soul and the beauty of her spiritual energy. In order for any man to master himself, he must first come in tune with the power and energy that have created him from his mother's womb.

Each man must master this type of teaching in order to elevate himself from this present earthly realm into another realm of life's spiritual existence. In other words, our present state of existence is here on earth, but our realm of elevation is on a different level than our existence outside of the earth's solar system. In other words, we as human beings are sharing the same space and time as other beings on this planet, but we are on different planes of our own existence, that is why sometimes, when we are walking, we feel that something either pushing us or we have the tendency to slip unexpectedly. When that happens, it means that your present space and dimension is being shared with another being who is extending in a different dimension and time where you both came into contact through the formation of matter. That is why we must remember that everything in this solar system is all controlled by the energy that created the nature of matter. Now the nature of matter is what creates our body to become a house for the human soul. We must use our own mind transgression as a process to elevate ourselves through the energy that is in the inner chambers of our soul and the energy that exists in our universe and solar system. We all are human beings with the potential to become our own primary God, but we must also give respect to the power that allowed us to be created in our mother's womb.

The Inspiration of the Woman's Energy Makes Her a God

When I mention energy that comes from the woman, I am not talking about the energy that created man from the so-called hands of a God. I'm referring to the energy that has created God into a being with a solid mass we call matter that is also from the procreation of the woman's womb. That same power that comes from the woman's womb is what also gave God the right to come into existence as a God. What happens is religious people cannot prove the existence of their God. Think about it. When a person asks a Christian a question about the existence of God, the Christian would respond, "Who created the world?" And they would say God. Then they want you and me to believe in a God with prayer and fasting, still and yet when you say you do not believe in God, most Christians use a conservative word called atheism to make you feel like you are doing something wrong or you are the closest thing to Satan while the Christians give other people the revelation that they are the purest and most divine people on the planet Earth, and only God knows the worst that they do.

Now the word *atheism* comes from *atom*; the atom is the first in existence when it comes to the creation of life. I would like to know where was the Christian during the first atom or atheist. Where was the Christian church when the first atom was created to bring life into existence? Some of the Christians would say God was the first atom that came into existence. I would say to the Christians, how did God decide how that atom is going to create Him, how did God transcend life without being able to think about life, and if God thought about life and brought it into existence, where did God's thoughts come from to create man? The reason why the question of life comes up is most people think that the energy of life was created only on earth, but the truth of the matter is that human life was created outside of our solar system and then transported into our solar system here on earth. Think about it. At this point and time, we were all created here on earth, but our true ancestors were created outside of Mother Earth from different solar systems. We sometime assume that people outside of our solar system look like they have three heads, big eyes, and long fingernails. The reason why we are given that type of a picture is it is easier for the people to accept the information about life being created some place else other than Mother Earth. People would accept life looking like it is uglier than life on earth. Why is it that life has to be ugly or less intelligent than we are in order for us to except the idea that life does exist outside of our solar system? That is because we assume again that we have all of God's intelligence and that he created us in the image and likeness of Himself. Think about it.

Remember, Christians, the King James Version of the Bible was edited in 1611. What happened to the authentic teaching of your God that you are to have faith in. Christianity is a new idea of the atom, or the energy that formed the atom that made people believe that God created all human beings. It is that same atom that created you and me from the power and energy of the woman's womb where the atom of every man is transformed into a human being. Religion, or your religious teacher, never taught you the cuneiform language of one of the original scripts. Can your ministers and preachers translate the Dead Sea Scrolls or even teach you how to translate the Dead Sea Scrolls from its original to the native tongue that you are speaking in today? Most of us do not know the Arabic or American language, so what you are being taught is a state of ignorance, with an emotional high that people refer to as Christianity. Christianity makes people a junky to stupidity. Most people in Christianity are more of a junky than the same junkies that are walking our streets today. Always remember that we all have to have a consciousness of life; we become junkies when we depend on something outside of our conscious in order to make life better and when we do want to elevate ourselves in life; but to just live life with no responsibilities, that is when we become junkies.

The Christians have always criticized people about how right they are but how right are the Christians? Now people criticize the authority of God that the Christians thought were authentic. The question comes to mind right now and that is how can someone have a belief, prayer, faith, and hope in a doctrine they cannot live up to in their lifetime; that is what I call a waste of time—to live up to certain type of knowledge you cannot comprehend with your own mind. I would tell Christians this, they are not even perfect people, every Christian or most Christians are hiding something in their life that they do not want anybody to know socially; that is why they are in a state of prejudging people. People would always sin; some people right now are sinning. No one, including myself, is perfect, but that does not give me the right to judge others and continue to do wrong. Remember in your teachings that God talked and sat among the sinners and ate and drank with the sinners. God did not turn up His face at the people; God did not even think He was better than other people. That is why most Christians cannot put themselves in God's shoes. Another thing, people believe in God just to hide their social issues; some of them want to be accepted by society. Some Christians hide their bad behavior through the positive teachings of God's word.

Now let me get back to the point about defining the power and energy that makes the women the Gods that they truly are. That same power and energy are the hands that shape man while he is inside the hands of the woman's womb to become a potential human being. That energy of the woman is what contributes to the women's spirit and soul, and that is what makes the woman the true God of love and procreation. That energy that is in our mother's womb is the same energy that helped shape and create this planet we call Mother Earth. People lack this type of knowledge: that is the same energy that is in the woman is the same energy that created the planet we call Mother Earth. That is why we need the gravity of the earth to hold us in our mother's womb while we are being created as men.

We must understand, as well as have knowledge of this type of information, that women are Gods, in order to find the truth that is within our own subconscious of life. What men and women in this society need to do is to stop limiting themselves in a state of belief, hope, faith, and prayer. What we need to do is start to elevate ourselves to become more conscious of who we are as a person existing in life in order to become survivors of our life. Because it is in the Christians' state of belief that they are able to create many theories that deal with the concept of God, again, that is why we have so many churches but no one knows what the truth is. Instead of trying to get the facts and information on the true energy that created God Himself from the woman's womb.

When I deal with the question who is God, I deal with this question because it even discusses who God actually is and His position in the universe and the planet we call Mother Earth. The truth of the matter is women are mothers that use their energy that comes from depth of their souls and spirit to create the gift of life, which are the human beings. The truth of the matter also is that is how we become who we are as individuals while we were in our mother's womb; it is all based on the woman. It is the life within the woman that makes her a true God.

I'm also able to go into the inner chamber of my life's soul and bring into existence my true nature and destiny in life. While those who have spoken about me, especially those people who do not know me but still choose to speak negative about me, have not had the courage or the opportunity to challenge their own subconsciousness, as well as their own fears, in order to find out if what they believe in is true or a man-made lie. People do not have the courage to find out who they are from a spiritual perspective, but people do have the damn courage to find a God they do not know anything about and still think that He is the most powerful being in the universe when the most powerful person in the universe is the woman who creates all of the men to be God's prophets. If people have travelled the path that I have traveled, they would experience the ignorance that have been taught to them in the world through religion. This life that we experience makes the women the true Gods of our existence, if men were honest and not dependent on their egos to dictate what they should be doing.

When we as men accept women as our true Gods, then and only then would people understand the true existence of life through the woman who is God, and they would begin to elevate the woman as the God that she has always been. Many people have talked about the woman being God, but not too many people who mention the women as being a God are able to express it entirely. People's mind is in a condition not to go beyond a certain school of thought, such as Christianity and Islam. That is why some people do not have any visions of who they are or where they are going in life. These are the people who complain and want people to have pity for them. These are the types of people that are walking a path and are still trying to find their way in life. The path that any man or woman wants to walk in should be the path for people to search for their inner soul and spirit.

Human Beings Have the Power To Be Their Own God

People do have the power to be their own God. People can become Gods by the power and energy that create mind transgression and transmedisoul. The one thing that we find very difficult to explain to people is that the mind of men and women can seriously comprehend a true reality beyond the walls and boundaries of any religion, universities, and even the life that we are presently living in now.

254 HUMAN BEINGS HAVE THE POWER TO BE THEIR OWN GOD

When people remove the wall of religion from their subconscious mind and try to go beyond the walls that religions have limited them. The reason why religions limits people's ability to think is to prevent people from becoming their own spiritual Gods, when people begin to understand that the true God in their life is themselves and not some God in the skies who is watching over them, waiting for them to make a mistake in order for them to burn in a lake of fire, they become inspired with just the gift of a better understanding toward life itself, and then they blossom into the natural order of things that causes them to better understand that life exists also within and outside of themselves. The people who went beyond the limits of what religion predicted them to know about themselves, they were able to elevate themselves to a different realm of their life's existence.

The reason why we are here is to elevate ourselves to be the Gods that we actually are, both spiritually and physically, instead of waiting for a God that we know nothing about or cannot comprehend, all because we were taught that the God in the skies is our true God. I do believe that someone created the human race, but I cannot believe that a male character achieved that task of being responsible for the human race's existence. Men and women are people who have to elevate themselves to be the Gods of the universe and planet Earth. This is the true realm of our life's existence, and that is to be our own God to ourselves and others, who need to reach that level of understanding, and to become the controller of our own life and existence.

People, ask yourselves this question, how could you be in the physical form of existence and use the spiritual world as a tool to communicate with a God you do not know anything about? The only people who should believe in God are the people who have seen Him and experienced him as God in the physical manifestation. What people do not understand is that the concept of God is only a theory that people created to fool the masses of people who actually believe in Him or God; people pray to Him, people hope for Him, and people have faith in Him. Think about it who is that God of Christianity.

When a person goes beyond all of the walls of the religious doctrine, what happens is that the true realm of life's existence becomes clear to him or her. This is the power that becomes a part of ourselves and it teaches us to become our own God. This is the potential that people are able to look forward to, and that is being able to be their own Gods. Again, when a person or people go beyond the concept and scope of God and religion, they can now recognize all of the lies that have been given to the world, again, to control the masses of people. The one thing people would never realize about themselves is that they have the potential to be their own God, but it is the fear within the teachings of religion that prevent people from becoming their own God. The many theories, and also His so-called doctrines, that helped create the image of who that God is are nothing but lies, all lies. When people go beyond the realms of religion, people begin to realize that they could become their own God, and the God that they have been worshiping all their life is actually themselves. That is why people must realize that the power and images of God's likeness is who me and you are. How does one God become so many people's images, so many people's churches' doctrine? It could be that we all become God through the powerful force that transcends from the woman's womb.

Transmedisoul comes from the power and ability to mentally transgress. I am glad that I have had that privilege to do so in my own soul. The positive thing about that is we all have the ability that is within our inner selves to use the power that allows men and women to use their mind to mentally transgress and develop themselves into the power of their own existence, which is that of being their own Gods.

The idea, the ability, of mind transgression could be achieved by anyone who is willing to burn the midnight oil that would allow a person to seek the knowledge they might need to create their own knowledge and wisdom to better understand their life. That knowledge and wisdom allow us to arrive at the true purpose of what our life's existence is all about. People who have college degrees on whatever level of their concentration need to realize that the knowledge they receive in any college or university is not enough to understand and elevate oneself as being the true God that you were created to be. Mind transgression is a personal thing that one shares quietly with themselves that would bring a person in their life to better understand one's own spiritualism of life.

"Mr. Grant, how can we be created and be a God at the same time?"

It is simple. Many people believe that because you are a human being, you cannot be a God. In other words, anything that is a part of matter cannot be a God, and some people do feel strong about that. What is never taught to us is that we are created to be Gods, not to be a human being. If men and women allow themselves to die without realizing that they were created to be Gods, then they have not achieved enough knowledge and wisdom to move on to the next stage of their spiritual existence, and sometimes, they have to come back into our solar system to relive their own experience as a human being.

Those people who do not elevate themselves as a God when they die, they will die in vain. One of the main keys to this life is to understand the person that created your energy force and bring that energy that is in you to be a potential human being. That same energy is what allows men and women to come into their own wisdom of life's understanding and the comprehension of self through their own existence in life. Being a God of yourself means being able to become very independent about life itself. For example, being a God means stop allowing people to think for you. Being your own God has nothing to do with being arrogant. It is being mature of one's self, and also being humble, being open, and helpful to people in need of your assistance. Being a God means that you should be humble enough where a child or an adult can approach you about any conversation about life. It does not mean that you are unapproachable or arrogant or better than a child or an adult, being a God of one's self is being humble and having a virtue of character.

The Power of the Ha'oba'cka'

The power that is able to create the energy that transcends into our mother's womb, that brings us into existence, is called the Ha'oba'cka'. The power of the Ha'oba'cka' is the life force of every man's creation that is found in the inner chambers of the woman's womb. The one thing that I find interesting is that people who believe in a God, or the God, would never understand the true significance of life's spiritualism as it truly is. The world that created the concept of spiritualism created spiritualism to go beyond the doctrine of Christianity, and that is because, I believe, the concept of spiritualism was created way before the

Christian-era existence. In other words, men or women cannot believe in spiritualism unless they are able to comprehend the true power that is the master of man's true creation that brings him into his own spiritualism and physical existence. That is the power that truly comes from the woman's spirit and soul.

Many men have used the religious doctrine to oppress the power that makes the woman the God that she is. So anytime a nation of people oppresses their God, especially the God of that nation of people, those people would never be liberated or be exposed to the truth they need to liberate themselves from the ignorant state that there are in. The progress of a nation depends on the love and care they have for their women. That is why the doctrine of religion needs to remove the chains that are preventing the woman's power from becoming the actual power of God. Our women, through the teachings of many religious doctrines, have now become the Gods that are oppressed. In other words, the God that the women believed in has now become her oppressor in life. This happens because men have now thought of a male concept of God. People on all levels and walks of life must give the woman back her true position as the God that she is.

In religion, we speak of a God that is supposed to create people along with the universe and planet Earth.

The one thing that we do not comprehend is what God's spirit looks like. We believe in God Almighty being a spirit, or what his actual form of existence looks like. The people who believe in the faith of God are the same people who have never seen Him. The one thing that we do not know about God is whether God is a man, but the earth is populated with people who actually believe that God is a man. So are we saying all men are Gods, or are we saying one man, who we know nothing of, is a God? If this is the case, why is the world in the chaos it is in? We have wars and hate that cause all of these wars to accrue.

I even came into a problem while trying to write this book about the true Gods on this planet are not the God thought of in the skies. While some women assume that I do not know or have enough knowledge and wisdom about women to write a book about the spiritualism and essence of a woman's creation. Some women mentioned to me that I don't have enough knowledge to write a book about women, especially about the spiritualism of the woman, to place it in a book. These same women have a difficult time experiencing their own spiritual growth as Gods because their lack of knowledge has been burning out the true flame of who God is, which is why the women reject the idea that they are Gods of the Mother Earth's universe. Then we discussed that maybe we are Gods, but with the small *g*. When I mentioned that women are Gods, trust me, it is with the capital *G* only.

When I call a woman God, the first thing I realize is that I am not a God. How can I be a God and worship the woman as a God? I sometimes say to Christians, why is it that you cannot comprehend yourself being a God that you know exist, is it because you are already worshiping a God? Some Christians are worshiping a God when actually, they are the Gods that they should be worshiping. Again, they never see or experience who the God is that they should know is God.

Many people have called me a God because of my position on spiritualism or, some would even say, because I want to be a God. Here is another statement I also entertain, and that is I cannot be a God because I am imperfect, and for me to be a God, I can only be a God to myself only and no other person. I also know that God also is imperfect in His own actions toward mankind. Because He killed the same people that He created and caused them to suffer, all because they disobeyed Him. Now if God killed people that disobeyed Him, God cannot be a God of perfections but a God who has the same human nature and instincts to do wrong and be wrong at the same time; He is judging people for their own being and doing wrong. If God is all-knowing,

God would know already who is going to disobey Him and place them in hell, why wait for generations and generations to come and go through the process of allowing people to live and die? Why not eliminate that step in order to save time, and those who are going to be faithful to Him, allow them to live on earth and then go to heaven without causing bad to influence good people.

Even when God uses Noah to drown the world, He knew that He made a mistake. What God did was, in the process of making mistakes, he tried to perfect His own mistakes by learning from them, something that most people do not admit to but judge others of it. And God never took time to complain about what He had done that was wrong. Instead, God took time to perfect His mistakes by saying, "I would allow man to fall by his own ignorance." The one thing that I want to express is that I am not writing to impress any women groups or liberated women. I'm writing to enlighten the people about the truth, and that is the woman is the true God of the human existence. Now everyone can accept what I'm writing as the truth or a different theory about the concept of God, but as long as I am able to spark your curiosity and hold your interest, I have done my job. I am not writing to start a religion or to say, follow me and I would lead you; that is not the case. As long as we can entertain each other in the words of knowledge and wisdom, that means that we have now reached the potential to create world peace and understanding.

I am writing this book to let people know that there is a deeper essence and substance to the woman than what we were told through the many religious doctrine and theories of men. The essence and substance of the woman goes way beyond the need for her to be loved, respected, motivated, and spoiled. The essence and substance of the woman's power is mostly spiritual and creative. I want to bring to the attention of my audience that we, even in our state of religious belief, overlook the true essence and substance that makes the woman the true Gods of the universe and planet Earth.

This book is written to recognize the spiritualism of the woman not to impress any woman's group, but to reach the hearts and minds of all women on any level in the world. I was not led to write this book for any woman's liberation groups because if you read the book, you would know that women are already liberated, as well as elevated to be the true Gods of the universe.

I was inspired to write this book because I was in deeper meditation; as the thoughts for this book rushed through my mind, I was bursting with the joy and inspiration to write this book. I was inspirited to write for the inspiration and betterment of man and woman to simply acknowledge the wisdom and beauty of the woman's mind, body, and soul. It seems that my inspiration was to bring the mind, body, and soul of the woman into a reality that would be expressed in a spiritual light of wisdom, knowledge, and atonement. The power of the women in this book is not expressed through any religious ideology but through the spiritual light of life's energy and wisdom.

Many women have said to me that they do not think that I have a right to produce any type of literature based on the spiritualism of the woman, especially the creation of the woman. As I started to analyze the question of the women's concern. Women that I let read the literature were shocked at the information they received and saw from the pages of the book. They said that they thought it was a book that was degrading or providing something, like a negative tone, about the power of the woman, especially on a spiritual level. I asked the question how somebody who is approaching something as positive about the power and energy of the women's spiritualism could produce something negative about the women's soul? Our society needs to tell the truth about what the woman's true identity is. By doing this, we can start to remove the veal from the many religious eyes, and people would realize that the true Gods of the universe and planet Earth are the women who are our mothers. That is why we call earth Mother Earth because she supplies all of our needs and wants. The same way the woman do on this planet we call Mother Earth. She raised men out of her womb, fed men from her breast, held men in the strength of her hands in order to protect men from any evil. Think about it!

I even had women mention to me that the Bible is a spiritual book guided by the authentic hands of God, and that is what makes it a spiritual book. So for any person to define God as a woman—that cannot be the case because the concept of God comes from the prophets of God. But all of the prophets of God came from the woman. My question to that woman is, it is not the concept of God that created the teachings of the prophets of God. It came from the woman being God. It was the concept of the woman being God that created the concept of God in the Bible as in the masculine form of existence to define who God is.

If the Bible is a so-called spiritual book, why does it violate the rights of the women? For example, many people do believe that the man carries the stronger gene because of his sperm cells, and because he is a man. Now how true is that when in actuality, the woman has the same sperm or substance that is in a man. That substance from man is embraced in the woman's womb for nine months. Now again, the woman is still being degraded as carrying the male substance for nine months in her body; she transcends and transforms the creation of life, and we still admit she has the weakest genes. The truth of the matter is the woman does not have to use the man's sperm in order for her to give birth to a child. For example, I strongly believe that women were able to give birth before man was created, but they were able to create themselves. Now here is my belief that the woman, in her desire for sexual pleasures when aroused, has the same substance and color as man's sperm; that alone is proof that the woman can reproduce by herself without man's sperm and was the first to be created. As generations skip turns, the male came into the creation of life. I also think that generation skips a turn, and during the time that it skipped a turn, the male was created. It increases the antigens and that causes man to become a part of the woman's creation. As the male child became an adult, man began to become more of the woman's creation, and that is what caused man to become more and more populated in the world. The more populated the generation, the more males become a part of life creation, and man becomes a part of life's creation. Let me elaborate about the woman; yes, it talks about the creation of man and woman and the creation as it pertains to the world. This same book we call the Bible still violates and degrades the power and energy of the woman's spirit and soul. This same book we call the Bible—the woman did not let me finish. She said, "We definitely have a need for a book like that." She said, with her own words, "I now could strongly believe you might have been inspired to write such a powerful piece of literature" because of my thought pattern and how my thoughts come together in order to write the book. This state became more of an inspiration to men, and it was through her words of inspiration that the book developed during our discussion.

The one thing that she did mention was the book was well written. She was impressed and said she loved the information in the book. She went on to mention how glad she was that a man recognized the essence and substance of the woman in the spiritual realm of life's existence. She also mentioned that for a man to recognize that much power in a woman's spiritual and physical character, he has to be in tune to a lot of knowledge, because she mentioned that no man in any church has contributed anything that powerful in words to the women of the churches.

I told her that if there were no women available to write about the power and strength of the women, it could best be accomplished by the sons or son of the woman. Who else knows about the true strength and power of the women than her sons or son? So the nature of life left it to the women's sons to write her history as a God, and that was I. The one thing that men need to realize is that mothers are women who are Gods, and their children are all children of Gods. The reason why I was able to write this literature was through the inspiration of the Ha'oba'cka' that allowed the woman to be God.

What I tried to explain to people briefly in the book also is how we first existed in the form of power and energy. That power was then transformed into a complete state of energy. Now that energy is the energy that created man from the existence and nature of life. The reason that energy was able to created man is simple; energy created man because energy always had a consciousness to create something from whatever matter embraces it. That consciousness is able to transform itself into the substance that is able to create man from the energy of life. That energy had to have a consciousness. That energy created man from the woman's womb because energy itself exists in the perfect state of a consciousness, and it is in that state of consciousness that we all exist as a living example of life's existence.

The energy of the woman is what created the man from the elements of the universe and planet Earth. Now our energy, or the energy of the woman, is like a magnetic current that draws what are needed to make up our life force and bring us into existence as human beings. All of this is done through the inspiration of our mother's spirit and soul. So the elements of the universe are what helped form and create the formation of either men and women into the energy of life. The energy that created man is a divine force that carries a spiritual energy with it that travels throughout the universe to create man from the inner chambers of the women's womb.

As the earth begins to take on its shape and form, every human being comes into existence through the authentic hands of the woman's womb. The energy of man and woman needs to be embraced into the body of a human being. This can only be achieved through the mind, body, and soul of the woman's energy. The woman is the vehicle that is constantly moving in the state of motion to bring man into a complete state of existence. The existence of man can only be a reality through the spirit and soul of the woman's womb. That is why I am proud to be influenced by the power and energy of the Ha'oba'cka'.

The Power and Energy
of the Ha'oba'cka'

What is the *Ha'oba'cka*? The *Ha'oba'cka'* is the spiritualism of the woman's spirit and soul. It is a power that has existed in the inner chamber of the woman's womb, and it is in the woman's womb that the power and energy of the Ha'oba'cka' becomes the transcending energy of life. That energy of life is what is being transformed into a human being. The power of the Ha'oba'cka' is what makes women the Gods of the human creation.

The *Ha'oba'cka'* is a transcending power that creates the force that exists as an energy that is able to transcend as a current to bring man into the true existence of life.

"Mr. Grant, how does the Ha'oba'cka' become the creation of man?"

The *Ha'oba'cka'* is the power that transcends from the authentic hands of the woman's womb in the form of energy. That energy becomes a magnetic current that pulls energy and matter together. Here is how, the power of the universe and the earth's gravity that pulls all of the elements of the universe and earth together in order to create man. Now that power, which is the universe's power and earth's gravity, is also able to transform itself into the energy that produces the substance from man and woman to create the matter needed to become the primary tool in order to create the process that causes the motion of transfiguration, which becomes a part of the human existence of life. *Transfiguration* is the basic changing of matter into a different structure of something else that something else sometimes creates—a different nature of existence and reasoning. What is most interesting is that the process of transfiguration is all defined in the woman's womb of creation and life's existences.

We must realize that the creation of all men comes from the energy of the woman's spirit and soul. It is the depths of the woman's soul that is the energy that becomes the power of the Ha'oba'cka', and it is the Ha'oba'cka' that is the energy and the spiritualism of each individual life's process of transfiguration.

It is the Ha'oba'cka' that produces the energy of life. That energy of life is created from the authentic hands of the woman's womb. That is why deep within the inner chamber of the woman's womb is a transcending force that gives birth to the energy of life that blossoms into the creation that produces the experiences one needs to exist in this life. That experience of life becomes the reality of man's own physical existences. Now let me further elaborate on the Ha'oba'cka' by breaking each word down that created and formed the concept of the word the *Ha'oba'cka'*.

H is for the heavens; *A* is for the smallest atom that created man from the authentic hands of the woman's womb; *O* is a representation of the omega, *B* is for the black hole in our universe that takes men and women into a dimension of time, space, matter, and existence; *A* again is for the alpha of man's and woman's existence when they were in the form of power waiting to be transformed into a state of energy that creates man from the woman's authentic womb; *C* is the energy that comes from the inner chambers of the woman's womb to create man from the very essence of life's substance, matter, and form.

K is for the power of knowledge that the woman teaches the man in his childhood years in order that he might become a powerful human being that is fully complete with knowledge and wisdom. The true reality of life comes in the state of knowledge and wisdom. There is a vision that comes into a man's spirit that makes that man realize that when people have knowledge and wisdom, they no longer have a need to pray, have faith, hope, and believe, but they have time to elevate themselves and become their own God. This knowledge and wisdom is what I used to elevate all men into becoming their own Gods. And *A* is for the atmosphere that forms us from the elements of Mother Earth and the energy of the air, which is the spirit of man and the soul of woman's nature.

The *H* is a representation of our heavens, from which we originated from while we were in the state of complete energy without our physical bodies. This is before we used the women's womb as our gateway to our planet we call Mother Earth. Before the planet Earth was formed, and the energy of our souls were placed in the human body from our mother's womb, our souls came into existence from the Sirius constellation. As time provided us with the information we needed to prove that space traveling existed billions and billions of years ago, before we arrived in our present form of existence that we are in right now as men and women. We were truly in the heavens existing as energy. Some of us, depending on what dimension we were in, had to survive as a solid mass or matter or a spiritual form of energy.

The *A* is a representation of the alpha. The *alpha* in this case means the beginning of our present existence here on earth. It also has a reference to the idea that the pathway of our existence from energy to substance to matter to form and then to a potential living soul is all accomplished through the spirit and soul of the woman's womb. It is through this process of life's energy that the integrity of man and woman exists, waiting to be concealed in the human body. This is why women are rewarded beyond their natural state of existence as a human being, transforming into a natural being as a God because women carried with them natural energy that is capable of transforming life from an energy force into a natural human force. That is why men all over the world have to admire their mothers, not only out of love but also out of the power that our mothers have in order to create the human existences of life, which comes from the power and energy of the women's sprit and soul.

The *O* is a representation of the Oha'nda'. The Oha'nda' is to let us know who we are through our acquired knowledge of our inner self or, as I would say, the subconscious of the inner self. Our power of self comes through the knowledge that produces the wisdom that creates our own inner self. This is how we start to develop in the inner chambers of the woman's soul. The chamber of the soul is the level or steps people advance to. The more advanced we become of our self, the stronger we develop to become our own individual selves that transcends us into becoming Gods.

When we completed this journey in the state of the Oha'nda', we are moving from the physical death into the spiritual realm of our existence. Death, as it is to us, is a step back into our original state of existence, which is the state of energy. Death means that we have completed this journey here in the physical life, but death in the physical life is not the end of men and women. Existence of our energy, which is the soul, continues into the realms of creation. Now the soul is, and has always been, the energy of the human existence. The soul is the energy that shows itself on every mother's ultrasound test or, as most people would refer to, the heartbeat of life. When we are able to look at the heart when it is in the state of its ultrasound, it has not formed enough matter in order to become the heart of man. As matter forms around the energy of the heart, it begins to beat and create the human body.

The Oha'nda' is the completion of 360 degrees of physical knowledge that we have completed while on the planet we call Mother Earth. The question that we all should ask ourselves as we progress in life, especially from our childhood into our adulthood, is why are we here? Why are we in the physical state of our existence, and why earth? Second is, when the tides of life become very difficult for us to face, and when this life begins to challenge the integrity of each individuals hearts, the path of life makes it difficult for people to bear. This is when people ask the question of why we are here on this planet. The one thing that human beings need to understand is that they have within their subconscious a spiritual power of energy that manifests itself through the vibration of the human soul and spirit that would create a positive change in our life.

That in itself is what brings men and women into their own self-awareness through a certain power call mind transgression. What is mind transgression? *Mind transgression* is a process that produces or is complete when men or women uses the transmedisoul to elevate themselves from the planet we call Mother Earth. People have within their own ability the free mental will to elevate themselves from the planet

Earth into the skies. So if we do not like it on this planet, we can then elevate ourselves from the planet we call Mother Earth, but all of this knowledge was lost; this was the kind of knowledge that people were cable of achieving through their own knowledge and wisdom. People were able to go into their inner self and transcend into nothing but energy for someone to descend himself or herself to heaven by breaking the laws of gravity through eliminating the physical body, which is the matter of the human creation. That is why when we die, our energy, which is the soul, continues to go beyond the earth's atmosphere, and it is there that it awaits a new human body for existence; that same energy again transcends into another woman's womb.

Now the reason why we are on this planet we call Mother Earth is simple; we have to choose the right information that would elevate us from the planet Earth and that is why it is important for all men and women to stay in tune with anything that would help us expand our knowledge and wisdom. Many people choose death as a way out because they forget how to use their knowledge as a means that we need in order to elevate ourselves to move on a different plane of knowledge and wisdom.

This is one choice I know that would hurt me because people do have the potential to elevate themselves from this planet by allowing the soul and spirit of an individual to leave the body and come back into the present body. But through the power of mind transgression, people can elevate themselves by breaking the laws of gravity and descending into the heavens. People in today's society do descend into the heavens. We call it dreaming. In our dreams, we are supposed to be unconscious, but people remember everything in their dreams. Why is that? It is because the spirit and soul travel as a consciousness of energy that allows human being to remember they dream.

There is another approach toward leaving the earth, and that is like how our original ancestors did it. They did it by using the power of mind transgression to concentrate on the power within themselves and bring about the processing of our self-energy that is in our bodies to develop a consciousness of energy that would become what the mind needed to create our true process of transmedisoul existence.

Mind transgression is using the energy of the mind to concentrate and focus on the energy that is the bright light of the inner chambers of our souls. The bright light of the soul is the consciousness of self or, as I would say, the inner core of the human's soul. The spirit is the physical energy that creates the thought one needs to transcend into their soul in order to bring their physical being in their own life's energy. This means that the individual must use his or her mind to go within his or her inner self by a process called transmedisoul. *Transmedisoul* is the process that the mind uses to travel the path in a state of motion. This motion creates an energy wave that brings the individual's own mind into a perfect state of meditation that begins to break down the physical matter into its own state called energy.

As the mind begins to meditate, it takes the weight of the body into another dimension where the physical body, through meditation, becomes light, sometimes weighing less than a bird's feathers. The ideas in the mind are causing the human body to become like a bird's feathers. This is what I call the energy of the burning soul of the human being, and it is also the perfect state of human purity. The energy of the burning soul is the power in the human body, where it all takes place of man being in tune with the energy and power that brought him or her into the experience of being a man or a woman. This is also the main source of where it all takes place, creation and life existing as one through the human body, and it allows man to find as well as fashion the essence and substance of his or her true self and life. All of this is achieved through the power of mind transgression and transmedisoul. We must remember that all lives begin in the authentic hands of the women's womb.

The main reason why people should learn how to use the power of mind transgression and transmedisoul is that this is the power that brings men and women into the most divine and omnipotent state that they can ever achieve here on the planet we call Mother Earth. The power that is created through transmedisoul and mind transgression is what is used to elevate man from his original state as a human being into a God. The only way that man can become a God is by first mastering and knowing himself or trying to learn things that teach him more about who he is as a person. The first thing one must experience is being able to spend time with yourself and communicate with yourself. All of this is in the power and energy of what I call the *Ha'oba'cka'*.

"Mr. Grant, why should we become a God?"

We are here on planet Earth to prove through the power of the Ha'oba'cka', that man in his state of confusion and sin can still become a God. Even as man becomes limited by his or her physical body, both men and women can still fight the odds of the earth's gravity and become elevated because in the subconscious of the soul, all men and women have the potential to be their own God. Women are created as Gods; men have to earn that gift of being a God, and man can only become a God when he first realizes that the woman is already his

God, and it is in the wealth of knowledge that a man can become his own God. As quiet as it is kept, it is in our nature to prove what our talents are, especially if our talents are being developed for us to achieve our potential as Gods. In doing that, we, as human beings, can elevate ourselves into being in a more godly and divine state of our existence, where we can help others to be their own God through their own talents.

The *B* is a representation of the black holes that exist in our universe. These black holes, as Mother Earth rotates at a certain speed and time, people in planes, boats, even rockets, are pulled into these black holes and taken into a totally different dimension because of the powerful current that are in these black holes. These holes are sometimes used to keep the Earth aborting at a certain speed. It is also in tune with the gravity of the earth's vibration and the power of the universe's atmosphere. The black holes exist to also take people into a different dimension and time. Some of the people who have had the opportunity to experience being pulled into through the black holes have returned to Mother Earth's existence. These people have developed their third senses of power and mental telepathy that is beyond our present existence.

Most of the people who had the opportunity to go into these black holes that were Christians—when they came out, most of them became atheists and had a stronger perspective on life. The problem arises when these people had such a strong belief in a God that they thought existed during our physical existence here on the planet Earth and thought that it is the only existence of man and woman's experience and that nothing else in our solar system matters. These people had the opportunity to experience other forms of life. Some of the people who go through the black hole have a difficult time readjusting to this life. These people who experience the truth, when they are explaining it, sound ignorant to the masses, so the masses of people do not believe them. Still and yet they are speaking the truth. When people go through the doorway of the black hole, which is the door of the unknown, they experience the true life of our ancestors' existence. The ancestors that people experienced as they go through the black hole is a God, but not the God that the King James Bible refers to as God. That is why if you read the Bible, it explains how Satan travels into heavens to speak with Jesus and God; there was a world that existed way before earth was created.

The *A* is a representation of our atmosphere. It is through our atmosphere that we transgress in the form of energy. As we transgress in the form of energy, we are able to embrace the matter that is in our mother's authentic womb. That power of the human creation comes from our mother's womb. The sun's ultraviolet rays are the solar energy that is the transformation of men's and women's souls. The rays of the sun draw itself to the power of the women's energy to form the spirit of man. That energy that is the sun's ultraviolet rays continues to exist as a part of life's energy. That becomes the true subconscious of the human soul and spirit. Now again, this process of life's existence is done through the ultraviolet rays of the sun.

All of the human creation becomes life because of the rays of the sun. It is the rays of the sun that is the energy that also transcends to become the souls of men and women that are embraced in the transformation of the women's body. In other words, our souls are the energy of the sun. Now our energy is the consciousness of our souls that return to its original state of energy through the process of evolution, or what some people would call creation or physical death. All of this is the true power of the Ha'oba'cka'. All of this is achieved through the authentic hands of our mother's womb. Remember that mothers are women who are the Gods of the universe and planet Earth. It is our own atmosphere that allows men and women to be constantly reproducing as human beings. Through the power of the sun's ultraviolet rays, the soul and spirit of all men are born from the woman.

The *C* is our own means of existence. We were first created from the authentic hands of our mother's womb. The womb of the woman is our only means of existence and survival of life. The woman's womb is what I refer to as God's authentic hands of creation. As much as women are oppressed or degraded through the doctrine of religion, Jesus Himself was created from the spirit and soul of the woman's womb. What is interesting is that God took it upon himself to create Adam and Eve who became sinners of His creation.

What is interesting is this same God took it upon Himself to bring Jesus into creation from the power of procreation, or, may I say, from the woman's womb. Now what is interesting is God, who is all-knowing, authentic, omnipotent, and omniscient, created Adam and Eve. Guess what, Adam and Eve, did they sin. Now why did Adam and Eve sin? Could it be because they were created from the authentic hands of God instead of being created from the authentic hands of the woman's womb? Also, remember that Jesus the Christ was born of a woman's womb without the help of man's sperm, and he did not sin while He was on earth, so to me, sinning is just a process of life where one is able to overcome through knowledge and strict discipline. Maybe the perfection of man comes through the creation of the women's womb instead of God's direct creation. Maybe that is why we should recognize the woman as the true God of the universe and planet Earth. Because she was the only person in existence that created a human being directly from her body, even in the state of sin, the woman is still capable of creating man.

The *K* represents knowledge, the kind of knowledge one needs for them to transcend into the heavens where we originally came from. With knowledge, one does not need to have faith, hope, prayer, or even a belief in a God because you know the truth about the thing or place you call God. For example, when we go on a trip, we have faith, hope, and sometimes we even pray about our trip, and the reason why I think we do this is we do not know what to expect from the trip; we are about to go on, so in order for us to feel comfortable about the trip, we have faith, we pray, and we believe that the trip we are taking is going to be a good one. The question is we do not know? When we get back from the trip, we really do not have any need to be concerned about the trip, and so it is with God we must believe in God, we have faith in God, and we pray to God. So when a person have faith, pray, hope and believes, that means you are not sure about the situation or circumstances that you are faced with.

So if man experiences God face-to-face like Lucifer did, would man become like Lucifer and say, I want to be my own God of my own existence. Think about it! I believe that when the nature of man can come face-to-face with anything that exists as His God, man, by nature, would have no more respect or fear for that thing to become more divine or still remain his God other than himself; so man, in turn, destroys that thing that he once respected and feared as his God, something like the woman who is supposed to be man's original God. The one thing mankind needs is the truth about the knowledge of our existence. When we as human beings understand this, then we become our own Gods in life. As long as we depend on some other force to be our God, trust me, it would be your God; it might become more of what we understand hell to be, and it would also control you and prevent you from becoming your own God. When you allow something to exist as your God, or a person to be your God, you become a slave to your own ignorance. Only you know what and who your God is.

The one thing people need to recognize is that God from the scriptures would never be revealed to the masses of the people because the God from the theological doctrine of Christianity does not exist and has never been in existence, only since 1611. The true Gods are determined through the knowledge and wisdom one has in store within them. The more knowledge and wisdom we have, the easier it is for us to understand life and live life to its fullest. The condition that our life created for us through our knowledge and wisdom, that is what determines how we are going to live in the physical world as well as in the spiritual world of our existence. Knowledge goes through these trends; we are educated but that does not mean knowledge. Education is what we have gathered from an institution with many philosophical ideas that seriously relates to other men's ideologies. It has nothing to do with how you view the world or how you are viewed in the world. That is why most people who have achieved their doctrine in many subjects would tell you they have not learned anything from a college or university that makes them a better or a smarter person. What we need to elevate us to be Gods is knowledge; in the state of knowing, a person learns to develop themselves and understand themselves for who they actually are and not through the eyes of other people.

The most powerful knowledge in life is to understand who you are; this is a process of where man elevates himself to be his God, and not the God of the Bible and the Christians, but the God of self. That is why God has not yet revealed himself to man and woman because the God that we are waiting for to take us to heaven or either hell is the same God that we are. We are our own Gods; our knowledge and wisdom is directed with a lot of discipline. That is why people would never experience the existence of God unless you yourself become God, because you are your own God.

That is why God would never reveal himself to anybody that believes in faith because what is faith? Faith is a true state of ignorance, and in this day and time, people cannot be in a state of ignorance or believe in a God that they do not know whether He exists or not. Why should people believe in something they cannot experience or see? Even the theory that created the concept of faith lies in the power of man and woman's ignorance. Ignorance is a form of negative energy that has been misdirected and is ready to destroy the world and the people in the world or the people that are oppressed because of their own ignorance. To have faith is a simple state of not knowing. In today's society, if a person does not know that their God exists, why should they have faith? As long as they know that they exist and they have to be their own God in their own spiritual existence, they no longer have faith in a God. Now to me, believing in God means that you should reach a certain level in your life where you should have some type of information about what is right and wrong. When a Christian begins to grasp what is right and wrong about life, that is when the Christian becomes responsible, as well as independent for their own self. What we need to recognize is that Christians must move on and stop depending on God for everything in life; Christians must give God a break and have enough courage to move on and mature and stop depending upon God for everything that they need and want.

To have hope means that I do not know. Anytime a person does not know, they are in state of ignorance. I, and a lot of other people, am hoping that through their hope, life is going to change for the better. The only time that life is going to get better or change is if you yourself actually change it or become determined enough to change your own life. Sometimes, changing your life means changing your environment, friends, and maybe family members. So hope is nothing more than a state of ignorance. The state of ignorance comes when people are in a state of hope, faith, and belief. And prayer also is a state of ignorance that comes because people are even afraid to move on with their own life. Think about it? To move on with your life creates a sense of security that most people are afraid to face.

If we reexamine our own existence, we would know one thing, and and that is we exist in the form of a human being, waiting patiently for life, but it is death that brings us back into our own state of existence, which is God in the transformation of death. We do not need faith to influence our belief or to better understand who we are. When people know something, they do not pray about it. Now if people know something, and that something is causing them problems in their lives, then people want to pray about what is causing them the problem. When a person has a problem, now let us be honest, what does prayer do for them in time of need? Let us be honest, I still do not know what kind of people serve God and have to pray to God in order to get a better understanding of Him, along with themselves. I still do not know what kind of God people are serving. If every time that people have problems, they are praying to Him (God) when they want His help. It seems to me that God wants a lot of people's attention, and He likes people to be constantly in a state of self-pity and feeling sorry for themselves. If God needs people's attention to be God, then God cannot be God that created man from the dust of the ground and breathing the breath of life into the soul man; this sounds like the women's womb in the cycle of procreation, breathing the breath of life into the soul of man.

Here is something to pay close attention to, people do not exist in the state of hope, belief, faith, and prayer; people exist in a state of reality, and that state of reality is what we can comprehend as our life to be and exist in as our life. People exist in actuality, in the true state of energy that creates our lives. That energy that creates our lives is our true reality. It is not a mere imagination of hope, faith, belief, or prayer. Now the power that makes one into a God, or God into God, does not exist in a vision of hope, prayer, faith or belief but in the state of knowing. People, love God as well as fear Him because He knows, or He is an all-knowing God, not because he prays, or he has hope, or is faithful; it is because God is a knowing God and not a God of dough. When you know you have knowledge, you then have a vision of life, then you begin to understand yourself; and when you understand yourself, you experience the light that becomes your true soul and spirit of life, and it is that light of life that is burning as the spirit and soul of man. The knowledge of self is the existence of our true energy of life.

Now prayer on the other hand is another way to pacify God. God does not need people praying to Him. God needs people to have knowledge, first of himself, and then of Him. Because, to worship someone other than yourself, you still have to have knowledge of self, which is you. And when you have knowledge of self, then and only then would you find out who your true God is, or who your Elohim is, as people would say.

The reason why people believe in God is simple, they do not have enough knowledge about themselves or feel comfortable with themselves in order to understand the importance of their inner self. Most people believe in a

God that they do not know exist, never see, never touch, but we wonder why we are frustrated in this life, is it because we believe in something that does not exist? And we damn sure cannot comprehend the existence of that God. I know very well that the woman exists, but I still cannot, and will not, comprehend her, but the woman who created every man to have the ability that he can comprehend his existence do not get the credit she deserves as his God. People, if you do not have the knowledge of self, then you cannot serve the God you were taught that created you, who is actually living in the heavens. It is that same God that allows his son Jesus the Christ to sit on the right-hand side of Him after getting Jesus killed and not wanting to save His Son from being crucified.

The other reason that people are so frustrated with life is that they have mastered a God they don't know about, and, truthfully, if he exists or not, and then, when people realize that they can achieve more when believing in themselves, they begin to recognize that God does not exist in the capacity that Christian people claims he does. This has happened through theology and the doctrine that makes up the theory in theology. The reason why people do not believe in God is because they do not have enough knowledge of themselves, or they do not feel comfortable with themselves to know what we have to do in order to be responsible to and for ourselves.

To believe in a God that we do not know means that we are giving our rights and dignity away to someone we know nothing about. When people give their rights and self-worth away, they have no character or identity or even integrity to go along with who they are. This is what I refer to fake Christians or fake people or people who do not have a real sense of who they are.

People wonder why they are frustrated, some even express their frustration by being mad at the world. Some hide behind the many religious doctrines while they are manipulating the masses, posing as ministers of this same God that has oppressed the masses of people. What most of these people do not know is God doesn't want people who are perfect; He wants people who know that they are real and truthful enough to know themselves and their mistakes and try very hard to better themselves from where they are at. If God wants men and women to become perfect, then that same God has forgotten that he also made a mistake that He regretted, and that was when God himself created man. Also, if God is perfect, the world would already be in its perfect state of existence. But that is not the case, the world is imperfect because God is also imperfect, so that is why the world had a need for Jesus the Christ to come into the world, or for God to come in the form of a man, to save the world from it imperfections of sins. What we do not try to understand is if God came for the sins of the world, why are people still sinning? That is why most theologians say that the story of Jesus is the best story that has ever been told, do you know why? Because the people believe in the story that Jesus, who is a human being, is the Son of God.

Maybe God does not exist as we thought He did. People have become master believers, master fathers, master of hopes, master of prayers for a God they do not know about. These are the same people who believe in God, and still to this day, these people who believe in God do not know if God is either male or female. Ask them and they would say it does not matter because the concept of God was developed out of the procreation of the woman being able to give life to the same planet we call Mother Earth.

Now we know that God cannot be a hermaphrodite. What is a hermaphrodite? *Hermaphrodites* are people with male and female testicles. We know that God cannot have those attributes, but how did God develop the nature of the woman from just being God in a masculine and feminine world now that man cannot procreate life? Maybe God was also created by a woman, and that is what allowed God to have first hand knowledge about women being able to procreate life. Also, the reason why

God was able to create the woman from the so-called rib of the man, and way before Adam and Eve were created from the hands of God, is that God represented the power of the women way before Adam and Eve were created.

That is why a man or woman with faith would never be God's chosen people because those people who believe in faith are still in the state of not knowing. People who have knowledge about knowing are easier to receive the influence of God because they are in a state of knowing. The path that every man and woman travels while walking to find the truth about knowledge. The first path that accrues is knowledge, the first path of self-righteousness, and it is in the state of all self-righteousness that the bodies of man and woman embrace the spirit and soul that created the human body.

Knowledge comes when a person actually know themselves and understand the energy that has created them, again, from the womb of the woman. The problems that accrue in our world today happen because of people's insecurity about themselves and their way of life. People, it seems, should no longer embrace even those people that have money and political, social, and economic influence; their insecurities have helped damage this society and blocked many people's visions from becoming their own reality.

People are living in a state of egoism than spiritualism, so that contributes to why we are living in a world that is full of oppression and hate. People do not support their each other as we should. People are too busy looking out for themselves and not others. We as a people must remember there is no one man that can build a house by himself. As much as we desire to be self-centered, we still cannot live in this vast world by ourselves; we need love and the support of each other.

You see, if man and woman were to master themselves, then we would not have so much hate, pain, and suffering in the world. Why do people hate so much; it is a very simple question. It comes from the idea that people want to be God's chosen people or God's chosen race. God of the religion is where all of the schools of hate have developed because people are looking for reasons to hurt each other's through world wars. What people, who believe in God, need to do is to stop trying to perpetuate hate toward people who might have a different perspective on God and develop more of their self-awareness and be more in tune to themselves. Hate burns up too much body energy and causes too much frustration, suffering, and pain. Hate even occupies too much of the brain's mass. Hate is a state of negative energy. What people need to understand is that believing in God is to realize that God never found man or woman through his or her religion.

God blesses people through their self-knowledge and discipline; the more knowledge a person has of himself or herself, the closer they become to the wisdom of their God. Who now is God? God is the power and energy of the woman soul and spirit that created the energy that brought man into the full physical manifestation of life.

The *A* in this case is a representation of the atom. An *atom* is the smallest participle of a thing that created and formed that thing into its own perfect form of existence; the energy that is the atom is knowledge that transformed a thing into its own nature and existence. This word *atom* is a very profound word because it means a thing that is coming into its own transfiguration. Now if we exist in the state of atom, does that mean that we exist before being in an atom? Yes, people existed before the atom stages. Maybe we all existed as an atom but in a different dimension during our life and time. I believe that our existence in the state of atom comes from when we were in the state of energy. Maybe in the atom form of existence, we have already existed as a separate entity of life. For example, if Jesus was the word, the word was with God, and the word was made flesh, Then Jesus as an atom existed on all of these plains of life, then He became a human being.

This is very important because in the book of Job, which refers to God and Lord, it also refers to the Sons of God, and not the Son of God. This means that God had other sons besides Jesus the Christ. What made Jesus the Christ the savior of the world when he existed as an atom came through the birth canal of the woman to become God, or God's son, and is still more favorable than any human being on the planet Earth. So then that could be that we all existed before in heaven with God and his sons or daughters.

Now in the first book of John, God is saying, "let us make man in our own image, and in the likeness of us." Some people believe that God was talking to Jesus the Christ. Whoever God was talking to, they existed way before mankind did because he said to someone, let us make man in the image and likeness of us. Now who was God speaking to? Was God speaking to Lucifer, who we call Satan? However, if we look at the situation, people already existed outside of this solar system. These people who existed outside our solar system are now transcended here on earth in the true state of energy. Energy is the power that is the manifestation of life in this solar system through the process of procreation.

Every human existence that blossoms into the fullest and energy of life always asks this question, "who am I?" If I may answer that question, I would say we are all a form of energy, wrapped in the substance, matter, and form of a human body, that gives us the gift of life that comes from the woman who is life. The concept of "who I am" even as I try to define it. The one answer I have for that question is the "who I am" comes from the power and energy of the woman's womb. Because it is the women's womb that gives men the true reason to define themselves in the context of "who I am," this is what contributes the idea that the women's womb is the authentic hand we call God. Even if we define the concept of God to be God, or even if we do not define the concept of God to be God, there is one underlining question that is still not answered, and that is "who am I?" I am a God only to myself, and also a human being in the nature of creation that causes me to exist in this life. Men, even with our egos, we have to admit that our definition of reality comes from the power and energy of the woman's womb. That is why, as a man, I can only define the woman to be my God and creator of life. Now who are we? The question that I keep coming back to now is in its original perspective about "who I am." I'm a person that is nothing more than plasma and energy, embraced in something called a human body, waiting to come into a human experience and be recognized as a part of the human existence. Or as some would say, I'm the energy of life that has been transmigrated from substance, matter, and form, and in the complete state of my human form is where I write about my own experience of my spiritual and physical existence of life. Maybe also, we are spiritual beings that was transformed into the physical manifestation of life awaiting death.

The human experience is also where men get their true understanding of who they are in the state of their own physical existence. In the state of energy, we are embraced with the substance of life. The chemical reaction of life is nothing more than man being in the state of substance. The state of substance is nothing more than the consciousness of the human being. Here is why. The reason being from the time that the substance accrued the power that makes substance comes alive as energy, and that energy that is coming alive is beginning to create life. Energy when it exists with substance determines the atmospheric changes, or what I would refer as the opening up the doors of the universe to bring the energy of life into our atmosphere through the power and process of procreation. The power of procreation transforms into the substance of life into the women's womb in order to create man's own existence. The existence of the soul and spirit is the energy that forms the personality of life from the umbilical cord of the woman; it is the umbilical cord of the women that transcends life in the form of energy that becomes the spirit of man's own existence.

It is in the spirit of man that his integrity is developed and formed. So the beauty of the man's mind could be influenced by the spirit and soul of the women's umbilical cord.

"So, Mr. Grant, are you saying that the evil of man comes from the woman?"

Here again we have to blame the woman for something or place her in a state of evilness or put her back in a negative light. No, that is not what I am saying, but I'm glad that you ask that question. A mother always wants the best for their children; it does not matter what walk of life they travel. Mothers always want the best for their children. Now if I respond to your question, I would do so in this manner, by making this statement, and that is that mothers always want the best for their children. Why do men do wrong? When we as men learn about our egos, we learn to dominate and control things; this in itself contributes to the many wars and killings that accrue upon this planet. It is not women's transcending energy that is doing this; it is man's external knowledge of dominance that is developing his ego. It is in the ego of man that he does evil things to innocent people as well as good people like you and me. What we as men should be questioning is why do we want to dominate the women, is there a certain strength that women have that mankind has a strong desire to dominate the woman? If I am not mistaken; it was the woman who fed all men from her breast and raised all men with the knowledge they needed in order to survive. Why should men dominate what created them from his mother's womb? Why do men want to dominate those that created them? Women created them as men and are the true Gods of the universe. Most men also abuse women physically. It is the egos of men that afflicts the abusive behaviors on women. But why?

It could be that men are jealous of the spiritual and physical strength of the woman. Women control men with something called the energy of vibration, as well as the energy that vibrates through the universe that transcends into the motions of love and lust. Women are the ones in control of the planet where the tears of the woman is protecting the ego of men from contributing to the many killings and wars that accrue. It is the power of the woman's spirit and soul that can stop the wars from escalating; but in the case of the women, they know the importance of life, and they know that it is wrong for them to destroy life because they've already been through the pain and suffering it takes for life to exist. Maybe that is what causes them to acknowledge life rather than to destroy life itself. Could it be that women suffer during childbirth because they already know what it is like to appreciate life rather than kill it by sending their children off to war? Maybe the key to true life is found in the essence of the woman's soul.

May the pain and suffering that comes from childbirth is the pain and suffering of the woman. Maybe the pain and suffering of Christ that He is supposed to bear is nothing more than a lie, because Jesus was never able to give birth to any child. Maybe it is the pain and suffering of the women who actually bear the sins of the world for every man that has existed upon the face of the earth. Think about it, who actually is the God of man?

What is even more interesting in life is before we came into our mother's womb, we chose our true parent from the spiritual world. Some people would say I did not choose my parent because they are broke, because if I had the power, I would have chosen wealthy parents. I damn sure did not choose the ones I have now because they are broke, and I hate being broke. Trust me, I would have chosen some parents with a whole lot of money. When a child chooses his or her parents, he or she must give the parents love and start to spend quality time with their parents. Trust me, money is important, but money cannot replace or take the place of one's spiritual awareness because our parents now become the transcending forces of life that are able to create the spirit and souls of life's existence.

What we have to do is use the process of mind transgression and transmedisoul to concentrate on the subconscious of our spiritual form of enlightenment. The spiritualism of the woman's soul is like a beaming bright light that is captured in the mind, body, and spirit of man. This is where the power of man's mind communicates with his spirit in order to develop and create his mental ability to elevate him on another level of the universe.

"Mr. Grant, why do people advance faster than others?"

Most men and women's experiences are not the same; we all experience things differently, and that is why we reach different levels of advancement at different times, but what is true is that we all can elevate ourselves.

Spiritualism of the woman's soul is one of the most powerful forces in the universe because from the women's authentic womb comes the true essence and substance of the human creation. The power of all human existence comes from the power of the Ha'oba'cka', which, in some cases, are the spiritualism of the women's spirit and soul. When the sun beams it rays upon the planet, the ultraviolet rays of the sun transcends into the women's body, and it is the energy of the woman that draws the ultraviolet rays of the sun into her soul, and it is the woman's energy of her soul that is able to transform at the sun's rays, along with the elements of the universe and earth, to bring man into a perfect form of existence, giving man an energy called the spirit of his own creation. The ultraviolet rays of the sun is what causes the true existence of men's spirit to blossom into the energy, substance, matter, and form of life. All of life's creation comes from the power and energy of the women's soul.

It is the power of the women's energy that brings the spirit of man through the cycle of nature's procreation process, which are substance, matter, and form. The power that is in the inner chambers of the woman's womb is the force that transcends itself into being the spirit of man. Here is how the soul of the woman begins to create the spirit of the man? First, the spirit of the man is the energy that transcends from the ultraviolet rays of the sun. Second, the woman's body observes the sun's ultraviolet rays of the sun and then transforms the rays of the sun into a beaming bright light of energy that has either, or in this case heat. Heat is energy that creates changes, and life itself comes into existence because the heat is able to create changes in the thing that is being absorbed by the heat. Also, heat creates the energy that comes from the sun's ultraviolet rays. That heat that comes from the sun creates changes and is able to transfer the energy from the women's soul into creating and fashioning the spirit of man.

Even when man is in his mother's womb, waiting patiently to be procreated as a human being, it is in the woman's womb that the earth's gravity becomes the energy of the woman's soul. It is the woman's womb that holds and embraces the body and spirit of man. All of this takes place in the inner chamber of the women's womb, where the power of the *Ha'oba'cka'* truly exists as the power and energy of all human life. The sun's rays that reflect the ultraviolet light is what transcend into the body of the woman, and it is the soul of the woman that transforms man's energy into light; and when man moves from energy into light, it is the woman's womb that transmutates man into the existence of life. The energy of the sun's light is what becomes the soul of man that we see on the ultrasound's test. This is where life begins to form the nature of man, all of this transcending, transforming, transgressing, and transmutating exist as an energy of the woman's womb. Now who is God of the universe and the earth? The spirit and soul of the woman's energy is the true God. Each transcending force is a process of creating all life, and it is in all life that we all are transformed by and from the sun's rays as the energy of life.

Who and What Is the True God

People always ask me this question and that is do I believe in God? When people ask me that question, it seems that it has to do with the idea of analyzing my perspective on life in general. Now that does not bother me; what bothers me is when people ask my position on God. Here is an honest statement; I do not know who God is, and I never experienced God who exists as the spirit of man. Nor am I depending on some prophets to tell or explain to me who God is because I have learned in my lifetime here on earth that I have to have my own understanding and interpretation of life, and that is when I myself can tell anyone who my God is. If people cannot interpret life for themselves, or even try to define the idea of who God is, what is their reason and purpose for living? Man can only define life based on how he interprets the understanding of life. The only God I know is my mother, who is my God and savior from the cradle to the grave; I would always remember my mother's love and mistakes. I then ask them which God are you talking about, the God we know as a spirit or the God who is my mother? They would say to me there is only one God. I would then say, which God are you talking about? They would say to me they mean Jesus the Christ's father. I would then say to them, "Do you mean that God, which is God is Jesus' father the God of the spirit?" The reason why I ask them if they mean Jesus' father is God is simple, there are many Gods. So I myself end up being confuse, although I want to know the God that everyone else seems to know or pray to; I never saw him, or was He introduced to me? Why should I waste my time believing in that God? People, I believe that people have faith in God because they do not know who God is.

In other words, who are the true Gods of your own life's existence? Not even God is the God of your own life existence because if a person puts a gun up to your head and pull the trigger. Now when I always respond to them with this statement: how could I believe in a God that could not help Him selves down from the cross. How can I believe in a God who denied His own son the help he needed to save his life? God could not even help His son while He was on the cross, and guess what? With His own son, Jesus, God said no when Jesus was being killed on the cross. Do you mean that same God did not stop the bullet that killed John F. Kennedy, Martin Luther King Jr., Malcolm X, and others who fought for the goodness of the people? Do you mean that same God did not stop the killer that killed Martin Luther King Jr., Malcolm X, and John F. Kennedy? If God did not stop the bullet that killed these people that were fighting for the human rights and liberties of the people who were being oppressed through violence, that means that God does not care about the people who love Him, or He, God, does not exist. The question that people need to ask the theologians is why, if God loves me, did God want me to be oppressed or fall victim to the hands of the oppressor? Why should I give God so much credit over my life as being the creator of my life when in actuality, my mother would never see someone killing me and not try to retaliate; many mothers have protected their children all on the account of *love*. It seems that God does not help the people who have faith in Him, or even believe Him, but for those who do not, it seems that God helps those people. What kind of God is this?

Instead He helps people who are not, and many people who are serial killers; these serial killers were able to live longer lives while innocent people's lives were cut short at the hands of these so-called criminals. These serial killers live after they killed all those innocent people. God never tried to kill or bring the other people back to life; God never came to support the poor and the weak because the weak is still the weakest, and the strong remains the strongest. I am not referring to what you read in the Bible or even God splitting the Red Sea. I am talking about someone who loves you because you love them and that they or He (God) created you. We look at these religious books to say that God is loving, but remember that God also killed a nation of people instead of personally trying to talk to them. Remember that the God you love would never protect you from any harm. For example, assume that you are at home, relaxing from a hard days work. You're sitting on the floor praying to God, or even walking on a beautiful day, and suddenly, someone breaks into your home or robs you while you were walking the streets or even on vacation. How about if you were also killed when you were burglarized? How come God did not save you or kill the robber that robbed you or hold the robber until the policeman got there? Instead, God let the robber go free and was never get caught, and now you are praying to a God that had all of the power in the world to help you, and He God never did. Now I know that my mother will not let that happen.

Just like giving thanks lets someone or people place a gun to your head. If you want to find out how much God loves you, then compare that love to the woman who is your mother, and trust me, you will get some interesting results. When God, or Jesus, said, "Let this cup pass," how could I believe in a God that needed help, and His God did not help Him, and again, that same God could not even help His son Jesus the Christ? That same God who was on the cross for so long, suffering with nails in his hands and being in some excruciating pain, needed the help from His other God to bring him down from a cross. Now that same God had nails in his feet and nails in his hands and thorns on his head, and His God said no; now that is a damn shame. Think about it, who is this God that we all loved?

This is the same God who could have helped the other God who called upon Him for help, and He refused to help His son who people call God. Now how could I worship a God that would not even help another God, or Himself, or the God who is His son Jesus the Christ, who called upon him for help? This God that called upon the other God for help refused to help Him and allow the cup to pass. That cup was the cup that helped cause the blood of death to God's son, Jesus the Christ. Remember that cup was not wine or something sweet to drink; it was the sadness and pain that came with death. It was known as the cup of death. The cup of death is just that, it is the death of another God not having His father to have compassion to save him from the cross. The cup of death is supposed to be the forgiveness of man and woman's sins through the blood sacrifice of Jesus the Christ the son of God. The death of Jesus now became the covenant of the New Testament church. Why did God who is all-knowing allow his son to die on the cross for the sins of the world? Did not God know that people were going to continue in sin if He God was all-powerful and all-knowing?

Many theologians mentioned that the death of Christ was the beginning of the New Testament Church. Why is that the beginning of the New Testament has something to do with the death of a God, or that of God's son, Jesus Christ, dying? What is happening here is that God is even submissive to the power of death that He, God, created Himself. Yes, I mean God is being submissive to the power of death even though he rose from the dead. If God is God, why does He also have to be submissive and subject to the same thing as me and you, which is death? People, you do not understand that this thing called religion is just a game, and the Christians are people like you and me are, the pawns on the chessboard. Religion passes judgment upon the emotions such as pain, and suffering of many people.

Now God is supposed to be the creator of all living things including men? Still and yet God is allowing the same people who killed His Son to still survive as good human beings. Because of the death of this God, a New Testament Church was created, and the people's names who were Christians were now saved to live an eternal life in the heavens above.

I have a question to ask the theologians, and that is why is it that the cross is always been respected as one the most powerful divine symbolism in Christianity, and that same symbolism is in two places in the world? The first place that it is found represents death of the physical life. The second is death of the spiritual life let me elaborate more. Each place the cross is found, it represents death. When you go to the church, the cross is being hung in front of the church where everyone can experience their own spiritual death. Think about it. The cross in or on the church represents the sign of a spiritual death, which is the killing of people spiritually, because people who are Christians or are in the church are believing in a spirit that they've never seen, experienced, comprehended, or even understood enough to know whether or not He is real, but people believe in this God. People, it is better to believe in yourselves; you actually know who you are, and when you know who are, that is the first step toward an elevation of one's own spiritualism of life. The second is seeing the cross in the graveyard. People, ask yourself this question, why is the cross found in the graveyard? That is simple, it is a sign of death; a person, Jesus the Christ, died on the cross. The cross is where Jesus died while hanging on the cross and asking God, who is his father, to let the cup pass, the cup of death.

This same God died at the hands of mortal men. This same God could not pass his own cup, and the God who could help did not help. Now it is difficult to believe that this same God is going to help me or have helped me when I am in trouble. Now think about the ignorance that we are faced with, and people have created these for us to believe in and worship. What makes you think that this same God is going to help you when you need help. This same God might allow our cup to pass also, by bringing death to people, even the people who believe, pray, hope, worship, and have faith in Him. If God did not save his son, what makes you think that God is going to save you or me from death. Whether we believe in him or not, look at the many people that God did not save who actually believed in Him. If you are a drug addict, homeless person, God did not save you. If

God saved you, He would not let anything bad happen to you that would cause people who are a drug addicts and homeless so much pain and suffering. People decided on what they want to do in life; we use God as an excuse to cover up the bad things we do that comes with our behavior. You were the one who decided on taking drugs, and now you are the one who needs to stop taking drugs because you are getting tired of taking them; the only God that is going to save you is you. Think positive and remain positive to your own selves. Just because you have the excuses to satisfy your bad behavior does not make what you are doing right.

"I pray to God, and God is going to make everything all right."

No, you are the one who is going to make everything in your own life well. If people were always finding excuses for doing wrong, they would never become successful in life. One way to stay positive is to change your environment and the negative people that are constantly in your life.

Now if God could not pass the cup that killed His own Son, what makes you or me think that he is going to pass the cup when it is time for us to die? This same God died at the hands of the mortal men, the men he was supposed to have created that he called Adam and Eve. Now if God could not save Himself, how could I have enough faith to believe in Him, or even take time out to worship Him as a God? Now you want me to trust God with my life? I do not think so; the only God I trust with my life is me, and sometimes, based on the circumstances that I am faced with, I even need help to be reinforced about my position in life. Yes, we all need help, but we do not need God or people to be your own God.

So if the God that I believe in could die on the cross, by the hands of the men he created, how could I believe in him? Why should I want to believe in a God that can be killed by the hands of men he created? The truth of the matter is God could not help himself. Now if you put me in the same position as God being on the cross, I could not help myself either. Trust me, I would be praying to someone for help, and if that person helped me, then that person or people would now be my God, this person or people would truly be my God because I needed them to help me. So why should I believe in a God that is incompetent to help himself and myself? So when we pray to God, we are actually praying to a God that is a spirit and is also unable to help Himself or Herself from being nailed on the cross. It seems that God is so far removed from people in this universe that it seems that he does not exist as God, or it could not be God that created the world, but a God that created ignorance in man to believe in. Still and yet the woman would never allow her son to die if she can help him, even if he was dying for the sins of the world. Here is the reason again, it is the woman who actually bears the cross that causes the pain and suffering that bring life into existence; only the woman knows what kind of pain and suffering it takes in order for that child to become an adult.

The God that we believe in could not help himself, or even help me if I was in the same position as He was in, especially when he was being nailed on the cross. This is the same God people want me to worship and have faith in, pray to, and hope for. Who the hell is this God of the universe and planet Earth that everybody worship and give so much thanks to? This God gets so much credit for His power of creation, still and yet I never see Him. The same God that the men killed on the cross is the same God that is supposed to have created the world. I was told as a young man that God is a spirit that dwells only in the wall of the heavens and the atmosphere of the universe. I was also told that no man or woman has the ability to see this same God physically and live to tell about the physical description of God. I now wonder if God does exist as people say he does. Yet this same God took time out of his busy schedule and transformed himself into a human being called Jesus the Christ, where everybody could experience seeing Him as Jesus the Christ. Now this same God created himself both physically and spiritually, by saying I'm, how could a man who, by nature, does not reproduce create life in the masculine and feminine form of creation by just saying "I am"? I wonder what was God thinking as He created the female? What nature of God caused Him to find room in His heart to create the female? Unless God was first a female before He became a male God by man's ideology?

This same God also chose to cry like a baby while being nailed to the cross because he could not stand the pain of suffering that He God said represents Him and the many people who believe Him that God is suffering. The question I would like to ask the theologians is if Jesus the Christ died for the sins of the world, why are people still killing and sinning? Here is another question. How could God, who is all-knowing, allow his son to die on the cross, to be brutally beaten, spat on, having thieves nail him to the cross and still kill his Son in order for Him to create a new covenant of life? This is the same Jesus the Christ who has contributed love to a world by healing the sick, making the lame walk again, and even preaching the word of God. Who is this God, this all-knowing God, that killed his son to save the world from sinning? Did God know that the world was going to continue sinning? If this is a God that is all-knowing, he still gave people freedom of will to either do what is right or wrong. God, who is omnipotent, omniscient, did not know that man was going to sin after his son died on the cross, such a brutal death; that incident gave me something to think about. Now to me, that means that Jesus' life was in vain because people are still sinning.

What God should have done is spend more time dying to prevent people from suffering, being killed, dying of torture by evil people; it might have been better if God would have died to prevent the oppression, hate, and death of many innocent people's nations killing nation for political, economic, and social power and control. I know God would achieve more if He died to prevent the many hate and oppression and killing of people in this world than to allow his son to die for the sins of the world. Also, on top of all this, God gave man a freewill to do as he pleases; something does not fit into the equation of Jesus the Christ dying for the sin of the world and God allowing man to have a freewill to sin or not sin. If God was intelligent, He would have known that same freewill is what caused Satan to be His own God, and now it has caused man to be his own God. If that is the case, that everyone's nature is to seek knowledge and wisdom, then knowledge and wisdom with a consciousness to do good has to be everyone's own God.

Remember, God, it was your own freewill that you gave to men that caused men to kill your so-called only begotten Son. At this point, I have to refer to the writings of William Shakespeare with one of his famous plays *Measure for Measure*, even a sister would do anything to save her brother's life. How come a God did not save His only begotten Son Jesus the Christ? There is no mother on this planet in her right mind that would see her son dying and not help him; if she can prevent her son's death, she will, but not God. Think about. Maybe it is because God did not have a Virginia to feel the physical pains it takes to bring life from substance and matter and then form it into a potential human being. The power of all life is the woman, and it is in the woman that created you and me in life. Because the woman, who is our original God, shed her blood every month while on her menstrual cycle, on her period, for the sins of the world, not even man who is an avatar can die by shedding his blood for the world. The laws of our existence do not allow that to happen. The only God that has ever shed their blood for the sin and pain of the world is the woman. Not Jesus the Christ. I know with my simple human mind that for man to have freewill, that is what is really going to lead the world into its own state of destruction and cause many innocent people to die at the expense of what they think is right for people to believe in and have faith in.

Now, people, do you know that the Bible came into its own completion in 1611? The Bible was even edited with the help of a King James and about forty-six of his councilmen. Some places in history mentions it forty-six councilmen. Someone mentioned that in the book of the forty-sixth Psalm, the person who actually edited the Bible was *Shakespeare*. Here is how you can find this out by going to the forty-sixth Psalm and counting the verse from 1 to 46 from the top and the bottom, and it would give the hidden code for the Bible and who actually edited the Bible, which should be *Shake Spare*. When they are put together, they spell *Shakespeare* and the history of the Bible goes on. That is why I would always say never believe, pray, faith, or have hope. People, we have to know, and in the state of knowing comes wisdom, and wisdom is what makes simple men and women Gods.

There is also a story that after these men edited the Bible, they were all killed. Why? Because they know the truth about the lie that causes the Bible not to be authentic; they had to change and remove from God's authentic writings. That lie was created to mislead the masses of people. Also remember that before Christianity came in to existence, the woman was being worshipped as God. So now, God being she could already be changed to the He form of worship. What happened is that the forty-six councilmen knew the lie that was to hide the truth, and it was that same lie that killed the forty-six councilmen. All that was written down and placed into the Bible, and the Bible became nothing more than a lie to the masses of people. Now I was told that in order for me to love God, I must first love my brother who I have always seen. One of the problems, I came to recognize, is the reason that I have hated my brother is because I keep seeing him all the time, and he became who I am, and that is a human being with a lot of mistakes in life.

The Struggle of God, Man, and Woman

Now as human beings, we struggle with many ideas in order to find out what actually is the truth about our life. Some of us struggle with idea of what it is about life that makes us human beings and most of all, who is our God and why are we here on Mother Earth? These are some of the questions that have caused many countries to go to war among themselves. These questions also caused many people to fight each other and created a lot of hate among countries.

What some people do not know is it was through my kind heart that caused me to actually dislike my brother, or just people in general who always take advantage of other people's kindness, because people actually do take advantage of not only me but other people who always extend their love and help to others. Now the question is why would other people take advantage of others? It's simple. We take advantage of others because we experience living in the same atmosphere with each other; we know each other's weakness and emotions, so sometimes, people would develop in their mind that it is right for them to take advantage of a person who gives them love and helps them out. It seems sometimes that if a person does not take time out to love and appreciate themselves, those are the people that would take advantage of others. Just because a person is materialistic or a Christian does not mean that they love themselves. People would always try to take advantage of you or me because the more we give of ourselves; it seems that it produces a weakness in me that causes other people to take advantage of me. Some people in society have taken advantage of me based on the kindness that I have given to them.

I do not want you to believe that I give all of myself to people and people did not give me anything in return. Let me be honest. Sometimes, people take advantage of

others because they did not know or understand at the
time that the beauty in life is to give the gift of love and
help others when they need it. I also had to learn how to
appreciate other's love and help that they have given me.
When a person give all of themselves, it does not mean
that they are weak, it means that they have an eternal
light of strength and wisdom in their souls where they
understand that the best way to understand life is to love
life and help each other when you can.

Most people, I believe, should learn from their
mistakes how to appreciate others who love them. I know
now how to appreciate the kindness of love, especially
when people give of themselves to me. What most people
must learn is it is only out of concern and love that people
give of themselves in order to help each other. People are
not obligated to help you or me, so when they do, they
are making life become more meaningful and valuable
to live. When people have reached that level of life and
understanding, it is not right for other people to take
advantage of loving people. What they really do not
know is that it is a sign of strength and power when we,
as human beings, know how to treat each other with love
and respect. This is how my mother treats me, with lots
of love and respect, and that is why we should treat each
other the same way. She has given me the power and the
strength I need to become a better human being; this was

not done by the God in the skies, only the God on the earth, which is my mother. People like what others can do for them as well as what they can get from others as well; I like people for who and what they are in life, not what people want them to be.

Maybe if I was to see God He might also take advantage of me also. Why would God take advantage of me, some people would ask. It is simple. From the time that God and man occupied the same space in the universe, they become equal as one, allowing themselves to be in the same substance, matter, and form. Maybe the idea of God being in heaven gives Him, from the theologians perspective, more control of man because maybe people have faith in God because God cannot be experienced by them or seen by them. This is what actually happens with Satan and God. They both occupy the same space, at the same time, and that allowed God and Satan to be created in the same substance, matter, and form that created both God and Satan to be equal with each other.

This is very interesting because from the time that Satan recognized that he occupied the same space and time as God in the same substance, matter, and then form, Satan wanted to be his own God. Satan wanted to have control over his own life and his own existence. All Satan wanted was to be like God and think on his own freewill, and God, it seems, being afraid of Satan's independence, decided not to let Satan or Lucifer out of heaven and place him among the men on earth.

Now if God had good intention for man, why did God place Satan among man to tempt man, even Adam and Eve; and God never removed the power of Satan, so in essence, Satan would always have the upper hand on men and women that exist in the flesh because He, Satan, has more powers than man, and just enough courage to make him a fool. What men need to do is realize that the God we are serving might not be the God we need to pray to or serve because he never appreciated or wanted men to be their own God. Here is why, instead, God cast Satan and his fleet of angels to the earth to live among men, and even marry the daughters of men. This means that Satan came to earth with wings, because all angels have wings. If we did have Satan's genetics, does Satan have the same genetics as man just like God does? Do God and Satan have the same genetics with man, because we were made in the image and likeness of God? We do not have feathers on our backs, why does Satan do? All angels have wings. We must remember that Satan was able to travel to and from heaven in his craft, or using his wings from the heavens, to the bottom of the earth. Satan's genetic or biological makeup makes him look like men, but Satan is known as an angel in heaven.

Now men became more of a God than God Himself because if we look at the conditions that man have been faced with, God is not being honest with man, because man is fighting a war that is spiritual while man is in the physical manifestation of his own existence. Most men cannot, and is not, able to recognize these principalities and things unseen, but the one thing man does know is that he is fighting a war without information of his enemy's strategies, and God is expecting man to win this battle. Still and yet man is being held accountable for an enemy that God placed before him. Man has never seen his enemy, but he has to defeat him. So from the beginning, God wanted man to fail the test that He placed before man, because their is no way man is able to win against Satan, not even in the Garden of Eden, because man did not have the power, the transcending power, that God gave Satan and Jesus. Satan always had the power to conquer man in the physical manifestation of life; that is why man cannot be perfect enough to fight the spiritual and physical battles with Satan, because at this time, man only knows what exists in the physical realm of his existence.

It was very difficult because when God placed man on earth, he had no powers to defend himself or his family against Satan, and that was when God allow Satan to have sexual intercourse with the daughters of men, because men themselves were not capable and did not have the power to fight Satan or even know the wisdom of Satan, so that is why it was easy for Satan to tempt man. When God created man, it seems that God placed man in a negative environment in order for man to become submissive to Him. Man was placed in an area that has nothing positive in it; what man was faced with was all the negative energy that created us to be a part of a major life force here on earth, and that is why the women play such a vital role as man's God. Because as man exists in the state of the physical manifestation of life, it is the women's energy of creation that gives man the knowledge and wisdom he needs to fight the wars against principalities and things unseen. Especially those things that are unseen to man in the physical manifestation of life. The process that moves man's creation from substance to matter and then form man is nothing more than a spiritual manifestation of life transcending in the physical existence of life, and that is what gives man the power to fight in the realms of principalities and things unseen to man. We are told that they are twenty-three or twenty-six chrome zone, but before we were born, we had to be the strongest of the other chrome zones in order to survive. Our survival depends on how well we fought the other chrome zones in our mother's womb. Now that was our first experience that exposed us to the spiritual wars between the many principalities and things not seen, and the knowledge we got from that experience in our mother's womb is what actually prepared us for the spiritual and physical battles that we continue to have in our physical life.

Still and yet it is the duty of man to elevate himself from the bottomless pit of life's oppressions to become a shining star like Jesus the Christ, having complete authority over his life. Now if man is able to liberate himself from the depths of the bottomless pit of life in order to become the God of his life, then man has the potential to be better than God, especially a God he never knew or knew well enough to be called God, or to worship or even have faith in. If God cared about men's condition, God would have created man with enough knowledge that would allow man to defeat Satan every time that Satan tempted man. Now what God you know would place a demon among helpless people here on earth for them to fight against the devil without giving them the right knowledge they need in order to survive about the spiritual and physical existence of life? Many people would say you have the Bible, and the Bible is the word of God, and God's word is able to fight anything the devil placed before man. We have the Bible, and man is still sinning. It is interesting to know that when we go outside of our mother's doors, we are warned about the dangers that lie a head, and it seems that she has always been right.

If God loved man, he would not have let men suffer at the hands of the devil. Look at the word that spells *Job*, which spells like it is *job*, because of the way people labor at their own jobs, reminding them of how God made Job suffer while being at the hands of Satan. God made Job lose his wife, family, and children, who have disobeyed and fought with God, to regain heaven, just to prove to Satan that Job was upright and faithful. Why does God have to prove anything to anyone if God is God? People do not want to experience the truth; or maybe I got it wrong, so wrong that what I am writing about is actually the truth.

Now if I met God like that, the question comes to mind is why would God place the devil among men, knowing that men do not have the power to compete with Satan's wisdom? This means that man was to sin, and be responsible for his own sins, while degrading the power and essence of the women's spiritualism. The one thing that puzzled me is why is it that God did not place Satan on Pluto or some other planet? Why did God place Satan on earth to test men and find out whether man is honest or not? Now if men do not pass those tests that God want them to pass, why does God send them straight to hell and burn people in a lake of fire for the duration of their life, which is man's soul? If the body of man goes to the Earth, why does his soul live forever in the lake of fire?

Now God, with all of his wisdom, should have known to place the devil on Mars, Pluto, or any other planet in the universe. Why among men who are powerless, letting Satan have intercourse or sex with the women of men in order to become daughters and sons of men? There is no mother that would allow a man or anyone to take advantage of her daughter or jeopardize their children's welfare, but not our Loving God 'cause He placed Satan among man in order to place man in hell; all of this took place in the book of Genesis. Many people would say that God gave us his word, which they make reference to the Bible, but the question I have for them is how much of that is true and how much of that is implemented by the theologians in order to control the masses of people and how much of the Bible is true enough for all people to actually live by?

When Adam ate the apple, all he wanted to do was recognize what was right and wrong. All Adam wanted to do was to know, and because of that, he became the father of sin. This to me does not sound like a God that created the world and is trying to save the world and the good and innocent people in it from the destruction that is about to occur. This sounds more like Satan, and Satan sounds more like God sometimes, when I try to evaluate who God actually is. It seems that when you seek knowledge in Christianity, you become Satan; you become the devil because you do not think like everyone else, and you want to be very much in control of your own life. Now do you get the message? Women, including my mother, want me to be independent, they also want me to be knowledgeable about life, and they do not feel threatened like God did when Adam and Satan wanted to be responsible for their own existence. Women who are educated—it also seems that men are automatically intimidated by their education. I love an educated woman; she helps develop who I am. Men, the same education that makes you intimated by women with an education, that same education is found in the woman. Also, the women, I believe, have more wisdom than men; I think they do. Now with these types of Christian perspectives in mind, I am faced with many problems trying to define who God is; I have more Christians coming to me, asking me questions that they cannot ask their own ministers. Most people believe that God is keeping track of their activities on Earth, especially when they are doing things wrong.

What most lonely people who are Christians do not realize is that God in the heavens does not care about anybody but Himself because he is a human being just like us. The theory of Jesus dying for the sins of the world is a lie. Jesus never existed as Jesus the Christ. Time will be our best teacher, and all the lies will be revealed to the masses of people. What people are taught to believe is that what is scripturally sound might not be always the truth. I believe we need to challenge the scriptures. If you were a person that was willing to apply these scriptures to your life, it would be of your interest to know and not have faith in the scriptures. Then you need to research them instead of believing in the scriptures through faith; as long as we can read and research, faith is nothing but a state of ignorance that many people believe in. People, in this life, we have to know what is right; we cannot live on the basis of faith and hope anymore.

The one thing that puzzles me about God's relationship toward man and woman is how a loving God caused so much destruction or left room for people to bring so much destruction toward the world and still allow people to love Him as a God of omnipotence. I strongly believe that people love God out of fear more than they love God out of their so-called deep-rooted faith, hope, prayer, and most of all, belief. This made me ask the question, what is *love*? As a young man having to attend church and growing up in Sunday schools, I could never understand what true love is, especially when it is coming from God. I mean not talking about the emotion one gets when they feel good or think that something good is going to happen to them and they love to feel the emotional high of the thing that they call Jesus or the damn power of Jesus. That is the emotional high that keeps the masses of people in a state of ignorance. Especially when these people have to shout and yell like a fool, these are the people that give others the wrong messages about God. The power of God is shared in the hearts of men, not in words but with the expression of love. Never preach a sermon to me; show me your sermon through the manifestation of your life.

I knew what true love is and where it is coming from; true love comes from the heart, arms, and tears of my mother's heart. People who believe in God do not want to admit that God's love is just a figment of their own imagination. No one on this planet can comprehend the existence of God or Jesus because they never see or experience God. For example, assume that someone told you that there is a rock that exists, and the same rock was on this planet for many years, and that same rock that you see over there has more power than what is in the world today because the energy from the rock is what created the world and the people in the world. Then all of a sudden, you are to love and have faith in the same rock, still and yet you cannot see the power of the rock, so you say to the person, "Where is the power of the rock?" And then the person says to you, "Have faith in the rock because the power is there in the rock, you do not have to see it in order to believe it. We feel the wind, but we do not see it. Remember it was that same rock that created the world, and it also created you and me." Now tell me what does this reminds you of? Even in the concept of the rock, we try to create the reason for people to love and have faith in that rock.

There are many different stories and experiences that people use to describe what God is like. For example, I think that God is like listening to music. Something like jazz, or the wonderful bars that created Bach, along with the wonderful music that he plays. It is a fake high; to know and have knowledge of that is what I call a natural high. I have experienced true love coming from my mother's heart. I experienced my mother working hard for me to have a better way of life in this world. It was my mother's desire and determination for me to have a better life, not God; I still do not know if God exists or not, but the actual act to achieve my highest goals in life had to come from me, and not some God in the skies. God is in heaven; it is not by the grace of God's love that I achieved success in life. The only time that I ever got hurt or even taken advantage of was when I expressed or showed love, or what I thought love should be. This alone should make people listen and pay attention to what and how people in society define what love truly is from their hearts.

Love to me is when a person opens the window to their heart to let others view their soul and life for who they are and how they are that could be love. We must also remember that love, because of its nature, creates room for a lot of pain and hurt that comes when people open the window to their soul just to give someone the opportunity to love them. Still and yet we do not know what love is. What then is love? From my perspective, it is an emotional weakness of nothing but pain and hope. It is here that the integrity of man and woman becomes destroyed.

"Mr. Grant, why would you say that the women know about love better than the men?"

A mother never leaves her sons or daughters. If that woman is in the right state of mind, she would give up her life for her family, and God did not for His only son, Jesus the Christ. The woman is the one who bears the pains of love. Our love, or, may I say, the pain that produces love, is what the woman bears, not the one that God or Christ experience. The man does not have this ability to procreate in the depths of those long pain and suffering. The woman is the true God who died on the cross for the remission of every one of her son's sins. I could not be the Son of God. Could it be that because men lack the pain of procreation, he cannot produce the love needed for constant peace? Instead, man creates the wars that kill the sons of the women. Women are the true Gods of the universe and planet Earth.

Here is how God allows man to define his true love. Even God dealt with people in a way that they might understand what true love is. God is simply saying how could you love me and not your brother or sister who you constantly see every day? Now let's analyze that statement coming from the Most High. What is God simply saying to people or Christians in general? He, God is saying, "Do not have any faith in me or security in me because I would let you down. Have faith in yourself not me." It would be better if we have all of our security in each other because we are all human beings that are affected by the inspiration of love and not God, whom you have not seen.

People, think about it! If man was to have faith and security in each other, the world would be a better place to live in, wouldn't it? Because people would become more consciously aware of each other's emotions, feelings, and properties; people would also respect each other more. People place all of their positive energies in a God that they never experienced or saw. Why do we do that? Why? What people or the masses of people do not want to admit is that the only love that is able to give love is that of the woman's. The woman is the true experience that gives life to this world because it all comes from the energy of the woman's womb. Look at the dangerous state the world is in with all of its evil and chaos. Look at how we use excuses to validate the many killings and wars that are even created through the egos of men that cause all of the damn chaos in the world today. That is why we must remember that the woman is God. The woman (mother) during child birth shed the blood of life and every mother is still shedding the blood for the sins of the world and Jesus did only once. And the woman sheds blood every month of her cycle. That is why the woman is God of the World.

The Vision of the Book
Women Are God

The book *The Ha'oba'cka'* would make a very important gift. The Ha'oba'cka' is a book that most men would feel proud to purchase for their female friend, such as a spouse, an intimate friend, or even just a friend on the job. The book could also be enjoyed and become a center of attention in many salons and beauty parlors. I believe that when people read this book, they would appreciate the honesty of its content. The book could be a tool that women can use to read the sincerity and honesty of a man's heart before she actually gets into a relationship with him, and most of all, it expresses his true spiritualism as a man.

When I explain the content of the book to people, I do receive some interesting responses about the book. One of the responses was how mothers have appreciated the information that I have gather together to create the book called *Women Are God*. Also, mothers have mentioned that the book is easy to read, but the depth of the manuscript is very powerful and shocking to read and accept. The manuscript discusses the truth about the beauty of the women's sprit and soul. The Ha'oba'cka' even embraces the woman's power and the essence and substance of her true beauty and spiritualism.

The depth of the book's spiritual message makes women feel good that a man has come to experience the true strength, sprit, beauty, and soul of the woman's existence. I was told that the book's spiritual insight comes from a man, and it was that spiritual insight of the man that most women who are mothers appreciate the book for. It make mothers recognize the depths of their spiritualism, as well as embrace the strength of her mind and her soul, and the appreciation a man has for their ability as mother's to procreate man into the existence of life.

Remember that the authentic hands of our mother's womb are the doors through which all men are brought into the existence of life, even if man admits it or not. The book *Women Are God* shows how women, like mothers, wives, sisters, and daughters, play a vital role in the procreation process of life, and also through the life of all men. Now at this point, I express, as well as elaborate, that women are Gods. The point where I try to admit that women are more than females, they are Gods, is the point that is not well accepted by most men because many men cannot accept that women have that type of power and strength in life, and that is to be their God. But the truth of the matter is that the woman is as, or more, powerful than man because she is the mother of all men.

The book takes a very harsh look at the reality of God, man, and the true spirit and soul of the women. It explains a lot of truth in it, and it also sparks the curiosity of many people's mind. It seems that each sentence gives an inspirational look at the reality of the woman being God other than God Himself being God, the God that we were taught of in Sunday school as children growing up. The book gives a new perspective on the creation of life, women, God, man, and the spiritualism of the woman.

I did have someone explain to me, after I discussed the content of the book, that they could not in their lifetime experience how an individual mind could even comprehend the idea that women are Gods, not on this planet we call Mother Earth, or on any other planet. What happened was after we discussed more of the information I used to complete the book, the individual begged me to complete the book because he mentioned that the book would become more of an appreciation to others. He mentioned that the information that we discussed is important for others to know. This same individual said I would have never looked at life from that perspective.

He then went on to say that it took a great mind to develop the inspiration needed to elevate the women from the way society has portrayed them into becoming a true God. Our society has portrayed the woman to be submissive to men; even in the world of many religions, the woman is taught to be submissive. It took another man's perspective to place the woman back on her pedestal, to be the God that she really is. The person did say that I did have the spark needed to raise some good philosophical and spiritual questions that hold true to the reality of life and the human existence. The person did say again that the words needed to be bound into a book. He even said that if the words were bound, this would be a book that people would constantly enjoy referring to once a year.

"Trust me, Mr. Grant, this would be a book I know people would always treasure and reread at least twice or more a year because as people mature in life, they need questions on life and God this book would bring people along in their maturity, and spiritualism in life.

"Sometimes in life, there is just one book that comes along and changes the course of history and how people think and view life. The *Women Are God* is that kind of book. Although, Mr. Grant, you are not known as a popular author, after this book you would be. The reason why I think you will become popular is simple. After reading your T-shirt on the Million Woman March, you have a style of writing that is very energetic, spiritual, and edifying, not too many authors have that gift as a writer.

"The Million Women T-shirts that you wrote have a powerful message, and if this book is a combination of that then the book itself has to be a powerful book. The author of the *Women Are Gods* has the ability to become one of the most successful authors in the world today because James E. Grant is able to bring in his book the sprit, soul, energy, and reality in his writing. The reality that the author uses to express his view of the woman being God would really make you think about life in general.

"I strongly believe that any book that deals with the woman being God and challenge the authority of the God and religion has to be an inspired by the author's love for women and his work. The author has to be inspired by the power of the something to bring this topic itself into a reality, as he has done so in this book. This is one of the most powerful manuscripts that any person has written about the power and energy of the women's spirit and soul, I think, by any man alive today. Mr. Grant, that information you gave me to read is a must thank you!

"Mr. Grant, I did discuss some of the information we talked about concerning your book with some people, and my date as well, because my boyfriend and I discussed about your information becoming a book. He got so interested in the information that he even teased me sometimes about the Ha'oba'cka'. After I had the opportunity to read the manuscript of the Ha'oba'cka', I did enjoy it—the manuscript in its rough draft—when you let me read it. I also gave it to my boyfriend to read, and from his response, it taught me a lot about my boyfriend's perspective on life and on women. I was glad that I gave it to him.

"What the manuscript and our discussion did for me in life, helped me to know my boyfriend a lot faster. It might have taken many more years for me to learn about him and his true spiritualism as a man. I even understood the depths of his spiritualism, something that I would not have had the opportunity to experience if I did not talk to you and had the opportunity to read your manuscript. I find that my boyfriend and I discuss the topics in the manuscript, and in doing so, we were able to discuss many topics on God, life, and spiritualism; the book work to ease the tension between us.

"The manuscript even allows my boyfriend to have a better understanding of me as a woman. This is a manuscript that has some very powerful words; I believe that women all over the world would definitely would enjoy and love reading it when it becomes published. Trust me, the author, James. E. Grant, did focus on the spiritualism of the woman's spirit and soul and her true ability as a woman.

"The manuscript, the Ha'oba'cka', expressed the true beauty of life, procreation, love, spiritualism, man, and God. This type of information is a must to have because it discussed a lot about the creation of life. Where men's philosophy and religion left off, the manuscript the, Ha'oba'cka', goes way beyond the ordinary mind of philosophy and religion. The book even let men realized where they should be mentally when it comes to understanding and interpreting the power of woman's existence through life's procreation cycle. I strongly believe that from reading your manuscript and talking to you about how you were approaching the information in the book, you have brought up some interesting points about God, man, woman, existence, life, and most of all, our reality. Dam! You made me think. If all of this was inspired from a T-shirt, I want a couple of those Million Woman March T-shirts.

These are some of the ideas and visions from the people that I have spoken to and who have had the opportunity to read the manuscript about the information I wanted to place in a book I decided to call the Ha'oba'cka'.

This book focuses on the power and strength of woman's spiritualism through our spiritual eye and our own physical existence. When I mentioned our own physical existence, I'm referring to how women bring men from the spiritual world into the physical world of our present existence today. Each man and woman's existence comes through the process and power of the woman's procreation cycle. The power of the woman's procreation cycle is simply defined as the power and energy of life and most of all, how that energy and power of life is being transformed into the mind, body, and soul of every human being's physical existence.

I analyze this by focusing on how the women procreate life, especially how the energy of the woman's soul is able to embrace the substance of man and then transformed that substance into life, from man into matter, and then from matter into form, and from form into the energy of life, which is what people recognize to be a potential human being. That energy of life that I am talking about is nothing more that substance being transformed into a potential human being. That energy of life is also the substance that comes from man as his sperm, and it is the sperm of man that becomes the energy of life as it transcends into the transformation of life. That energy of life is what creates and fashions man into being a potential human being. Now in order for man to come into existence, he desperately needed the mind, body, and soul of the woman's energy to transform him into a solid form of a human being.

Men must remember, by placing their egos aside, that the creation and process of life can only be achieved through the inspiration of the woman's womb and the existence of man's sperm. All of this is done from the power and energy of the woman's procreation cycle. I would go on to prove that mothers, who are women in their physical existence, are nothing more than the Gods in the spiritual manifestation of life. I really do not think that I can achieve anything else in this world that would surpass my being an author trying to prove that women are Gods. Trust me, this attempt would probably become one of the most important things that I could ever achieve

in my lifetime because it is the power of the woman's soul
that gives me the power and the energy of life to exist. It is
that same power and energy of life that makes all women
Gods, and it is that same power and energy that created
me and you from the wombs of our mothers.

When you read this book, you would then realized
why I, as a man, feel so privileged to be led by the power
of the Ha'oba'cka' to be the spiritual force that was used
on this planet we call Mother Earth to produce such
a powerful literary book as the Ha'oba'cka'. That is
authentic enough to discuss the power of the women's
presences as the God; that she is of the universe and
planet Earth. I feel that this book has given me more
insight into the inspiration of the woman's world and
her energy. It allowed me to recognize her strength and
being as a woman, and I hope it does the same for you
as it has done for me.

Through the power of the Ha'oba'cka', I was driven
to write this book, it seemed, by the same energy that
have created me from my mother's womb. Approaching
this book has brought me into a world of harmony and
enlightenment and it made me more in tune with the
universe, and now I have a better appreciation for the
cosmic world, along with our world we call Mother
Earth. Working on this book produced in me a certain

particular information that have transcended from the universe and into my own mind, body, and sprit, like something I have never experienced before. It seemed to be an inspiration that has been waiting to enhance the condition, lifestyle, social, and most of all, religious perspective about life.

"That experience that was revealed to me seems to be hidden from men and women for many years, and at this time, the best place to reveal this information was through sprit of James Grant. Why James Grant? Because James E. Grant was available and humble to the powers that caused him to be in tune with the universe's energy and earth's gravity. Now the one thing that I was told was that the vibration of the universe's energy sends in the form of wave was the current that transcended itself into the energy of the man or woman that was in tune to the universe, and the planet Earth. I had to stay in tune to the universe and earth, every second, while I was writing this book, in order for me to receive the information I needed to complete this book. The universe influence me to call the book Woman Are Gods: The Ha'oba'cka' comes as a series of book that talks about the spiritualism of life and death.

"Mr. Grant, could you please explain to me how you were inspired to write this book call the Ha'oba'cka', because what has happened is people have mentioned that they have been inspired to do something, but in reality, how do we know that they were truly inspired? Sir, I cannot speak for anyone else; I can only speak for myself. What I can tell you sir is when I felt the inspiration and spiritual guidance to write this book, it was a process that took place within the inner chambers of my soul.

My first inspiration came from a T-shirt that I created for the Million Woman March; many radio stations interviewed me about the T-shirt. Second, everything that I did from that day on kept reminding me of writing things down in a journal in order to explain what was on the T-shirt. I was being used because of the inspirational message that was on the T-shirt and my ability to constantly stay open to the vibration of the universe. While writing this book, I developed a sense of compassionate sensitivity and understanding about life.

Then I felt a vibration that vibrated very loudly in the inner chambers of my soul. That vibration controls all of my thoughts and my focus and my awareness, and then I could not move. The one thing that was mentioned to me is what would happen if an incident in the world occurred and was never reported to the masses of people. Something says what happened if that thing was known to people but they concealed it, and now that same information is being transcended through you, Mr. Grant, as a force in the universe. Then something quickly said what happens if it was the ultimate truth of the world? What people do not know is the truth about the human creation and universe that have been seriously concealed from the masses of people. What happens if people were being led in the wrong direction about life, God, and their existence? What happens if creation did not begin in the Garden of Eden? What happens if the woman is man's true God? What happens if the woman is really our God in life?

The universe then chose me because I wanted to challenge the concept of what really happened, who was God, or was I my own God, but I then was faced with the true reality of life, and that is that the women on this planet we call Mother Earth are our true Gods of the universe.

Now I know that I was in trouble, but then something said that you were not in trouble, because depending on your level of spiritualism, and knowledge the universe chooses you or someone else to be the inspiration for the masses of people to understand and comprehend. These people that are in tune with the same energy as you are they are able to understand or accept your work also as the chosen one of the universe. The chosen people that the universe knew and used from the time that they were in their mother's womb to enlighten the masses of people, in order to wake them up from the valley of the dead dry bones, the only thing that can give life to the dry jaw bones are the words of spiritualism. The dry bones were dead. The only time that the dry dead bones began to come to life was based them receiving knowledge of life, that woke them up to become a living breathing soul. This knowledge of life is what brings people from being human beings into being a God of themselves and their own existence.

Index